BORN
TO
LOVE

JAX BURROWS

VINCI
BOOKS

By Jax Burrows

The O'Connors

Worth Waiting For
Healing Hearts
Never Too Late
Born to Love

This book is dedicated to midwives everywhere.

Vinci Books

vinci-books.com

Published by Vinci Books Ltd in 2026

1

The publisher and the author have made every effort to obtain permissions for any third party material used in this book and to comply with copyright law. Any queries in this respect should be brought to the attention of the publisher and any omissions will be corrected in future editions.

A CIP catalogue record for this book is available from the British Library.

Paperback ISBN: 9781036708061

The EU GPSR authorised representative is Logos Europe, 9 rue Nicolas Poussion, 17000 La Rochelle, France
contact@logoseurope.eu

Chapter One

Josie O'Connor should have noticed earlier that the weather was closing in. The temperature had dropped, and the sky was heavy with light grey clouds full of snow. She shivered and turned the heater up in her Mini Cooper, then turned the radio up to sing along to one of her favourite Christmas carols: Away in a Manger.

Her mind had been elsewhere when she had left the South Yorkshire home of Harriet, a midwife Josie used to work with before Harriet took maternity leave.

Josie had hugged Harriet, congratulated her, and given her all the Christmas presents she had bought for Harriet, her husband Frank, and Chloe, the latest arrival. Her new baby was adorable, and Josie felt mixed emotions as she held the tiny, soft, wriggling human in her arms. She was happy for Harriet, of course, she was, but jealous of her too. She had everything Josie wanted. A loving husband, a gorgeous baby and a future as a wife and mother.

Josie was determined to get home that night. Her twin brother, Jay, and his new wife, Caitlin, were returning from their overseas travels and, much as she wanted to see her beloved twin again, she had a bone to pick with him. Jay and Caitlin had married on a beach in Bali with two witnesses. Josie hadn't been invited. She was hurt but understood the reasoning behind it. She would never have done that to him though. When she married, all the family would be there to celebrate with her. First, of course, she had to meet the right man.

Josie turned the windscreen wipers on to their highest speed and looked up at the sky which had decided to shed its load. It was getting dark already and Josie knew she'd have to put her foot down if she was going to beat the weather. The wind had increased, and snow swirled and danced in front of the car. The wind pushed at the car as if trying to knock it over, so Josie decreased her speed, despite her anxiety to get home to Leytonsfield as quickly as she could.

Josie had two choices: she could head to the motorway which would probably be the best option or take the Woodhead Pass route, which was scenic and would take longer but was Josie's preference. She loathed driving on the motorway, feeling safer on the A roads.

In fine weather, the surrounding moors looked beautiful and Josie loved the drive to Harriet's, but in bad weather, they were dark and dangerous. At present, she could hardly see them through the snow which was building up to become a blizzard.

She was still trying to decide which way to go when she saw a man step into the road in front of her car. If she hadn't been driving so slowly she might have hit him. He had a dark jacket on and wasn't wearing anything reflective. He was waving his hands for her to stop, and his face was white in the light from the headlights.

Josie moved into the side of the road and pulled on the handbrake but left her headlights on and the engine running. She had heard of scams where people stopped cars in such a way then either robbed the driver or stole the car. Sometimes both. Josie was aware of being alone and no match for a man if one attacked her. Maybe it was time she invested in self-defence classes.

She lowered the window slightly, but not enough that the man could put his hand through. He bent forward and Josie could see the desperation in his eyes.

'Please… we need help. My wife's in labour and the baby's coming. Can you help?'

Josie forgot her fears immediately and got out of the car.

'Have you phoned an ambulance?' she asked.

'Yes, but since then the baby's head… well, I think I can see the head. Can you help her?'

So, the baby's crowning. Josie left her headlights on as they might give her precious light to work with and moved swiftly to the car where a woman was writhing and crying in pain. Her partner had pushed the front seat of the car as far back as it would go, and the woman was reclining on it with her hands resting on her belly. There was fluid on the seat and the floor of the car, indicating that the woman's waters had broken.

'What's your name, love?' asked Josie.

'Brenda,' the woman gasped. 'Is Mike there?'

'Yes, but I'm a midwife and can help you deliver the baby. There's not enough room for both of us in here.' Josie laughed but the woman was too busy breathing through another contraction to join in.

'May I examine you?'

Josie took the woman's groan as a yes and, kneeling in

front of her, pulled her patient's maternity leggings and panties, which were at her knees, further down and took them off, handing them to Mike who had clambered into the driver's seat and was watching Josie's every move anxiously.

The car was a Nissan but surprisingly spacious and Josie was confident that she could help Brenda deliver her baby safely, provided the cord wasn't around the baby's neck or they weren't dealing with a breech or brow presentation.

Josie felt Brenda's belly and was relieved to feel that the baby was in a good position; head down facing Brenda's back. She then examined the business end as one of the consultants she worked with called it, and the baby was definitely on its way.

'Is she alright?' asked Mike with a tremor in his voice.

'She's fine,' said Josie.

'Arghh!' said Brenda as another contraction twisted her inside out.

'Push, Brenda, that's it—you're doing well.'

Josie was aware that this poor woman was delivering a baby in a blizzard with no pain relief. She felt overwhelming admiration for her. Women were so strong when they had to be. Mike, however, looked as if he was about to pass out. He needed something to do.

'Why don't you ring the ambulance service again and tell them things have progressed since your first call?'

'Right, I'm on it.' Mike climbed out of the car and Josie breathed a sigh of relief. Now she could concentrate fully on Brenda.

Mr Charles Atkins was spending Christmas alone in his brother's cottage in the Peak District. An isolated, lonely place that suited Charles's mood perfectly. He had swallowed his pride when Andrew offered him the retreat and forgot the animosity he felt at the obscene amount of money Andrew earned in his private practice in London. He was desperate to get away and the offer of the cottage was exactly what he needed.

The plan was to pretend Christmas wasn't happening and drown his sorrows in copious amounts of whisky. To that end, he would need more of the stuff as well as essentials such as bread, milk, baked beans, and coffee. If he needed to eat he could exist on beans on toast; he'd done it before as a medical student. Then it wasn't lack of money that forced him to eat frugally, but the long hours he had spent on the wards, studying for exams, and trying to keep body and soul together. He had never had the time to eat properly.

Charles stocked up with provisions and booze in the small supermarket in the village. He ignored the Christmas music being played, the brightly coloured tree in the corner, and the tinsel strewn over everything in sight. Christmas. Bah humbug!

The snow was falling heavily now, and the pavements were already becoming treacherous. He glanced over to the pub on the other side of the road. Andrew had told him all about the village and its inhabitants and the pub sounded as if it was worth a visit. As it was the only one in the centre of the village, it was a warm, friendly place apparently, where everyone knew everyone else in the typical intimacy of village life. He would have liked to have ordered a pint and sat in front of the roaring fire that Andrew had assured him burned merrily all winter, but in his present mood, he wasn't up for making small talk and being cheerful. He was better off alone in the cottage.

Charles drove his four-wheel-drive Subaru carefully down the winding road that led out of the village. Moorland Cottage, as Andrew had named it, was conveniently within walking distance, which was useful in good weather, Andrew had told him. Now, however, with visibility at almost zero and the temperature falling, Charles was glad of his car.

He was nearly back at the cottage when he passed two parked cars, both with headlights blazing. The Mini had no one in it, but the Nissan, which had the interior light on, contained two women who looked to be engaged in a sexual act in the front. One woman was bare from the waist down and the other woman was kneeling in front of her, and... at the long, drawn-out cry of the first woman, Charles realised his mistake. He would recognise the agony in that cry anywhere; he'd heard countless women in labour emit the same sound.

Charles parked up ahead of the Nissan and got out. He noticed the man next to the car on his mobile.

'Can I help at all?' asked Charles.

'Uh, I don't know. I've phoned the ambulance and it's on the way. The lady says she's a midwife.'

'Right. I'll just see if there's anything I can do.'

Charles put his head around the open door. 'Need any help?'

The midwife who was encouraging the pregnant woman to push, frowned and glared at him. 'There's nothing to see here. You could talk to the husband if you want to do something to help.'

Charles was taken aback by her abrupt manner but considering the unusual circumstances and the fact that she didn't know he was an obstetrician, Charles decided not to take umbrage.

'Okay, if you're sure.'

'Push, Brenda, the baby's nearly out. Push down into your bottom. Yes, that's right, good girl.'

'Be careful that the cord isn't around the baby's neck.' Charles couldn't move away despite the midwife's orders. He was ready if she needed him to step in.

The midwife glared at him. 'I've checked.'

'Good. Be ready to catch her; once her head and shoulders are clear, she'll come out like a cork out of a bottle.' The midwife ignored him.

'Come on, Brenda, that's it... you're doing great, just one more big push.'

'Aaarrrgggh!'

'She's here. You've done it. Oh, she's beautiful, Brenda.'

The baby let out a lusty cry and waved her tiny hands at the world, as Josie deftly lifted her and put her on Brenda's chest.

Charles had a lump in his throat as he beckoned the man to come forward. He did, with tears streaming down his face.

'Come and meet your daughter,' said Charles.

'Oh my goodness, Bren, you did it. Oh, I love you so much. Can I see her?'

Mike came forward and kissed his wife then stared at the baby in awe.

Charles removed his woollen jacket and took off his Aran sweater, then put his jacket back on. 'Here, take this to wrap her in. It's warm and soft.'

'Thank you.' They wrapped the tiny girl in the sweater and stared at her in rapture.

The midwife had got out of the car and was bending

and stretching to ease her aching muscles. Charles recognised the signs of fatigue in her face, something he'd experienced himself after attending a long labour. She'd been squashed into the footwell of the car which can't have been comfortable for any length of time. He felt a surge of admiration for the midwife and the new mother.

'Congratulations. Lucky for them you came by.'

'Thanks,' she said. 'I wish the ambulance would turn up, I'd be happier if the cord could be cut and she was checked over by the experts.'

A siren in the distance getting closer made them both look up in the direction of the sound.

'Looks as if your wish is granted,' said Charles.

Fifteen minutes later, Brenda, Mike and the baby were safely in the ambulance and on their way to the hospital, and Charles and the midwife were huddled together in an increasingly violent snowstorm.

Charles felt cold without his favourite Aran sweater and was eager to get back to the cottage to start on the first bottle of whisky.

'Right, I'll be on my way. Have you got far to go?' he asked.

'I live in Leytonsfield in Cheshire.' Now there's a coincidence, thought Charles.

'Be careful on the motorway in this weather.'

'I'm thinking of taking the A628. I avoid motorways if I can, especially in weather like this.'

'The Woodhead Pass would be worse—if they haven't closed it already.'

Charles wasn't happy about this. She was in a Mini Cooper, a car not built for serious weather conditions. She'd be tired after delivering a baby in difficult circumstances. It was his duty to try and dissuade her.

'Why not come back to the cottage for a while and see if the blizzard eases. You can stay the night and leave in the morning.' It would only delay his date with the whisky bottle by one night.

'I need to get home tonight. It's Christmas Eve tomorrow and I don't want to be stuck here over the festive season.'

Charles fumbled in his inside pocket and produced one of his cards. 'Here, take this and ring me if you get stuck. Don't take risks, it isn't worth it.'

The midwife squinted at the card in the dim light and then looked at him. 'Mr Charles Atkins. Obstetrician and Gynaecologist.'

'And you are?'

'Josie O'Connor.'

'Midwife extraordinaire.'

She smiled. It was the first time he had seen her smile and Charles realised she was extremely attractive with her hazel eyes and long dark hair.

'Right. I'll be off. Nice to meet you.' Josie got into her car and started the engine. Charles watched her drive away with mixed feelings. The last thing he wanted this Christmas was company, especially that of a beautiful woman. He wanted to be a miserable so and so on his own and forget his problems for a while. But, on the other hand, he hated the thought of anything happening to Josie because she'd stopped to help a complete stranger.

Charles hoped that, if the road was closed, she'd ring him. Perhaps he'd postpone his binge drinking until later just in case.

Chapter Two

An obstetrician. Of course, he had to be an obstetrician, didn't he? No wonder he knew all about the dangers of birth, such as the cord around the baby's neck. Only someone who delivered babies for a living would be able to retain such a cool, self-assured demeanour when faced with a woman in labour. He must have delivered hundreds of babies. Well, so had she and the baby was safe and well, as was the mother. Because of her. She should be proud of herself.

Josie tried to concentrate on the road, which was proving harder with each mile she drove. The weather was getting worse the further she travelled.

By the time Josie had reached the turnoff for Manchester and the A628, she was too late. The familiar red metal sign telling motorists that the road ahead was closed sat firmly in the middle of the lane. She had no choice but to turn around and go back.

Josie took her phone out of her pocket to let her mother know that she may be delayed, but there was no signal.

Sighing with frustration she turned her car around and headed for the motorway. She'd drive slowly and carefully. It was fine. She could do this.

Driving back the way she had come was harder as she was heading into the wind and the blizzard was obliterating her view of the road. She knew she should stop and ring the doctor to help her. It was madness to drive in these conditions and common sense told her she was putting her life— and other people's—in danger. But Josie was stubborn and desperate to get home. She wanted to see Jay again.

She drove on, slowly crawling along the narrow country road. She could only see a few feet ahead of her in the full beam of the headlights; large snowflakes hit the windscreen and were angrily swept away by the wipers. She could see nothing on either side but a white swirling mass. She knew there were fields, dry stone walls, copses, hills, and streams. The Peak District was a beautiful place in summer. Now it was the stuff of nightmares.

Hypnotised by the white world she was enclosed in, Josie didn't notice that she was drifting into the middle of the road until a car coming in the other direction sounded its horn to warn her. She pulled the steering wheel over to the left as hard as she could and skidded on an icy patch of road, the Mini ending up in the ditch with the wheels spinning uselessly.

No, oh, bugger! I don't believe this. Josie thumped the steering wheel in temper. Then broke down and cried.

When her hissy fit was over, she wiped her tears away with the back of her hand and listened.

The engine had stalled but the radio was still playing. A children's choir was singing *In the Bleak Mid-Winter,* their voices pure and sweet. Josie joined in. She loved singing and had always been in choirs from schooldays to university and then the hospital choir at Leytonsfield General, and it distracted her from the predicament she was in.

The blizzard was as fierce as ever and Josie felt the first stirrings of panic. Whenever she was in a tricky situation or had a difficult decision to make, she thought of her gran, her mother's mum, a lady of infinite common sense and wit. When she'd died at the age of ninety-two, Josie didn't think she would ever get over it. Her mum had told her that Gran was watching over her and she could talk to her at any time. So she did.

Okay, Gran, I need your help. She knew what her gran would say. Phone the doctor, he didn't give you his phone number for nothing. Ring him.

Josie took her phone out of her pocket, forgetting there was no signal, and stared at the blank screen. Okay, so find a public phone box. To do that, however, she would probably have to walk to the nearest village as she hadn't noticed one on the drive to where she was now. Where was she? She didn't know. She'd kept on the same winding road, except for turning around at the junction to the Woodhead Pass, so if she kept walking, she'd surely end up back in the village.

Josie had a choice—she could stay in the car and hope another motorist came by who she could flag down. Or she could get out of the car and start walking back to the village. She was warm where she was but how long would that last? It was freezing out there and what if she wandered off the road and lost her way? She could get stuck in a snowdrift and then what? Death from hypothermia?

Okay, Gran, what's plan B?

Josie waited for inspiration. Then she peered out of the windscreen as she thought she spotted light. Yes… there were headlights coming towards her. She quickly opened the driver's door and gasped for breath at the cold and the strength of the wind. She had no thoughts now of serial killers or people trying to rob her. Her gran had sent this person to rescue her.

'Are you okay?'

Josie recognised the voice. Then she felt relief when she saw his face. She had never been so grateful to see anyone before. It was the doctor, and he was sensibly carrying a torch.

'I had to pull the wheel over with some force and skidded on a patch of ice.'

'Right. Get your things and get in the car. There's nothing we can do about the Mini until the snow melts. It looks as if it's stuck fast.'

When Josie clambered out of her car, she saw what he meant. Her little motor was almost completely buried in a snowdrift with more snow covering the top and side. If she'd stayed in the car much longer, she would have been buried too.

She did as the doctor said and relished the warm interior of the four-wheel drive. She bet he had snow tyres as well. There were no carols playing on the radio though.

'Have you got a suitcase or overnight bag?'

'No. I wasn't planning on staying the night. I've only got the clothes I'm wearing.'

'Right.'

The doctor climbed in, put his seat belt on and proceeded to perform a perfect three-point turn.

'Thanks for coming. How did you find me?'

'Process of elimination. I knew you had to be somewhere between the village and the turn off for the Woodhead Pass. It wasn't difficult.'

'How did you know I needed help?'

'I made a lucky guess. The blizzard is getting worse, the

forecast is dire. A Mini Cooper is no match for these conditions. I shouldn't have let you go. I blame myself.'

Josie bristled at that. 'It was my decision, not yours. You can't blame yourself. I'm a grown woman.'

'You may be a grown woman, but you weren't thinking straight. You were desperate to get home and nothing was going to stand in your way. Common sense had flown out of the window. No, I should have insisted you stay overnight or at least until the roads had been gritted.'

'I'm glad you didn't try insisting. I'm grateful for your help but no one tells me what to do.'

The doctor gave her a sideways look with the hint of a smile. 'Would you like me to stop and let you out? Or take you back to your Mini? Or would you prefer to accept my help?'

Chastened, Josie realised the truth of what he said. She needed his help and she'd have to accept it, at least until the roads were open again.

'I'm sorry. I'm grateful and, of course, you're right.' Josie hated to admit it, but she needed this man, at least for the next twenty-four hours.

'Apology accepted.'

Josie kept quiet and stared ahead at the snow. It was mesmerising watching it dance in the headlights.

They turned right off the road and the doctor pulled up outside a stone cottage. The side of the cottage faced the road and the front looked out over the moors. The views would be spectacular in daylight.

'Right. Let's get inside,' said the doctor.

They were glad to move from the freezing cold into the warmth and light of the cottage.

'Oh, this is lovely,' said Josie gazing around her. The living room was small with low ceilings and exposed wooden beams. There was a three-piece suite in brown leather, adorned with brightly coloured cushions, that looked comfy and inviting. A television sat on an oak stand, and there was a bookcase and a coffee table. But the thing that drew Josie's attention was the cast iron wood burning stove in the corner of the room.

'Oh, I love these,' she said moving towards it and holding her hands out to the blaze.

'Careful, you'll get chilblains if your hands are cold,' said the doctor who was standing in the doorway watching her.

Josie moved away. How long would she have to stay here with Dr Grumpy? Nice as the cottage was, she wanted to be at home with her family. But he was putting himself out to help her and she needed to be more gracious.

'I just wanted to say again how much I appreciate your help.' That came out all wrong. It sounded stiff and too formal.

'You're welcome. I wasn't going to leave you out in the snow.'

'No, but still… Dr…?'

'Atkins, but you can call me Charles seeing as we're going to be sleeping under the same roof.'

'Right. I'm Josie.'

'Yes, I remember. Would you like me to show you to your bedroom?'

'Yes, please.' She hoped he wasn't expecting her to go to bed yet, it was far too early, and she hadn't eaten for hours.

Josie followed Charles up the narrow stairs, the wood creaking with nearly every step. You couldn't sneak home in the early hours in this cottage, thought Josie, the house itself would give you away.

'Sorry it's only a single bed, and the room's quite small.

The wardrobe is minute too, but I imagine you won't mind that. At least you can hang your coat up.'

'You're not selling me this room, Charles.'

Charles laughed and his face lit up. His eyes sparkled and laughter lines appeared. He looked completely different when he smiled. It was a shame his default setting was miserable.

'Sorry. I'm not used to the idea of a visitor yet. I had planned to spend Christmas here on my own.'

'Really? Whatever for?' Josie was amazed that someone would choose to be alone at Christmas. 'Don't you like Christmas?'

'Normally I don't mind it, but this year... it's compli-cated. Anyway, how about a drink? Tea or coffee? I'll make it while you settle in and have a look around. I'll lend you a T-shirt to sleep in if you want.'

'Yes, thank you. Yes to the T-shirt and either, I drink tea and coffee. Anything really. Whatever you're having.'

'Right. Okay then. There should be a new toothbrush in the bathroom and a flannel. I'll hunt out some towels. Use whatever's there.'

'Yes, I will, and thank you again.'

'No need to keep thanking me. Right. Come down whenever you're ready.'

'I will.'

Charles left and Josie listened to his footsteps running lightly down the stairs. She sat on the edge of the bed and closed her eyes. This wasn't on the agenda. She had taken some annual leave to welcome Jay and Caitlin home and spend some quality time with her family. She was looking forward to a normal O'Connor Christmas at her parents' house. For the last few years, she had been on duty so felt she had earned Christmas and New Year off.

Not only was she away from her family but she was disturbing Charles's plans. But why on earth would anyone choose to spend Christmas alone? Whatever the reason, he must be annoyed to have an unwelcome guest drop in. No wonder he was grumpy, she would be too if her plans had been scuppered in such a way.

Josie sighed and looked around the bedroom. The bed was comfortable enough even though she hadn't slept in a single bed since she was a teenager. The room was tidy, and the bed linen smelled fresh. She stood up and gazed out of the window but all she could see was snow still swirling around. Visibility was almost nil.

Time to go downstairs and join Charles. She took off her coat and hung it in the wardrobe. It looked lonely hanging there on its own. She closed the wardrobe door and made her way to the kitchen.

'You said anything, so I decided hot chocolate would be a good drink for this weather.'

'Fantastic, I love hot chocolate. And you've got marsh-mallows as well. Thank you.'

Josie sat at the kitchen table, sipping her hot chocolate. Charles sat opposite her. The wind howled around the cottage. It could be worse, she could still be stuck in her car in a snowdrift. Or out on the moors, lost and alone.

'I know you said not to keep thanking you, but… I am grateful.'

Charles smiled and nodded.

They sat in silence, both lost in their own thoughts. The blizzard continued to howl, and Josie wondered how long she would have to stay here, in an isolated cottage with Dr Grumpy. Then, as if she heard her gran's voice, the words appeared in her mind; Angels come in many forms.

Chapter Three

'Are you hungry?' asked Charles.

'Starving. And I need to phone my family. Where can I go to get mobile reception?'

Charles glanced at Josie, sitting huddled on a kitchen chair, her hands wrapped around her mug of hot chocolate. She still looked cold, even though the cottage was warm. How long would she have lasted in her car in this weather?

'I'm afraid there's no reception at the moment. You'll have to wait until all this blows over.'

'I need to contact my family, they'll be worried about me.'

'I had a listen to the forecast and the blizzard should be over by tomorrow. Nothing to be done about it before then, I'm afraid. Reception in the cottage is always patchy so you may have to move higher up. I'll drive you to the village tomorrow, but for now, just sit tight, and try not to worry.'

'Okay.'

That was easy, thought Charles, he'd been expecting an argument at the very least. But Josie looked done in and he wondered if he could persuade her to have an early night. Then he could have some time to himself. The whisky binge would have to wait though. A good host doesn't get drunk as soon as his visitor has gone to bed.

Josie frowned and sipped her chocolate, with a faraway look in her eyes. She was his guest and he needed to start looking after her. Hopefully, if it stopped snowing and the temperature started to rise, they could dig her car out of the ditch, and she could still make it home before Christmas Day.

'Right. How about something to eat? Do you like pasta?' Charles was conscious of how limited his food supplies were. If Josie stayed after tomorrow he'd have to go to the village for more.

'I love pasta. Can I do anything to help?'

'Do you like cooking?'

'No, I hate it. And I'm incredibly bad at it. My mum always tells people that I can't boil an egg. Which, of course, is true.'

'Well, in that case, no. You could sit in the living room if you like, you'd be warmer there.'

'Or... I could sit here and talk to you.'

The last thing Charles wanted to do was to talk. He wasn't sociable at the best of times and this Christmas was going to be one of the worst he'd ever spend, but, in the spirit of being a good host, he smiled and nodded.

'I must warn you, I'm not much of a talker.'

'Oh, that's okay,' said Josie, 'I can talk for both of us. I could talk for England, in fact. At least that's what my twin always tells people.'

'Tell me about your family.' Charles realised that, if he could keep chatterbox Josie chattering, then she may not notice if he said little. The secret of being a good listener was to get the other person to talk. He had a feeling Josie wouldn't need much encouragement.

'Okay. Well, my dad's a GP and my mum used to be a midwife until she had us. I have two older brothers, both consultants and my twin is a paramedic. And the next generation of O'Connors is growing now. Riordan and Zoe's son Tom and daughter Abigail, Casey and Lexi's daughters Jade and Lucy and there are three dogs who are also related.'

'And your twin?'

'Jay. He got married in Bali to a fellow paramedic, Caitlin. I'm still angry with him for not inviting me. Not that I could have gone because I didn't have the money for fares and probably wouldn't have been able to get the time off.'

'And what about you, Josie? Are you a career woman or planning on marriage?'

'Why can't I be both?'

'No reason.' Charles realised the conversation was sailing into tricky waters. Fortunately, the meal was ready. He put their plates on the table and poured them a glass of white wine each.

'This smells delicious.' Josie was already tucking in as he sat down.

'Sorry, it's only cheese, mushroom and tomato for the sauce. If I'd had more time I would have infused the milk with onion and garlic before making the cheese sauce, but it would have had to chill in the fridge first. There wasn't enough time.'

'I have no idea what that means but… don't worry, this is perfect.'

Charles laughed. It looked as if he was head chef for the duration of Josie's stay. That was good, as it would keep him busy until he could wave goodbye to her and resume his solitary Christmas.

When the meal was over, Josie offered to wash up, but Charles steered her into the living room to finish the wine and sit next to the fire. She didn't take much persuading.

When he had cleared up and wiped the surfaces down he joined her.

'Do you want to watch television?' Charles asked.

'Do you?'

'No, not particularly. I hardly ever do as I never seem to have the time.'

'I'm happy just to sit here. It's so peaceful and I feel relaxed after that lovely meal. And the wine, of course.'

'Good. You must be exhausted.'

'Not too bad. Since I became a midwife, I've learned to exist on less sleep than most people.'

'Sounds familiar,' Charles muttered.

'So, Charles, what about you? Why are you here on your own? Is this your cottage or are you renting it?'

So it begins, thought Charles. The questions.

'It belongs to my brother. He's a Harley Street specialist and has more money than you or I could earn in a lifetime. He's not married and has no children that he knows about. He offered me the cottage for Christmas and New Year when I told him I needed a retreat.'

'Why?'

'Why what?'

'Why do you need a retreat? Or is that too personal? Don't answer if you don't want to.'

Charles didn't want to answer. In fact, he didn't want to talk at all. But he had the feeling that Josie wouldn't let it go. She seemed tenacious. She was definitely stubborn. He may as well get it over with.

'In January, my wife of eighteen years left me for another man. A rich businessman and they, and my daughter Megan, who is sixteen, are spending Christmas and New Year skiing in the French Alps. It's the first Christmas I won't see my daughter and it's tearing me apart.'

Charles drained his glass and filled it up again, offering the bottle to Josie. She was looking at him with sympathy in her hazel eyes and he looked away. He didn't want pity or platitudes, he simply wanted to be left alone to drown his sorrows.

'I'm so sorry, Charles. No wonder you want to be alone.' Josie refilled her glass.

'Yes… well, best laid plans and all that.'

'I'm even more grateful to you now. Don't worry, I'll be out of your hair tomorrow. When the snowstorm is over, and they've treated the roads, I'll be on my way. I'm truly sorry. I know how bad I would feel if I couldn't see my family over Christmas. Even when I'm working I get to see them at some point.'

'I'll have to get used to it I'm afraid, but this is the first Christmas I've been on my own.'

'But what about other family? Your parents?'

Charles smiled inwardly. If Josie knew his family she wouldn't ask.

'My parents are in America for the holidays visiting friends.'

'Your brother?'

Charles laughed. 'He's in Amsterdam with his new woman.' And he's the last person he wanted to be in the same room with, never mind for the whole of the festive season.

Before Josie could ask about friends—Charles didn't

have many—he stood up and stretched. Hopefully, she'd take the hint and go to bed. But she stayed where she was, gazing at him in an appraising fashion.

'You're staring at me.'

'Sorry.' Josie looked away and then looked back at him. 'I was just wondering why you didn't tell me you were an obstetrician when I was helping Brenda.'

'You were doing a splendid job and didn't need me butting in. I was there in case you needed me. You didn't. And there wouldn't have been enough room for the two of us plus a labouring woman in the car.'

Josie grinned. 'Yes, that would have been cosy.'

They laughed and Charles sat down again.

'I wonder what kind of a Christmas Brenda and Mike will have with their new daughter?'

Josie stared at the fire and she looked sad suddenly. He deliberately hadn't asked her any questions about her private life. She didn't wear a ring so probably wasn't married. She hadn't mentioned a significant other. Not that he was interested.

'Sleepless nights, endless nappies. Relatives popping in at the most inconvenient times. That's what I remember when we brought Megan home.'

She turned to look at him. 'You must have been young when you had your daughter?'

'I was twenty-five and working crazy hours. Clarissa did most of the heavy lifting when Megan was young.' His wife had complained that he didn't do his share, but a junior doctor didn't have spare time, they worked, ate if they were lucky, and slept. Megan hadn't been planned or he would have arranged it better.

'Why didn't you have more children?'

'Clarissa didn't want any more.'

'Did you want more?'

Charles squirmed slightly under Josie's direct gaze. She was starting to ask questions he didn't want to answer. The breakdown of his marriage was still raw in his mind and he didn't want to think about what might have been. He had enough trouble dealing with realities.

'Would you like more wine?' Charles asked.

'Sorry, I'm asking too many questions. No thanks. I think I'll go to bed if that's okay?'

'Of course. Do you have everything you need?'

'Yes. Thanks again for everything, Charles. Goodnight.'

'Good night, Josie, sleep well.'

'I will. I'll sleep like a log now.'

When she had gone, her footsteps making the stairs creak, Charles sat and stared at the flames. Talking about Megan as a baby made him miss her more than ever. She'd been a sweetheart as a young child, and up to the age of about fourteen, when things started to go wrong in their marriage. After that, when she grew into full stroppy teenager mode, he found it harder to reach her. She called him embarrassing when he tried to talk to her, and he felt he had to play the stern father on more occasions than he was happy with.

Now, with her living apart from him, he was scared she'd forget him, preferring Clarissa's new boyfriend, Todd Wilcox, who showered her with gifts and expensive holidays and pandered to her every whim. He'd tried to talk to Clarissa about it, worried that Megan was becoming spoiled by getting everything she asked for. Clarissa had accused him of being jealous and told him to leave them alone as the three of them were a happy family unit and he had no part in their lives.

Clarissa could be very cruel, not caring that she was

stabbing him in the heart with her offhand manner and her inability to see it from his point of view. He was Megan's father and he loved her. He couldn't care less about Clarissa and what she got up to, but Megan was his daughter and that would never change. And he was prepared to fight for her if he had to. He only hoped that, between the two of them, Clarissa and Todd didn't succeed in turning Megan against him.

Charles realised that he was getting maudlin again. If he'd been on his own with his whisky supply, it wouldn't have mattered. But he had Josie to look after, so he made his way to bed.

He was tired but he couldn't sleep. He thought of Josie and how calmly she had helped Brenda give birth. He idly wondered what the couple would name the little girl. His thoughts drifted to his daughter and he hoped she was enjoying the skiing.

The wind was still howling and the snow still falling. Charles eventually succumbed to sleep, and his dreams were strange and disturbing.

Chapter Four

Josie woke up early the next morning, hoping to see blue skies and a picturesque scene of moors with the snow glittering in the morning light. Instead, when she peered through the small window she saw snow falling. Not swirling as it had been the previous night but falling gently and layering the world in a fluffy white eiderdown.

Despite her disappointment, Josie was mesmerised by the silence of the scene and the way the individual snowflakes drifted out of the sky to blend in when they landed. Nature was wonderful and Josie was transfixed until her mind returned to the problem of getting home.

If the snow didn't stop soon, she stood little chance of being able to dig her car out of the snowdrift in the ditch and it may need some work doing on it before it was up and running again.

She dressed quickly and made her way down to the kitchen where Charles was making coffee.

'Good morning. Did you sleep well?'

'I did thanks, the bed was comfy, and I must have been more tired than I thought.'

'Breakfast?'

'Lovely.' Josie sat at the kitchen table and sipped the coffee that Charles had poured for her.

'What do you normally have for breakfast? I'm afraid I don't have much in and intend to brave the weather with a trip to the village later on. I might wait until the snow stops though.'

'I'll come with you and try to phone my parents. In answer to your question, I'll have anything you've got.' Josie couldn't believe how hungry she was and would have relished a full English, but Charles probably didn't have the means to make one for her.

'How about scrambled egg on toast?'

'Sounds good.'

Charles set to, beating eggs, and adding salt and pepper. Josie watched him for want of anything better to do. She knew it was time she learned to cook but she had no interest in it at all and hoped that her Mr Right, when he showed up, would like cooking as much as Charles obviously did.

Charles heated some butter in a pan and slipped two rounds of bread into the toaster. Then he took a small bottle of something dark out of the cupboard and put a few drops in the beaten egg.

'What's that?' Josie was interested suddenly. Maybe it was poison, and he was going to dismember her and bury her body on the moors. Josie had always had a wild imagination and had read enough crime novels to know all the different ways serial killers operated.

Charles turned to speak to her. 'It's soy sauce. I only use a drop, but it improves the flavour. You'll hardly taste it I promise.'

'Okay.' Josie wondered why he bothered to use it if you couldn't taste it but wasn't going to argue the toss. She wasn't in a good mood. She desperately wanted to get home and, if it didn't stop snowing, she might have to spend Christmas Day here. She needed something to lift her spirits —like blue skies and no snow.

Charles placed the scrambled egg on toast in front of her and suddenly life looked better. Eating was one of her favourite hobbies and Charles was a great cook. She cut a corner off the toast and egg and put it in her mouth.

'Oh my goodness, that tastes amazing.'

'Good. My soy sauce trick is still working.'

'It's lovely, Charles. Aren't you having any?'

'No, I've already eaten. Another coffee?'

'Tea please,' said Josie with a mouth full of food.

It didn't take Josie long to clear her plate. She sat back with a contented sigh. Charles put a pot of tea on the table with milk and sugar and two mugs.

'That was absolutely gorgeous. I think I should pay you for all this food. Will you accept something from me?'

'Don't be ridiculous,' Charles said crossly. 'It's a poor show if I can't help a fellow human being out during the, supposed, season of goodwill.'

'Supposed? Sounds as if you don't believe in it.'

'It's like I said, I'm not in a good place at the moment and if you hadn't shown up I'd… well, let's just say I wouldn't be in the kitchen cooking.'

'So where would you be?' Josie felt cold suddenly. Surely he didn't mean he'd do something stupid? He was a doctor. But then, the suicide rates among doctors were rising.

'Charles,' Josie said carefully, 'what exactly would you do if I wasn't here?'

'Get drunk and stay drunk until New Year's Day.'

'Nothing worse than that?'

Charles frowned. 'Like what? Run about naked in the snow?'

Josie giggled. 'Sorry, it's just that, when you said you wanted to be alone… ignore me I've got a vivid imagination.'

'Whatever are you talking about? What else would I be…' Then the penny must have dropped as Charles sat down opposite her. 'You thought I meant I was planning to take my own life?'

'Well, no… yes, maybe. I don't know. We don't know each other. I have no idea what you're feeling so how could I possibly know what you were planning.'

Charles smiled and his eyes sparkled. He leant over the table and covered one of her hands with his. Josie felt a tingle down her spine. His hand was warm, and it felt strangely comforting. The O'Connors were a demonstrative family and were always hugging and kissing. Josie needed physical connections with people, she thrived on it.

'Josie, thank you for your concern, but let me reassure you that nothing is further from my mind. I have my own way of dealing with problems and getting drunk is one of them. Not the most mature or grown up and doesn't solve anything in the long run, but it would have helped me get through Christmas.'

'Until you woke up with the hangover from hell.'

'That's the price I would have to pay, yes.' Charles withdrew his hand and stood up, collecting the used plates and mugs then stacking them in the dishwasher.

'So, I'm stopping you getting drunk?' Josie asked.

'For now. There's always tomorrow. Anyway, let's talk about something more cheerful, shall we?'

'Can we have the radio on?'

'Of course.' Charles turned it on but there was just a political discussion on the station it was tuned into. Josie got up and changed it until she found Christmas carols.

'That's better.' It was *Once in Royal David's City* and she sat down again and started singing. Josie knew she had a good voice. She'd sung solos in the choirs she'd been in many times. Charles, however, had his back to her as he cleaned up the toast crumbs and didn't seem to be listening. She sang louder. For some perverse reason, she wanted him to tell her she had a good voice. She didn't know why. They were strangers and meant nothing to each other, so why she should feel that way, she didn't know.

The O'Connors all sang, with varying degrees of skill. Her father and Casey belted out tunes with no regard for the key signature, while Riordan and her mum had lovely voices and the three of them often sang in harmony when preparing the Christmas dinner or clearing up afterwards. Jay wouldn't sing whatever she threatened him with, but the kids were happy to join in. Even the dogs threw back their heads and howled when it all became too much. That set them all off laughing until their sides ached.

The carol ended. Charles applauded and cried, 'Bravo!'. Josie felt a warmth inside her that was nothing to do with the heating in the cottage or the breakfast she'd just eaten. 'More!' he shouted, and Josie grinned at him.

'Okay.' The next carol was *Bethlehem Down*, and Josie sang the soprano part because that carried the tune. She often sang the alto part and wished now she had her family to sing with her as the harmonies of the different voices blended beautifully. But she did her best, closed her eyes, and gave it everything even though it was an emotional carol. The story of a young girl and her first born.

When it ended, Josie felt the tears in her eyes and turned

her head away so Charles couldn't see them. He was moved too as his eyes were sad and he sighed deeply.

'That was beautiful, Josie, you have a lovely voice.'

Then the news came on and they both listened to reports of political strife, violence, and crime.

Josie got up and went into the living room. She sat quietly, composing herself and feeling sadness descend on her like a blanket someone had dropped over her. She wasn't melancholy by nature, in fact, she always described herself as a glass half full kind of person but until it stopped snowing, and she was on her way home to her family, she would find it hard to stay positive.

After a while, Charles came in and stood in the middle of the room. 'I know this smacks of desperation, but we could play a game if you like.'

Josie wondered what was coming next. Strip poker? 'What kind of game?'

'Well… Andrew, my brother, stocked up for families for when he rents the cottage out in summer. In case of bad weather. Scrabble, Monopoly, Ludo…'

'No computer games?' Josie had really enjoyed playing the Game of Thrones video game with Jay and Tom, and she prided herself on her prowess at world building.

'No, I'm afraid not. They're in that cupboard if you want to have a rifle through.'

Josie got up and looked through the cupboard. The first thing she picked out was a thousand-piece jigsaw of London. She didn't feel desperate enough yet to tackle that, so she searched for the Scrabble. There was also Trivial Pursuit and Jenga, but Josie decided to keep those for later while hoping that they wouldn't be needed.

Occasionally she glanced out of the window to check the weather and it was still snowing.

There was nothing else for it, she would need to be calm and patient. The snow would stop in its own time. And Charles was doing everything in his power to make her feel at home, despite the fact that he was longing for solitude and the space to get stinking drunk in.

Josie set up the Scrabble game and waited for Charles to sit down opposite her at the kitchen table. They both chose a tile and Charles got the higher number, so he selected his seven tiles, then offered the bag to Josie. She picked her letters, and they were off.

Josie felt strange playing Scrabble with Charles when she'd only ever played it with her family. Her favourite rivals were her mum, Tom, and Riordan who always won because he had a mind like a computer.

'Are you competitive?' she asked Charles.

'Extremely,' he said not lifting his gaze from his letters. He had a frown on his face and looked as if he meant business.

Josie took the opportunity to study Charles. He had a good head of dark brown hair which complemented his blue eyes. His eyes were his best feature. He was attractive for an older man. She had worked out that he was forty-one. Ten years older than herself. He had been twenty-five when Megan was born, and she was sixteen. Which totalled forty-one. Nothing wrong with her maths, she thought as she returned her gaze to her letters.

Josie had an appalling hand. She couldn't make anything from it. Charles went first. He put a short word down that gave him a good start. Josie followed and managed to get rid of an X but Charles won the first game easily.

'Another game?' Charles asked.

Josie glanced out of the window. It was still snowing.
'Okay.'

An hour later and Josie won her first game. She celebrated by doing a happy dance around the kitchen with
Charles watching with amusement. Then she stopped dead.

'It's stopped snowing!' she cried and they both went to
the back door and opened it to get a closer look. The snow
was up to their knees. 'What do we do now?'

Charles sighed. 'We get our warmest clothes on—I can
lend you boots, socks, and a warm sweater—and start shovelling. There's a shed over there and we need to get to it. I
have the longest legs, so I'll go.'

'We should have taken the shovels out earlier,' said Josie
helpfully.

'Hindsight's a wonderful thing,' muttered Charles as he
ran up the stairs to get changed.

Chapter Five

Charles waded through the snow to get to the shed. He had borrowed a pair of boots that must have belonged to Andrew and found a smaller pair for Josie. He also handed her a sweater that was far too big and a pair of thick socks; she was going to need them as shovelling snow this deep was hard work and her feet would get cold.

When he arrived at the shed after high-stepping across the snow he realised the door opened outwards and he would need to clear the snow in front of the door to get inside. He spent a frustrating time removing the snow with his gloved hands and cursing that he hadn't had the foresight to put the shovels in the cottage. Josie was right, which was equally annoying.

Eventually, he got the door open and picked up two snow shovels, then tramped back to the cottage.

'Who do these boots belong to?' said Josie, flexing her feet inside wellington boots that protected her legs up to her knees. They were bright pink with blue spots and Josie was studying them dubiously.

'Oh, I don't know, one of Andrew's women I imagine.'

'Does Andrew have lots of women?'

'Does a bear shit in the woods?'

Andrew's women were a sore point between them. Charles believed in fidelity which was why it had hit him so hard to find out that Clarissa had been seeing Todd behind his back. Andrew, however, was a narcissistic bastard who used women and then tossed them aside when he'd finished with them.

'I see,' said Josie still studying her boots.

'Right—let's get shovelling.'

It was hard work and they both became hot and sweaty with all the effort. Soon they fell into a rhythm and worked well together clearing the path from the cottage to the shed, the cottage to the steps down to the road and a path from Charles's car to the road.

The gritters hadn't been out and the roads were icy. Few cars had passed the cottage since yesterday and Charles knew he'd have to drive carefully to the village if he didn't want to end up in a ditch as Josie had.

'Shall we stop for a drink?' asked Charles, straightening up and feeling his back complaining with twinges in his hips and neck.

'Yes, good idea. We've done a lot though.'

Josie didn't look any worse for her manual labour. He wondered if she worked out or ran. She was physically fit, and her cheeks were pink with the exertion. She grinned at him and he realised she was enjoying herself. He grinned back which turned into a chuckle.

'What are you laughing at?' Josie asked.

'I'm laughing because you look as if you could go on all day and I'm aching all over and exhausted.'

'That's because I'm younger than you by ten years.

We're a different generation. And I'm used to physical exercise. Being a midwife is a demanding job.'

'Don't you like older men?' Now why had he asked that? Because he was conscious of being over forty, that's why.

'I've never been out with an older man,' said Josie smiling at him.

'You don't know what you're missing,' Charles said.

When Josie didn't reply he hoped he hadn't embarrassed her and propped the shovels up against the wall.

'How about a quick coffee and then I'll drive you to the village so you can phone your family?'

'Great idea.' Josie took her boots off and sat at the kitchen table.

After the coffee, they rugged up again, put their boots back on and drove to the village.

Charles inched the car forward until it was on the road, then drove at a snail's pace, concentrating hard on keeping the wheel as steady as possible.

Josie was singing again, another carol that he wasn't familiar with.

'That's nice,' he said when she had finished.

'It's called *What Sweeter Music?* and it's one of my all-time favourites.'

'It's lovely.'

Josie was happy now that she was going to contact her family. Charles fervently hoped she'd be able to get home for Christmas as it obviously meant a lot to her to be with them. He envied her that closeness and wondered how Megan was doing. Perhaps he'd send her a quick text to wish her a good holiday and tell her how much he was missing her.

As soon as Charles had parked up, Josie was out of the car and phoning her family.

'Mum, it's me.'

'Oh, my darling, thank goodness. We've been worried sick. We phoned Harriet who told us you'd left but that the blizzard had closed the roads. Where are you?'

'I'm sheltering in the cottage of a man who stopped to help when I was delivering a baby. A woman was giving birth in the car and her partner flagged me down to help. Then the doctor turned up. An obstetrician would you believe?'

'Oh, Josie, that sounds like an adventure. Trust you to find a labouring woman to help. And this doctor—where does he fit in?'

'He was driving past but wasn't needed. She gave birth to a little girl and all's well. I'm staying in his cottage until I can get my car out of the ditch.'

'Why is your car in a ditch? Are you okay? You're not hurt? Oh, Josie, I wish you were here with us. Jay and Caitlin are back, tanned and besotted with each other. When can you get home?'

'I don't know to be honest. But I promise you it'll be sooner rather than later. Charles is trying to find a garage to rescue the car and check it over. Hopefully, I'll know more later today.'

'Charles is the doctor?'

'Yes, Mr Charles Atkins. He's been wonderful.' As Josie said it she realised how true it was. Charles couldn't have done enough for her. She'd turned his plans for Christmas upside down and eaten him out of house and home.

'Well, take care, my darling, and come home to us safe and sound, won't you. We all send our love to you and will wait for your call. Goodbye, sweetheart.'

'Bye, Mum. Love you. Love to everyone.'

Josie couldn't help the tears that ran down her cheeks. She brushed them away angrily. She'd get home somehow, even if she had to walk. The thought of spending her free days off stuck in a cottage with a stranger when she should be home in the midst of the family was tearing her apart, although Charles was beginning to grow on her, and she owed him so much for his kindness.

Josie looked up and down the street to see if she could spot Charles. There was no sign of him, so Josie stayed with the car and studied the village.

The supermarket was small but seemed to be the only place to buy essentials. There was a hairdresser, a butcher, greengrocers, a gift shop which was closed, and, intriguingly, a clothing shop. Josie had been in the same clothes now for two days and wondered if she was starting to smell. She needed a shower and a change of clothes badly, especially after the exertion of shovelling snow when she had been sweating like a pig. It had been fun though and challenging to keep up with Charles. She should have admitted to him that she had started to ache too, but pride had made her keep quiet and let him think she was fitter than she was.

Not wanting to arrive home looking like she'd been sleeping rough, she nipped across the road and bought some essentials; panties, a nightie, two T-shirts, and a sweater. At least that would suffice in the event that she had to stay another night. She also bought a pair of driving gloves that would do for Charles's Christmas present in the event she had to stay. That prospect depressed her, so she gazed out across the snow-covered moors instead.

The village was high up and the view down the valley was beautiful. Dry stone walls snaked their way through the fields, dividing the land up into segments that looked like a mosaic of white. Trees and cottages were tiny in the distance and the snow-topped hills sloped gently up, providing the perfect backdrop.

'Nice view, isn't it?'

Josie turned at the sound of Charles's voice.

'It's beautiful, like a Christmas card.'

'Yes. Right. Do you want the good news or the bad?'

Josie really didn't want bad news but needed to be brave and face whatever Charles was about to tell her.

'Bad, I suppose.'

'Okay. The Woodhead Pass is still closed and will stay that way for the foreseeable future. The motorway is open, however.'

'Great. And the good news?'

'I had a word with the mechanic who owns the garage up there.' Charles pointed up the hill. 'He is willing to dig your car out and get it on the ramp to see if it needs any work. We need to give him the key. You do have it with you, don't you?'

'Yes.' Josie fished around in her handbag and pulled out the key. 'When does he think he can do the car?'

'He can retrieve it this afternoon and get to work on it. Obviously, as it's Christmas Day tomorrow, he may not be able to have it roadworthy until Boxing Day.'

'Right. Let's go.' Josie was eager to get the key to him. The sooner he started the work, the more chance she had of getting home for Christmas. Hopefully, it wouldn't need much work and, if the mechanic could work on it this afternoon, she might be on her way today or early tomorrow morning.

They strode off up the hill. Charles had his hands in the pockets of his jacket and stared at the ground as he walked. Josie looked at every shop and cottage they passed, taking it all in. It was a lovely little village, especially with the snow sparkling in the light.

They arrived at the garage and gave the key to the mechanic. He said he couldn't promise anything, but he'd do what he could. Josie thanked him profusely and they walked back down the hill to Charles's car.

'We need to do a shop,' said Josie.

'Yes, I was thinking that. How about a quick drink first? The supermarket is open until six tonight, so we have plenty of time.'

'Okay. How many pubs does the village have?'

'Only one, the George and Dragon, but Andrew assures me it's a nice pub.'

'Right.' There wasn't much else to do except wait for the mechanic to fix her car and Josie was happy to mingle with the locals.

They were met with warmth, laughter, and the smell of beer when they walked through the doors.

'What are you having?' asked Charles.

'You should let me get these. I have so much to thank you for. Okay?'

Charles shrugged. 'Okay then. I'll just have a half of bitter please.'

Josie stood at the bar waiting to be served while Charles went to find a table. The pub had an olde worlde theme, with exposed wooden beams in the ceiling, stone flagged flooring and a huge black fireplace which held a cast iron wood burning stove, similar to the one at Moorland Cottage, but bigger. Every wall was covered with pictures, mainly of tourist attractions and scenic views, and Josie studied them as she waited.

Food was being served and Josie's stomach rumbled at the delicious aromas wafting from the kitchen. It seemed hours since she'd had her breakfast and with all the shovelling, she needed to refuel.

Josie ordered two halves of bitter and asked for the menu. The barman grinned and pointed to a blackboard propped up on the bar. There were only two meals on offer; roast pork or roast chicken and all the trimmings.

'We usually have a more varied menu but it's Christmas Eve and only the regulars come in today, with the exception of you two. People on their own who don't have anywhere to go and don't fancy being with strangers are grateful for a roast dinner.'

'Thanks,' said Josie and joined Charles.

'Cheers,' Charles said as they clinked their glasses together.

'Cheers,' replied Josie. 'Are you hungry?'

'Now you come to mention it, yes. How about you?'

'Starving. We could have a meal here then we won't have to bother later.'

'Good thinking. But I'll get these. Pork or chicken?'

'Pork I think, with apple sauce.'

'Your wish is my command,' Charles said as he stood up and wandered over to the bar.

As they waited for the barman to bring them their food, Charles kept glancing at his phone. Eventually, he got the message he was waiting for.

'Is that your daughter?' asked Josie.

'Yes. She's having a great time apparently.' Charles put his phone in his pocket.

'That's good.'

'Yes.' Charles looked sad and Josie wasn't sure what to say to make him feel better. Fortunately, they didn't have to wait long for their meal, and they tucked in as if they hadn't eaten for days.

The roast dinner tasted as delicious as it smelled, and Josie sat back after she'd eaten it and groaned. 'I feel stuffed now. But a pleasant stuffed if you know what I mean.'

Charles finished off his last roast potato and put his knife and fork together neatly on the plate.

'That was a good idea of yours, Josie. Whatever happens for the rest of the day, at least we've both had a decent meal.'

All Josie wanted to happen was to have the Mini fixed and back on the road and a clear run home. She gazed out of the window and studied the sky. The blue had gone to be replaced with pale grey. There was more snow up there. The question was, how long would it be before it started falling again?

Chapter Six

Charles and Josie wandered around the supermarket with a basket each. Charles headed to the alcohol section and Josie selected cheese, crackers, fruit, chocolates, and other snacks.

Charles was just about to put another bottle of whisky in his basket when Josie joined him, holding a frozen duck.

'I was thinking,' she said slowly, 'in the event I can't get home today, what are we going to eat?'

'Eat? We've just had an enormous roast dinner.' Charles looked at the duck and back at Josie.

'No, not today, for tomorrow. If I'm still at Moorland Cottage. That is, if I'm still welcome.' Josie smiled tentatively. Charles melted a little.

'Of course, you're welcome, you know that. What do you like to eat with your duck?'

'Whatever you want to cook.'

'Is the right answer.' Charles smiled. If Josie had managed to leave before tomorrow, he'd cook the duck for himself. No reason why he couldn't have a decent Christmas dinner before he got too legless to move.

When they left the supermarket they had two full to bursting carrier bags each of provisions. Charles had bought all the basic ingredients for a meal plus essentials including bread, milk, eggs, tea, and coffee. Josie, however, had stocked up on Christmas items including tinsel and a small Christmas tree that would look great standing on the bookcase in the living room. At least Josie thought it would. Charles wasn't bothered either way.

They hurried back to the cottage and put everything away in cupboards and the fridge.

Charles noticed that the shed was still open. He should lock it as it contained expensive gardening equipment. He'd taken his boots off, but Josie still had hers on.

'You wouldn't do me a big favour, Josie, and lock the shed would you?'

'Of course.'

Charles handed her the key then continued to put the food away.

'Look what I found.' Josie was outside the kitchen door and looking pleased with herself. 'It's a toboggan or sledge, I've never really known the difference.'

Charles came to the back door and examined the wooden structure. It was just a piece of wood turned up at the front and didn't look safe to his eyes.

'So it is,' he said.

'So… let's try it out. It won't get dark for another hour or so and there's a hill not far from here. What do you say?'

'You can have a go if you like and I'll watch.'

Josie's smile disappeared and she looked disappointed. Charles felt like the Grinch. He really didn't want to do anything Christmassy as it reminded him too much of being alone. Drunk and alone was okay. Sober and alone was agony. But as he looked into Josie's eyes and thought about everything she might be missing out on if she couldn't get home to her family, he realised how selfish he was being. He could give her this; it was the least he could do in the circumstances. She was away from her family at Christmas because she stopped to help a stranger. She was a good person.

'Oh, don't look at me like that. Okay, you win, I'll have a go too. But if I break my neck I'll blame you.'

'Hurray,' sang Josie and did another happy dance in the snow.

Charles couldn't help laughing at her dancing around in those ridiculous boots.

They carried the toboggan between them across the road and up the hill to the top. There were families and couples there already, all screaming with laughter and having the time of their lives.

'How does this work?' asked Charles.

'Have you never sledged before?' Josie asked.

'No, never. I've watched the winter Olympics on television but imagine this is different. You'll have to tell me what to do.'

'Okay. It's easy. We both sit on it and it runs downhill and then stops.'

'How do we get it started?'

Josie thought about that. She had only ever done it with her brothers who had fought to be the one in control of the sledge. She had just sat on it like the Ice Queen and given her orders. She had no idea how to get it started.

'You don't know, do you?' asked Charles with a grin.

'Of course, I know. I'll sit in front of you and put my feet on each side to stop it moving. You sit behind.'

Charles was looking at her in a supercilious way as if he was sure her plan wouldn't work. Josie was determined it would.

'Come on then, hop on.'

'Okay.'

Charles got on the sledge gingerly as if it was about to take off like a rocket. When he was settled and holding onto the sides for dear life, Josie put her feet up on the sledge and leaned back into Charles. The sledge took off slowly and gathered speed as it went. The snow was just the right consistency for a smooth ride and Josie laughed out loud with the simple pleasure of it.

When they arrived at the bottom, they got off, laughing.

'How was that?' asked Josie.

'Not as bad as I thought it would be,' Charles said. 'In fact, it was fun.'

'Come on then, let's get back to the top.'

They climbed back up the hill again and the second time they took off smoothly and sped down the hill even faster. Josie realised that this time Charles had his arm around her waist. He was preventing her from falling off rather than making a move on her, but she relished the closeness of their bodies and the feel of his strong arm holding her.

As they climbed the hill for the tenth time, Charles's phone rang. It was the mechanic, and he didn't have good news.

'He's managed to get your Mini out, but it needs a bit of work and he won't be able to do it before the day after Boxing Day at the earliest.'

'Damn.' Josie's good mood evaporated like ice in the sun.

Just at that moment, snow began falling again. The sky was heavy, and the light was fading fast.

Without a word being spoken, they both started to walk down the hill. Josie toyed with the idea of asking Charles to drive her home and stay for Christmas. But that meant the roads would have to stay open and the last thing the good doctor would want to do was spend Christmas in the company of strangers. It was far too much of an imposition and she wouldn't embarrass them both by suggesting it.

No, there was nothing else for it. She was spending Christmas at Moorland Cottage. At least she'd get a Christmas dinner.

When they arrived at the bottom of the hill, Josie realised she needed to phone her family.

'Look, I'm just going to go back to the top and phone home. Do you mind waiting?'

'No, of course not,' said Charles.

'I won't be long.'

Josie walked swiftly back up the hill until she got a signal. She would have loved to have spoken to her brothers and her dad, but they were all working today, and she didn't want to disturb them; the price they paid for having Christmas Day off. So she phoned her mum.

'Hi, Mum, bad news I'm afraid. The mechanic can't fix the car until after Christmas. The roads are closed and it's snowing again, so I'm stuck here.'

'Oh, darling, I'm so sorry. Well, never mind, at least you've got a nice place to stay and the doctor sounds like a good sort.'

'He is.' Josie wiped away a tear that had escaped, despite her determination not to cry. 'We've been sledging and we're having duck for Christmas dinner, so you don't need to worry about me, I'm fine, and I'll be back as soon as I can.'

'Okay, my love. I'll give your love to the rest of the gang. We'll be thinking of you tomorrow and will raise a glass to you and Mr Atkins.'

'Thanks, Mum, we'll do the same to you lot. I love you, Mum.'

'Love you too, Josie. Take care.'

When the call had ended Josie closed her eyes and concentrated on the snowflakes that fell onto her face and melted, blending in with her tears. She loved her family so much and had been looking forward to Christmas Day for months.

Okay. What would Gran say? She heard her gran's voice as if she was standing next to her. *It could be worse. You're staying in a lovely cottage with a sexy doctor and having duck for dinner. Stop complaining. You could be dead in a ditch.*

Josie laughed out loud. So Gran thinks he's sexy. Josie thought of Charles's arm holding her on the sledge and the way his eyes crinkled at the corners when he smiled, which wasn't often enough. He had lovely eyes, clear blue and expressive.

Josie studied Charles as he stood patiently waiting at the bottom of the hill, the sledge at his feet. The sledge he hadn't wanted to go on but did for her sake. He was cooking for her and Josie was sure he'd let her win that last Scrabble game.

Gran was right. It was about time she started being grateful and making the most of the situation rather than wishing for something she couldn't have.

Josie started running down the hill and Charles watched her in amazement. She nearly collided with him but managed to stop herself. Would he have caught her in his arms if she hadn't?

'Did you phone your family?'

'Yes and told them the bad news. But then I realised how much I've got to be thankful for. Because of you.'

Charles nodded slowly. 'Like I keep telling you, you don't have to thank me.'

'Yes, I do. I don't know what I would have done without you.'

'Well, it's nice to have some company.' Charles was looking uncomfortable and, to spare his blushes, Josie decided it was time they got Christmas started.

'Come on, Charles, let's get home and put the tree up.'

Chapter Seven

Charles was deep in thought, mainly about Josie. She had said "let's get home…" Was that something he should be pleased or worried about? It wasn't her home, nor his. It belonged to his brother. But it wasn't Andrew's home either. It was a rented cottage, bought with the express purpose of making his brother more money than he already had.

It was, however, their home until Josie's car was back on the road. And therefore, the two of them, together, should do as Josie suggested and make the most of the situation.

Josie was an extrovert, and he was the complete opposite. Normally, he would have been horrified at the idea of spending Christmas Day with a woman he had only known for two days. Especially when she was stopping him from getting off his head. Strangely enough, the desire to render himself semiconscious wasn't as strong as it had been before he met Josie. She had done the impossible and cheered him up.

Josie had put her small tree on the bookcase, and she was busily festooning it with tinsel and a few small baubles that were all that the supermarket sold. She had managed to find a star for the top and Charles reluctantly thought it looked quite good.

The radio was broadcasting the Nine Lessons and Carols from King's College Chapel and Josie was singing along to the carols. Some were the old favourites and a few Charles had never heard before.

The fire was blazing merrily, and the snow was falling gently, obliterating their footprints, and smoothing the world into a pristine white carpet. It was peaceful and Charles pondered the thought that he had never had a traditional Christmas. Even as a child, Christmas had been spent overseas; in hotels, on cruise ships or at the large houses of family friends where Charles had sought a quiet corner to escape from the forced jollity.

Clarissa had also spurned Christmas spent at home and instead had opted for flying off to the sun. In the early days of their marriage, she spent Christmas alone or with friends as Charles, as a young doctor, was always on call. When he became a consultant, and Megan became a pre-teen, Clarissa had still opted to go abroad.

Tomorrow would be a first for Charles. A traditional Christmas dinner, carols, a tree... he wasn't sure how he felt about it, but Josie seemed to be happy and he would make it his mission to give her as close to a normal Christmas as he could.

Charles wandered into the living room and sat down on a couch to watch Josie finish decorating her tree.

'What d'you think?' She stood back and Charles smiled as he looked the tree up and down.

'I think it's splendid. You've done a great job considering you didn't have much to work with. Well done.'

Charles hoped Josie didn't think he was patronising her as that wasn't his intention.

'That's a compliment coming from a man who hates Christmas.'

'I don't hate Christmas, Josie, I just hate the fact that my wife has left me, and my daughter is being spoiled rotten by another man.'

Josie sat next to him and took his hand in hers. 'I'm sorry, Charles. I'm sure she'll never love this other guy as much as she loves you. You're her father and nobody could take your place.'

Charles wished he could be as optimistic as Josie was. Perhaps she was right, and he was worrying over nothing. He gave her hand a squeeze and then let go.

'Right, how about a movie night? There'll be plenty of Christmas movies on TV,' Josie said brightly.

'As long as it isn't that black and white one with a man running through the streets wishing everyone Merry Christmas,' said Charles, 'I can't stand that film.'

'Right. Okay,' said Josie miming striking something off a list. 'Not *It's a Wonderful Life* then. I'm guessing you wouldn't want *The Wizard of Oz*?'

'If I had a pound for every time I've seen that film with Megan, I'd be a rich man. She loved it.'

Josie had switched on the TV and was surfing the channels. 'Oh look… my favourite film of all time, *Love Actually*.'

Charles fought to stop himself from groaning out loud. 'Okay, we'll watch that.'

'Do you like this movie?'

'I've never seen it.'

'Oh, you'll love it.'

Charles doubted he'd love it, but he was prepared to watch it for Josie's sake. He had perfected the art of pretending to watch something while dozing or thinking of something else entirely, while he had kept Megan company as she devoured endless children's TV. He'd been bored stiff at the time, but now he'd give anything to get those days back. A time when his little family was happy and living under the same roof.

'Charles?'

'Sorry? What did you say?' Josie had obviously been asking him something, but he hadn't heard a word she'd said.

'I asked if we should crack open the Prosecco.'

'Good idea, I'll do it.'

He poured them both a large glass and returned to sit next to Josie on the couch.

The film wasn't as bad as he'd thought it was going to be. In fact, it was quite funny in parts. Josie giggled all the way through it and, when it had ended, Charles realised they had drunk a whole bottle of wine between them. Charles was feeling depressingly sober, but Josie had flushed cheeks and she was slurring her words slightly. She was also sitting too close to him.

Charles didn't think he'd ever spent as much time alone with a woman he hardly knew. It was a strange situation, and her closeness was stirring feelings in him he'd rather not have. Josie was sweet and pretty, a mature woman in a lot of ways: capable, sensible, and caring. But in other ways she was like a little girl, giggling at silly things and happy dancing when she got her own way.

He had to admit, though, that she was good for him. She'd stopped him getting drunk which, although irritating, would turn out to be a good thing when he looked back on it.

He wondered what it would be like to kiss her. He

shouldn't be thinking about that. She was his guest, and he had a responsibility to look after her.

'I think it's time for bed,' he said.

'Are you propositioning me, Charles?' said Josie leaning towards him.

He backed away from her and stood up.

'No, of course, I'm not. How can you think such a thing?'

'I'm joking, don't get your knickers in a twist.' Josie stood up too and frowned at him. 'You know what your problem is? You have no sense of humour.'

'Well, thank you for putting me straight on that score. I'm going to bed now. Goodnight, Josie.'

Charles ran up the stairs and sat on his bed listening for Josie's footsteps. There was only silence. He went to the bathroom to clean his teeth and could hear that the television was still on. He climbed into bed and shut his eyes, but sleep was a long way off.

He realised now that Josie had only been teasing him, but his reaction worried him. He wanted to take her to bed. She was getting under his skin in an inconvenient way. What would have happened if he'd taken her in his arms and kissed her? The inevitable, that's what. Would that be so bad? Two people comforting each other wasn't wrong, was it? The sooner Josie could get her car fixed and be on her way, the better.

Josie woke the next morning with a headache. It took her a while to come round and shake off the deep sleep she'd been in. She got out of bed and padded to the window to look at the snow. It must have been falling all night as it was thick and unblemished, the path to the shed nearly obliterated. Tiny footprints of birds searching for food patterned the ground.

The blue sky was cloudless, however, and the light was clean and pure. It was a gorgeous day. Christmas Day. 'Happy Christmas, everyone,' she whispered, wishing her words could reach her family who would all be together at her parents'. Their house would certainly not be silent that was for sure. The kids would be giddy with excitement, the adults relaxed and happy in each other's company.

Josie sighed and got dressed slowly. A painful memory of her behaviour the night before stabbed her brain. *Did I really say that? What will he think of me?* She would be on her best behaviour today and help Charles with the cooking. She wouldn't hog the TV and they would do what he wanted to do.

The aroma of food greeted her as she ran down the stairs to the kitchen. Carols were playing on the radio.

'Happy Christmas, Charles. That smells good.' Josie wanted to hug him or kiss him on the cheek. The O'Connors always gave each other Christmas hugs. The kids loved them and had a competition to see who could keep the hug going the longest.

'Happy Christmas, Josie. We're having a full English. Is that okay?'

'Fabulous, can I do anything to help? You must let me help with the dinner as well, you can't do it all yourself.'

'I'm sure I could find you a few jobs, like peeling the veg.'

'Fantastic,' Josie said as genuinely as she could. She hated peeling veg.

'There's a fresh pot of tea on the table.'

'Great.' She poured them a mug each. 'Charles, I need

to say something. I'm really sorry I embarrassed you last night. I blame it on the Prosecco.'

'Ah, so it's my fault then, as I gave you the Prosecco.'

'No, I didn't mean—'

'Ha, ha got you. I was only joking.'

'Very funny. You don't have any paracetamol, do you?' Josie's headache was getting worse and trying to be cheerful wasn't helping. She wanted to go back to bed. After she'd eaten, of course.

'Hangover?'

'Yes.'

Charles opened a drawer in the kitchen dresser and tossed the packet of paracetamol to Josie who caught it deftly.

She took two with a swallow of tea that was too hot and burned her mouth.

'I'm aiming dinner ready for about two. Breakfast will keep us going until then. Is that okay with you?'

'That's fine.'

He put two plates laden with food on the table and sat down opposite Josie.

'I hope you're hungry.'

'I'm famished.' Josie tucked into the eggs, sausages, tomatoes, mushrooms, and fried bread. It was delicious. Charles was a great cook and it augured well for the roast duck. 'This is amazing. Thanks.'

'You're welcome. So… how do the O'Connor family celebrate on Christmas Day?'

'My father and mother go to church. I sometimes go with them to avoid having to do any cooking. We open presents, then eat Christmas dinner. Afterwards, after a quick rest, we go for a walk with the dogs. Just a normal family Christmas really but it's special because it's one of the few times that we get to be together.'

'Are your parents religious?'

'No, not especially, but with my father being a local GP, he likes to show his face at Christmas and Easter. The patients kind of expect it.'

'Tell me more about Leytonsfield.'

'It's a small market town. I've lived there all my life and it's home. The people are nice and there's a lot of things going on.'

'What about the hospital?'

'I don't know much about its history, but it used to be the workhouse. It's been rebuilt a few times.'

'Do you like working there?'

'I love it. Both my mother and gran were midwives and it's all I've ever wanted to do. The maternity unit is my second home.'

Charles finished his meal ahead of Josie and put a small parcel wrapped in Christmas paper on the table next to her. 'Happy Christmas, Josie. It's not much but I wanted to give you something.'

'Thanks, Charles. Yours is under the tree. I'll just get it.'

Josie gave Charles the driving gloves. He had given her a beautiful silk scarf in pastel shades.

'That's gorgeous, Charles, I love it.' She put the scarf around her neck and watched as Charles tried on the gloves. 'Do they fit?'

'Perfectly. Thanks, Josie, that's kind of you.'

After loading the dishwasher, Josie set to peeling the carrots and potatoes. She wondered what else Charles would ask her to help with, as she was still feeling hungover and needed to sit down.

'Do you like Baileys, Josie? I bought some for us to have before dinner.'

Great. Hair of the dog. Just what she needed. 'Yes, please. Good idea.'

He poured them a small glass each and handed one to Josie. 'Cheers,' he said as they clinked their liqueur glasses together.

'Cheers, Charles,' Josie replied and drank half in one go.

'You're supposed to sip it,' said Charles laughing.

'Are you?' Josie asked in mock innocence, 'I never knew that.'

They laughed and Josie felt her hangover dissipating. Perhaps Christmas Day in Charles's company wouldn't be so bad after all.

Chapter Eight

The meal went well, and Charles was pleased to see that Josie ate everything on her plate. The duck was cooked to perfection, with mouth-watering crispy skin, and the accompaniments of mashed potato with caramelised onion, carrots and roasted chestnuts cooked in butter and rosemary took the meal to the next level.

Charles had bought a bottle of champagne to drink with the meal. There wasn't much of a choice in the supermarket, but it made Josie's eyes sparkle and didn't taste too bad. Charles had drunk a lot worse and they managed to finish most of the bottle between them.

'Oh my goodness, that was gorgeous,' said Josie sitting back with her hands on her stomach.

'I'm glad you enjoyed it. Would you like dessert? I've got a small Christmas pudding with brandy sauce if you fancy it.'

'That sounds great, Charles, but… could we have it later? I'm stuffed.'

'Of course.'

He got up and started to clear the table.

'I'll wash up, seeing as you did all the cooking,' Josie said looking as if she never wanted to move again.

'I'm just loading the dishwasher, you sit tight.'

'Tight's the word. It's a wonder the button on my jeans hasn't popped.'

'All the more reason to sit still for a while or you'll get indigestion.'

'Yes, doctor,' said Josie.

When all the pots and pans had been put in the dishwasher, they moved into the living room with the last of the champagne.

They watched another movie—a tearjerker about a child trying to get his separated parents back together again. Charles felt it was too close to home and Josie wiped away tears at the end when they were all reunited.

'That's pure escapism,' said Charles, 'it doesn't happen in real life.'

'It must happen sometimes. I bet your daughter would like you and your wife to get back together.'

'I'm not so sure. Her stepfather spoils her rotten and gives her everything she asks for. She's becoming materialistic, just like her mother.'

'But you're her father. Surely she loves you more than him.'

Charles sighed. 'It's not as straightforward as all that. Megan has always been closer to her mother as she saw more of her. I worked long hours and didn't spend enough time with her.'

'Didn't Clarissa work?'

'Before we married she worked as a sales rep for a drug company. We met when the company was hosting a conference. It was wonderful in the beginning. She seemed to understand the life of a junior doctor and never complained if I was too tired to go out or had to work a double shift unexpectedly. But when Megan was born things changed.'

'How?' Josie was listening avidly, so Charles offloaded. It wasn't often he found someone who listened as well as Josie did.

'Clarissa has never been a natural mother. Megan wasn't planned and Clarissa found it hard to switch from a professional woman to a stay at home mum. She was desperate to get back to work and Megan was looked after by a nanny until she went to school. I would have liked more children, but Clarissa said no. She worked part-time so she could take Megan to school and pick her up in the afternoon.'

'Did that arrangement work?' Josie tucked her legs under her and watched his face as he spoke.

'It worked up to a point. Clarissa started working longer hours, so Megan attended an after-school club. I tried to give Megan as much of my time as I could, but... well, you know what it's like.'

'Yes. It's hard. Trying to get a good work/life balance is difficult, but I think much harder for people in the caring professions. You can't just down tools at five o'clock.'

'Exactly. Clarissa got fed up with me phoning and telling her I wouldn't be home at my scheduled time. But I'm a doctor, it's not something you can switch off at the end of the day.'

'Wow, we are getting serious,' Josie said. 'How about a coffee and mince pies?'

'Sounds good, but what would be even better is a liqueur coffee and mince pies.'

Josie grinned. 'Now you're talking.'

As they made their way into the kitchen, Charles

realised it had got dark. And it hadn't snowed at all. Maybe Josie would be able to get home the following day if the roads were open and the gritters had done their job.

They returned to the living room and feasted on store-bought Christmas cake, mince pies and liqueur coffees made with whisky. Charles hadn't yet had the chance to open his whisky, so put generous amounts in their glasses.

'Whoa, this is strong. Nice though,' Josie said.

So nice, that they had another, and then decided to forgo the coffee and just drink the whisky. Charles knew they were mixing their drinks, but it was Christmas Day. Tomorrow they would be back to their normal sensible selves.

———

Despite missing her family, Josie was having a good time. Charles was a marvellous cook; the duck had been delicious, and she had eaten more than she usually did. And now they were sitting on the couch in a lovely warm cottage, sipping whisky and talking. Charles had opened up about his family and Josie appreciated his honesty. For a private man like him, he must trust her to be able to tell her things close to his heart. The drink helped of course.

The curtains were still open, and the only light inside came from a small lamp on top of the bookcase and the flames from the wood fire in the cast iron stove. Strange shadows danced across the walls and the only sound was the crackle of the fire.

Charles had turned the television off, and they sat in silence, cocooned in warmth and sleepy from all the food and drink. Especially the drink. Josie didn't normally drink whisky but was enjoying the one she was sharing with Charles. Must be a good make, she thought dreamily.

Christmas Day was nearly over and tomorrow she would probably be on her way home. Josie thought of what her family would be doing at this time and wished she could ring them, but that would mean walking to the top of a steep hill in the dark and she was too comfortable where she was.

Charles was quiet and she wondered if he had fallen asleep, but when she turned her head to look at him, he was watching her.

'Penny for them?' asked Josie, looking away.

'Not worth that much,' answered Charles.

'Go on, what were you thinking about?'

'I was just thinking how enjoyable today has been. Thanks to you.'

'I've enjoyed today too, Charles. You really are a wonderful cook, that meal was amazing.'

'As good as your mum's?'

'Don't tell her I said so, but… yes.'

'When I was quite young, I used to help my gran with her baking. She was a ninja in the kitchen, she made the best pastry I've ever had. She taught me to cook and for a short time I was intent on becoming a chef.'

'Wow, a bit different to being an obstetrician. What changed your mind?'

'My father. He said cooking wasn't a profession and I should follow in the family's footsteps and be a doctor.'

'Was he very assertive, your father?'

'He was, but it wasn't just that. Andrew was the favoured son. Five years older than me, he never put a foot wrong as far as our parents were concerned. He had always wanted to be a doctor and everything he did was to that end. I tried hard my whole life to please my father and I suppose becoming a doctor was partly as a result of that.'

'Was he pleased?'

Charles shrugged and shook his head slowly. 'No, not really. He was pleased I'd done what he wanted, but I never became a world-renowned Harley Street specialist like Andrew. I'm just a common or garden obstetrician. One of many.'

Josie felt a rush of sympathy for him. She couldn't imagine having parents who favoured a sibling. All four of the O'Connors were treated equally and loved unconditionally. She had never felt pressure to be a midwife; it was simply something she had always wanted to be.

Josie took Charles's hand and this time he left it captured between hers. She sat like that for a while, intending to get up and make some tea. She realised that Charles was watching her again and this time she didn't break eye contact.

Josie put what happened next down to the drink, the ambience and having spent so much time in close proximity with Charles. A heady combination of factors that drew them together, slowly, and surely, until their lips met.

At first she was startled but then, as the kiss deepened, her arms snaked around his neck and his hands pulled her closer. She was conscious of his body pressed against hers, hard, male, and strong. It wasn't a wild passionate lust-fuelled kiss, more of an in-the-moment one, that either of them could have stopped at any time. Neither of them did.

Josie didn't resist as Charles's hand slid under her blouse and squeezed her breast gently. She didn't resist as he undid the buttons on her blouse and then caressed her stomach.

'Do you want me to stop?' Charles whispered against her skin.

'No.' Josie didn't want him to stop, she wanted to make love, it seemed the natural end to a perfect day. She didn't want them to just go their separate ways after sharing Christmas. The day hadn't felt like real life. It was a day out of time, surreal almost. They would never see each other again and all the usual conventions didn't apply at that moment. And Josie had drunk more than she usually did. She was aware of a feeling of mellowness that made her want to throw the rule book out of the window.

'Shall we go upstairs?' Charles's voice was husky letting Josie know that he was turned on.

'Yes, let's.'

Charles took Josie's hand and led her up the stairs to his bedroom. It was colder upstairs, and the curtains were open, bathing the room in pale moonlight, but still warm enough for Josie to undress slowly. Charles stood and watched her, so she slowed her movements down even more, teasing him as she stripped. Charles's expression was unreadable, but his gaze never left her as she put on a show just for him.

'You're beautiful,' he whispered as he watched her every move.

'Thanks. Now it's your turn.' She unbuttoned his shirt and ran her hands over his chest. He had a small amount of wiry hair around his nipples and his pecs. Josie ran her fingers through it then stroked his stomach as he had done to her. Charles closed his eyes and groaned. Josie loved finding out where a man's erogenous zones were.

Keen to continue the search, she undid the belt of his trousers and slowly pulled the zip down. He was hard and ready, which turned Josie on even more. Charles impatiently removed the rest of his clothes.

They stood, gazing at each other, drinking in the details

of their naked bodies. Charles's stomach was flat, and his body was toned. He was fit and Josie drank him in, her breath catching when her gaze went lower and she realised he was even more turned on than she had thought.

She put her arms around his neck and kissed him. This kiss was more passionate, and Josie felt herself being drawn into a state of heightened sexual awareness. Her nipples were erect, and she was wet. She wanted him now with a sense of urgency and she kissed him deeply. Charles returned the kiss and walked her slowly backwards until her legs hit the bed. They tumbled on to it still kissing. Josie clung to Charles as he kissed her face, her eyelids, nose and cheeks, before returning to her mouth.

There was a sense of urgency now as their mouths were locked together. Charles rolled her onto her back and started to move down her body, stroking and kissing. Her breasts were especially sensitive, and she loved the rush of lust that moved through her body as he sucked on one of her nipples. She moaned and writhed under him which prompted him to change to the other nipple and she cried out with the feeling of his mouth, sucking her breast.

Inappropriately, she wondered if breastfeeding gave women the same feeling. Not the right time or place to be wondering something like that. Then Charles brought her back to the present by moving further down her body, still exploring the touches that made her react. By the time he'd kissed and licked his way to the place that was demanding his attention, she was on the verge of begging him to take her like a heroine in a romantic novel. But Charles had other ideas and his exploration continued in her most secret and feminine place. She was so turned on by now that it didn't take long for her to orgasm and she cried out with the force of her climax.

Josie hadn't had sex for a long time and her orgasm lasted longer than usual. Charles was the perfect gentleman and held her until she came back down to earth. Then he swiftly entered her and thrust into her carefully.

'Is this okay?' he murmured.

'Wonderful,' she gasped. It was more than okay. Charles was a good lover, holding himself back until she orgasmed again and thinking of her needs before his own. She put her legs around his waist to bring him in deeper. He responded by thrusting harder and it wasn't long before they both came, crying out their release and lying together, wrapped in each other's arms until their breathing returned to normal and the air became chill.

Charles pulled the duvet over them both and then sighed deeply.

'Wow. That was incredible.' Charles still had his eyes shut and Josie cuddled up to him.

'It was,' Josie agreed.

They lay together, drifting slowly and peacefully into sleep.

When she woke they were both in the same position. But the room was colder now, and the moon was obscured by cloud. She lay still, gazing at the sky and thinking about the sex she had just had.

Josie didn't normally sleep with men until she had known them a while and got to trust them. With Charles, she felt she had known him longer than two days and instinctively knew she could trust him. He had been so kind and supportive, letting her stay in the cottage, cooking delicious food and listening to her talking about herself. He had also shared knowledge about himself with her. She felt they had a connection and was a bit sad that they would never see each other again once the snow thawed.

Charles was sleeping deeply, and she studied his face. He was a good looking man, older than the men she was usually attracted to. She'd never been out with a man who had children, let alone a teenage daughter. In the normal course of events, she wouldn't have looked twice at him, and it would probably be the same for him. This made the situation more unreal, as far from ordinary life as she could get. But she knew she wouldn't forget this Christmas. She had wanted this year to be special and thought she'd be spending it with her family, especially Jay and his new wife, Caitlin. Instead, she had spent it with a stranger and ended up in his bed.

Life has a habit of surprising you. Josie heard her gran's voice again. Words of wisdom from beyond the grave. Thanks, Gran.

Josie yawned and closed her eyes. Dawn was hours away yet and she was warm, relaxed, and lying next to a sexy man. What better way to end Christmas Day?

Chapter Nine

Charles was up early the following day. The temperature had risen, and the snow was starting to thaw. Icicles hanging from the roof of the shed were melting, the water dripping slowly onto the ground.

Charles lit the wood fire, then started preparations for breakfast. He had slept surprisingly well and felt refreshed and content. Having survived Christmas unscathed, with the help of a certain dark-haired midwife with a gorgeous smile and expressive hazel eyes, who he had left sleeping in his bed, he was feeling rather pleased with himself.

Their lovemaking had been passionate and sweet, made more precious as it had been unexpected. It came out of a pleasant day spent in each other's company, good food, the warmth of the fire and too much alcohol. Charles didn't regret it at all but wasn't sure how Josie would feel. Hopefully, she would take it the same way. Neither of them was in the market for a relationship. He was older than Josie and came with considerable baggage. The last thing he wanted was to get involved with someone. He needed to get his life together and concentrate on building a good relationship with his daughter. They were his priorities.

Charles wiped the mushrooms and put the sausages under the grill. He had a decision to make about his future. Staying in London was not an option. Everyone knew that Clarissa had left him, and he felt a complete failure as a husband and a man. He needed a fresh start somewhere different, so he'd looked further north. After having several interviews in prominent hospitals in Cheshire and Yorkshire, avoiding the major cities, he had narrowed the shortlist down to two hospitals. One was near Leeds and one in Cheshire. Leytonsfield Hospital to be exact. Once he had discovered that Josie worked at Leytonsfield Hospital, he had thought more carefully about accepting that job. Would it be a good or bad idea to work with a woman he had slept with? He couldn't let that be his criteria for choosing where to work.

Charles was just scrambling the eggs when Josie came into the kitchen.

'Good morning,' he said cheerily.

'Morning,' she answered. She sounded upbeat and Charles wondered if it was because she'd be heading home today. It could be because of their lovemaking and Charles hoped that was part of it.

'How are you this morning?'

'Fine. You?'

'I'm fine but you look a bit pale.' Then he remembered the amount they had drunk the previous day. 'Do you have a hangover?'

'I do. If you've got any more of those paracetamols, I wouldn't mind a couple.'

'Of course.' Charles put the plates on the table and the box of paracetamol with a glass of water.

'I had a text from the mechanic earlier, he's bringing the Mini round later this morning. The Woodhead Pass is still closed but the motorway is open.'

'Good. I'll be off soon then. Out of your hair.'

'You're not in the way, Josie, I've got a lot to thank you for. If it wasn't for you, I'd probably be in a drunken stupor by now. You've saved me from myself and I'm grateful.'

'Well, if it wasn't for you, I'd be dead in a ditch, so we're even.'

Josie was eating her breakfast slowly, but with little enthusiasm. When he had finished his breakfast, Charles studied her.

'Are you okay? You seem a bit under the weather.'

'I think I'm just a bit tired that's all. Christmas is more or less over now, and I go back to work tomorrow.'

'I'm sorry about the way things have worked out for you, but you should be proud that you helped a woman give birth safely and you've kept me company for which I'm grateful.'

'I know. It's been a good Christmas thanks to you.'

'It's not because of last night, is it? Do you regret it because I don't?'

Josie looked at him then and her beautiful eyes were tearing up. 'I don't regret it, but… I don't usually have one-night stands. I don't want you to think I'm…'

Charles leaned over the table and took one of her hands to bring it to his lips, kissing it before letting her hand go.

'I don't think you're anything but a kind, lovely woman who I have had the pleasure of spending Christmas with. It was nice, making love. I slept like a log.'

Charles smiled and Josie smiled back. He realised with a jolt that he was going to miss her. Her singing, her smile, the way her hair smelt of lemon shampoo.

'I'd better put my belongings together in case the mechanic shows up. It was good of him to work on Boxing Day.'

'I get the impression he was glad of an excuse to get out of the house.'

'Oh dear, poor man.'

'Do you want anything more to eat?'

Josie shook her head. 'No thanks.'

Once Charles stacked the dishwasher, he pulled on his boots and shovelled the snow from the path to the shed. Hopefully, there'd be no more snow until after the New Year when he'd be gone from the cottage. He cleared the snow on the path down to the road as well. Physical work was cathartic, and he certainly needed something to take his mind off Josie.

She'd be gone soon, and he'd be alone again. That shouldn't bother him, he liked being alone. Except that, now the moment was upon them for parting, Charles didn't want her to go. They'd fallen into a routine over the last couple of days. Charles wouldn't have believed he could have lived with a complete stranger and felt so comfortable with them, but he had with Josie. They'd talked about personal things and spent the night together, the ultimate intimacy. He wanted them to part on good terms at least, before they went their separate ways and got on with their lives.

When he'd finished clearing the paths, Charles left the shovels in the kitchen and removed his boots. He wandered into the living room where Josie was sitting staring into space. She turned her head as he came into the room.

'So, what are you going to do with yourself, Charles, once I've gone? I do hope you're not going to hit the whisky.' She had a twinkle in her eye but sounded serious. Was she still worried about him doing something stupid?

'I can promise you that I have no thoughts of getting drunk at all. You've made me realise what a stupid idea that was.'

'I'm glad to hear that. Okay, I know I drank too much and paid the price with a hangover or two but getting drunk to drown your sorrows never works. The problem is still there, and you feel as sick as a dog. Not a good idea.'

'You're quite right. But to answer your question, I might wander down to the George and Dragon for a pint and a pie later and chat to the locals. See what kind of a Christmas they've had. It would be nice to meet them in case I ever come back here. It's a good place to escape to for a summer break.'

'Great idea.' Josie looked thoughtful for a moment and Charles hoped that she'd come with him and go home later, but she obviously wanted to get home to her family.

Just then, the doorbell rang, which made them both jump as they hadn't heard it ring before. They both started laughing.

'That'll be the mechanic. Time to leave,' said Josie.

'Right. Well. Goodbye, then, Josie, and thanks.'

'Goodbye, Charles, and thanks to you too.'

They hugged a little awkwardly and Charles kissed her on the lips.

After settling up the bill and chatting to the mechanic about the weather and road conditions, Josie got into her Mini and started the engine. Charles watched as she drove away. She looked back once and waved. Then she was gone.

Despite looking forward to the moment when he was

alone again and free to get drunk, now that it was here, Charles found the silence oppressive and the cottage full of memories of Josie and her laughter. He missed her singing. He put the radio on, then turned it off again.

He wasn't ready yet to return to the reclusive introvert he had been before he met Josie. He craved company and didn't want to be on his own, so pulled his boots on again and locked the cottage. A brisk walk to the village, a meal and a drink in the George and Dragon, and people to talk to, that was what he needed.

Tomorrow would be different. He'd be back to his normal self tomorrow.

Josie headed for the slip road onto the motorway as the Woodhead Pass was still closed, according to the mechanic. The bill for the car was sky high, but then the man had worked over the festive season to get it finished for her, so she shouldn't really complain.

In fact, she should be happy that she was on her way home at last and joyous that she could spend the rest of Boxing Day with her family.

So why were tears rolling down her cheeks? Why did she feel hollow inside? She knew why. Because sex to Josie was special. She didn't do one-night stands, love 'em and leave 'em or friends with benefits, never had sex on a first date— or even a second or third come to that. Sex was something reserved for that special person. However, she wasn't a virgin and had known what it meant to be infatuated with someone, was no stranger to heartache and had been dumped by men she thought she had a special relationship with. She wasn't stupid and knew the score where men were concerned. But she had her standards and stuck to them. Usually.

Josie turned onto the motorway and kept in the slow lane at a steady speed, ignoring the lorries and bigger cars that thundered past her. She wanted to get home in one piece.

Josie had let herself down. Charles had given her every opportunity to stop. He would have been a gentleman about it, and they could have watched another movie. Josie had the feeling that Charles wouldn't have been bothered. He was a lovely man who she had spent two pleasant days with. She'd never see him again and under no circumstances would she Google him to see what she could find out about him. Definitely not. She'd forget him now and try to erase the memory of the night they had spent together. It had been wonderful to be made love to by a strong, sexy, caring man and she would cherish the memory. It was what she had needed, to be loved physically, even for just a few hours. But she was certain that Charles had already forgotten about it.

Josie put the radio on, pleased to see it worked as well as before and it was still on her favourite station. She turned it up and sang along to the familiar tunes.

As she got nearer to home, she started to relax. The motorway was clear of snow and the only white she could see was on the tops of the hills. Back to normal. Early shift tomorrow. A party at Casey and Lexi's place on New Year's Eve with the whole family and a few friends. It wouldn't be long before the last couple of days were just a fading memory.

Josie drove on, but every now and again, she heard

Charles's voice, or his laugh. A scene from the past two days would sneak into her thoughts as if she was watching a film. The toboggan, the meal in the pub, the Christmas dinner that was one of the best she'd ever had, shovelling snow together. It had been a good Christmas and, as she drove, Josie smiled.

Chapter Ten

'Hello, darling, at last. Come here and let me hug you.'

Josie was enfolded in her mother's embrace and never wanted to leave that warm and love-filled place. The sound of her twin's voice as he waited his turn to greet her, made her turn from her mother and grab Jay, hugging him to her as if she feared she would never see him again.

'Hey, Josie,' he whispered so only she could hear. 'Sorry, you couldn't come to the wedding.'

Josie had rehearsed in her mind how their meeting would be and all the things she'd say to him about her hurt feelings and how she would never get married without inviting him. But now, holding him tightly, his familiar scent enveloping her, all she could think about was how much she loved him.

'I'll let you off this time, but please don't do it again,' she whispered back.

'No chance of that.'

'Is that our girl?' her father asked as he wandered into the kitchen with Casey and Lexi following him.

'Hi, Dad, Happy Christmas.' Josie fell into his arms and promptly burst into tears. She never cried, keeping herself in check and holding it together; a lesson she'd learned from looking after pregnant women who were ill, or their babies were, or—the worst-case scenario—the baby hadn't survived. A midwife blubbing all over the place was no good to anyone. She had to be the strong one until the crisis was over. Alone she was then able to give vent to her grief.

Over the last three days, however, she'd been like a sprinkler.

'There, there, darling, it's okay. You're home now,' said her father patting her gently on the back.

Josie loved how her father reverted to the one he had been when they were tiny. It didn't matter that she was a professional woman who was responsible for people's welfare and hadn't lived at home since she was eighteen, she was his little girl and always would be.

'Sorry, I'm being silly. I just wanted to be with you this Christmas so much.'

'Well, you're here now and we're still celebrating,' said her mother. 'We've got all your presents under the tree still, despite Jade wanting to open them for you.'

Josie laughed and hugged Casey and Lexi.

'Of course, we've eaten all the food, so you'll have to make do with beans on toast,' said Casey.

'No problem,' said Josie, 'I've hardly stopped eating since Christmas Eve.'

'Was he a good cook, this doctor?' her mother asked.

'Actually, he was… not as good as you, Mum, but he did all the cooking.'

'Well, that's a relief,' said Casey. 'At least one of you could cook.'

'Where are the kids?' Josie asked as Jay stood with his

arm draped across her shoulders. Josie knew he'd be wanting to get her alone so he could talk to her twin to twin.

'Zoe and Caitlin have taken the kids and dogs for a walk. Riordan's on call today.'

'That's why the house is so quiet,' said her father. 'Come and tell me all about this man you spent Christmas with.' He steered her into the living room leaving the others to help Eloise make tea.

After her mother filled the large, brown teapot that had been in the family for years and poured everyone who wanted one a mug of tea, the rest of them moved as one into the living room and sprawled out on couches and comfy armchairs. Her father had his favourite chair and everyone else fitted in, squashed up together on the sofas.

Josie spent a pleasant half hour explaining how she'd helped a woman give birth in her car and Charles just happened to drive by and stopped to help. She played down being stuck in a snowdrift and how she'd escaped an icy death but told the story in a humorous way that had them all laughing at the antics on the toboggan and eating an enormous meal in the George and Dragon.

'Doesn't sound as if you had a bad Christmas to me,' said Casey. 'Someone to cook for you, village pubs and open fires, getting drunk and watching TV together.'

'It wasn't a bad Christmas,' said Josie, 'in fact there were moments that I'll never forget, and I'll always be grateful to Charles, but the truth is I wanted to be here, with you lot, my family, the people I love.' Josie stopped as she was in danger of tearing up again.

'And we all missed you, darling, so much,' said Eloise.

'Yes, we did. Jade kept asking when Auntie Josie was coming home,' said Lexi.

'But the main thing is that you were safe and looked

after and you're home now,' said her father, always the pragmatist.

Then all conversation was forgotten as Caitlin, Zoe and the kids and dogs came home. Jade and Tom raced each other into the living room to see Josie first. Tom hung back and let Jade win. She threw herself into Josie's arms and kissed her.

'Auntie Josie, I love you and I missed you,' said the little girl. Josie hugged her, breathing in the smell of vanilla and the outdoors.

'And I missed you too, my gorgeous niece,' said Josie fighting to keep a smile on her face and her eyes dry.

'Your presents are under the tree,' said Tom, giving Josie a quick kiss on the cheek. He was growing up and becoming more mature and self-conscious every day.

'Right. Who's going to help me open them?'

'Me!' shouted Jade.

After Josie had wished Zoe and Caitlin Merry Christmas, she and Jade carefully opened all her presents. There was a good selection of smellies, including her favourite hand cream which she used a lot of in her job, perfume, jewellery, chocolates and a scented candle. The family had made a pact several years back that the adults would buy each other token gifts and spend most of their Christmas budget on the children.

Jay and Caitlin were sitting together holding hands. They were tanned and looked totally loved-up. Josie allowed herself a second to feel jealous then quickly brushed it aside. Her turn would come, she had to be patient.

Casey was cuddling Lucy and Zoe had taken Abigail upstairs for a nap as the toddler could hardly keep her eyes open.

The family dispersed after a while. Tom and Casey

played computer games, Eloise went into the kitchen to prepare the cold buffet that was a Boxing Day tradition, and Zoe helped Eloise.

Josie was back in the warm embrace of her family. She wished she could entice Jay away from Caitlin so they could talk properly. Twin talk was done in private. They had always hidden away from the rest of the family when they had serious things to discuss. But Jay looked as if he was glued to Caitlin's side and wasn't going to move any time soon.

They all had someone. Even Tom had a girlfriend although he blushed and turned away if anyone mentioned it.

Josie was the only one without a partner. Was this it? Was she fated to live her life alone? An unmarried, childless midwife devoted to helping other women achieve the thing that she wanted so badly. Being an auntie to the kids was wonderful. But Josie wanted her own children. The thought of never knowing how it felt to be a mother was unbearable.

Josie wondered what her gran would say. She pictured the old lady and mentally asked her the question, *When will my prince come, Gran?*

Silence. Nothing. Nada. Was Gran asleep? Do people sleep in heaven?

Josie yawned and settled herself further into the couch, laying her head back and closing her eyes. Then she got a picture in her head, totally unbidden, of Charles watching her, his blue eyes burning into her soul.

Really, Gran? Mr Charles Atkins is my prince?

'Did you say something?' asked Lexi who was sitting opposite her with Lucy on her knee.

'Me? No, did I say something out loud?'

'Sounded like "Prince". I didn't know you were a fan.'

'Oh yeah,' said Josie. 'I've always loved Prince.'

'Me too.'

Josie wondered what Charles was doing. Had he managed to get falling-down drunk on his whisky, or was he cooking something delicious? Whatever he was doing, she hoped he was okay.

———

Charles returned to the cottage after an enjoyable couple of hours in the George and Dragon. He had eaten a simple meal of pie and chips and downed three pints of best bitter. He'd chatted to some of the locals, talking about the weather, the plans for a bypass to ease the traffic congestion, and how long the Woodhead Pass would stay closed.

The cottage was warm with the fire burning low and quiet when he returned. Too quiet. Charles's plans had changed; he no longer wanted to spend the festive season, or what was left of it, alone in isolation. He no longer wanted to get drunk and become a sad, pitiful loser who his daughter would be ashamed to know.

He felt as though he had been given a new lease of life and no longer felt like a victim of circumstance. Okay, so his wife had left him and was with another man. Well, good riddance. He would do everything in his power to improve the relationship with his daughter and spend more time with her. He would show her that he was just as good a father as Todd, without showering the child with material possessions to prove his love.

He packed his things and tidied and cleaned the cottage in an attempt to leave it exactly how he had found it. Then he went to bed, even though it was still early. Tomorrow he was going back to London and would phone Leytonsfield

Hospital to accept their kind offer of a post as obstetrician on the maternity unit.

He wasn't going there just because of Josie, although she had helped him to make the choice. Leytonsfield was just what he needed for a fresh start. A pleasant market town, within easy reach of all the major cities in the north-west. He'd already worked his notice in the London hospital, so he was free to start work whenever they wanted him to. From his point of view, the earlier the better. He just needed to vacate his London apartment and find somewhere to live in Leytonsfield.

Charles went to bed that night feeling more positive than he had for a long time.

Chapter Eleven

Two hours into her shift the following day, and Josie felt as if she'd never been away from the maternity unit. After the handover with the night staff, when the midwives were allocated the women they were looking after, it had been full on and Josie hadn't stopped.

There was a woman who had come in to be induced as she was past her due date and should have given birth before the festive season had begun. She had been given hormone pessaries to start the labour process and her waters had been broken, bringing the baby's head into direct contact with the cervix which, hopefully, would encourage the mother to have stronger contractions. As the woman had given birth before, Josie was hoping this would be enough to cause her labour to start without any other intervention.

There was a mother with pre-eclampsia whose blood pressure had to be checked regularly, and another had come in with contractions who was booked for an elective caesarean. Fortunately, there were also some whose labour was progressing satisfactorily. They were happy to sit on the bed and be waited on by their supportive partners. Josie was keeping her eye on those between looking after the more serious cases.

A lunch break was out of the question, so Josie nipped into the kitchen for a quick cup of tea and a handful of biscuits. When she had eaten her meagre lunch, trying not to think of roast duck and chestnuts, she hurried out again to resume her duties.

As she passed the nurses' station, she noticed a young woman who was obviously pregnant, but not about to give birth, loitering around the desk. She looked lost and was wearing baggy jeans and a sweatshirt. She wasn't carrying a handbag and didn't even have a winter coat.

'Excuse me, are you okay?' Josie approached her quietly as the poor girl looked petrified.

'No, I need help.'

'You're pregnant. How far along are you?'

'Six months.' The girl had long, lank blonde hair that looked as if it hadn't been washed in days.

'What can we do for you?' Josie feared the worst. Was this young girl losing her baby?

'I need help. Please?'

'Okay, come with me and we'll have a talk. You can tell me everything.' Josie took her into a small, private room and she sat on a chair and stared at her feet. She was wearing flip-flops and her feet were tinged with blue. Josie took a blanket and wrapped it around the girl's shoulders.

Josie said nothing, waiting for the girl to speak when she was ready. After a short time, she looked up, tears rolling down her cheeks.

'I don't have anywhere to go. I'm scared he'll find me.'

'Who is he?'

'My boyfriend. He doesn't want the baby and I do.'

'Okay. Are you living with him?'

'I was, but I've run away. He said he was going to kick me in the stomach to stop the birth.' The girl put her hands over her bump protectively.

When Josie heard that, she had to count to ten before speaking. Her anger was percolating below the surface of her calm, but she wasn't going to show her emotions to this poor, young girl. She needed strength and support now and the knowledge that she was in safe hands.

'You're being very brave, you know that don't you?' The girl shrugged and stared at the floor again. 'You've done the right thing to come here and ask for help and we will help, I promise.'

'Thanks.'

'Are you hungry? Would you like some tea and toast?'

'Yes, please.'

'Right. You stay here and I'll make a couple of phone calls after making it.'

Josie left the girl hunched on the chair, staring into space. If Josie was face to face with the dirty, vile, scumbag, she'd… well, she wouldn't be responsible for her actions. How dare he make a young girl pregnant and then threaten violence just because he was too pathetic to face up to his responsibilities. What kind of a man was he?

Josie hurried to the kitchen and made the tea and toast, adding a plate of biscuits as she doubted the poor girl had eaten for a while.

She told another midwife that she would be away from her mothers for a short while and asked her if she could check on them. The other midwife smiled ruefully and said she would. Everyone was overworked, but no one turned their back on a woman in need.

'What's your name, love?' Josie asked as she put the tray down and passed her the plate of toast.

'Mandy Hughes.'

'How old are you?'

'Nineteen.'

'Okay, I'm just going to make a phone call, then I'll be back.'

Mandy nodded, her mouth full of toast. She was eating as if she was starving hungry. The poor lass had really gone through it.

Josie phoned the shelter for women who were victims of domestic violence. It was run by two middle-aged women, Hannah and Nina. At present, Shelley, another victim of domestic abuse, was working there in place of Nina who had gone down south to nurse their aunt who was terminally ill. Shelley was proof of the healing power of the refuge as she had turned her life around after spending several months at the shelter, but was now living with her new boyfriend, Andrew, and planning on training as a counsellor.

When Josie phoned, Hannah answered and said she would collect Mandy later that afternoon.

'Good news,' said Josie as she returned to the room where Mandy was drinking tea and looking better for the toast and biscuits. 'I've got you a place in a women's shelter. They're lovely people and you'll be safe there. Hannah is coming to fetch you later.'

'Thanks,' said Mandy, 'I really appreciate it.'

'Do you want to talk? Tell me about what you've gone through?'

Mandy shook her head and Josie felt relief. She had patients to attend to and anyway, Hannah and Shelley were the best people to talk to her.

'Have you had any antenatal care?'

'No, he wouldn't let me. He said we weren't having the baby so there wasn't any point.'

Josie took a deep breath and tried not to explode in indignation and rage. The utter bastard.

'Well, we'd better get you checked over then. Make sure everything is going to plan. Okay?'

Mandy nodded and Josie felt a wave of affection for this poor girl who had already suffered so much. She'd managed to get away from the monster that this man must be, and Josie would make sure that everything went well for the rest of her pregnancy and labour. She deserved the best that they could offer her.

The end of Josie's shift came and went and still Hannah hadn't arrived. Josie phoned the shelter again and Shelley assured her that Hannah was on her way, so Josie waited to make sure Mandy had been collected.

Hannah was caring, but a woman of few words. She was straight and to the point. Mandy looked happy to go with her after Hannah assured her they would keep her safe. She needed that assurance now; the poor girl must be terrified of her ex. Hopefully, she'd never have to see him again.

When Josie got home to her empty flat that night, she collapsed on the couch and gave in to her tears. Why was there so much misery in the world? Why were some men so vile? She wished there was someone to talk to. Before he got married, Jay would have been the person she rang. Even if he'd been too busy to meet her, they would have had a long phone conversation and she would have felt better just from hearing his words of wisdom. For her twin was wise. He was funny, caring, dedicated to his job and the kindest person she knew.

Born holding hands, as her mother had told her, they

had been inseparable since their lives began in the womb. But now, Jay was married, and Caitlin was his priority. Which was right and proper, exactly how it should be. She would be the same if she got married. Her husband would come first. Which was why it was so important to meet the right person. Josie had no intention of suffering a marriage breakdown, like poor Charles, and divorce.

Josie wondered how Charles was. It felt strange to think she'd never see him again. After being together for two days, she felt they had got to know each other quite well. *You had sex, how much closer can you get?* Gran was awake again. Having sex doesn't bring you closer unless that person means something to you. Any fool can have sex. Gran didn't reply.

Josie sighed and got up to have a shower and make herself a meal. Or… she could have takeout. It would be quicker and taste better. All she wanted was her bed as she felt exhausted. And she was on another early the next day.

Josie loved her job but sometimes she found it physically and mentally draining. But she knew she'd never do anything else. She'd helped Mandy today and that was a positive thing. As Jay was dedicated to being a paramedic, she was dedicated to being a midwife. And the price she paid was tiredness and sometimes feeling low. Get a grip, she chided herself. She'd got so much to be grateful for and she was sitting there feeling sorry for herself.

Josie picked up the phone and pressed the button for her favourite Indian takeaway. A hot curry, pilau rice and naan bread. Her spirits lifted at the thought.

Chapter Twelve

Two weeks later, with Christmas a distant memory, Josie was back on the early shift and arrived at the unit well before her shift started. She did a quick tour of the ward and said good morning to the women, then returned to the office for the handover where the senior midwife delegated the workload and told the midwives where she wanted them to work that day. The midwives also found out about any women due inductions or caesareans, and any staff changes in the department.

After handover, Josie was just heading out to the ward, when a man dressed in scrubs, came in and stopped her in her tracks. She couldn't believe her eyes and wondered if she was hallucinating.

'Ah, good timing, Mr Atkins. This, ladies, is our new obstetrician and gynaecologist, Mr Charles Atkins.' Helen, the senior midwife, smiled widely as she introduced him.

Charles shook hands with the midwives in turn until he stood in front of Josie.

'Josie, we meet again.'

'Do you two know each other?' asked Helen suspiciously.

Josie couldn't take her eyes away from him. *Their new obstetrics and gynaecology consultant. Why the heck hadn't he told her?*

'Josie?' Helen was frowning at her, so she'd better speak up.

'Yes, we have met.'

'Josie was helping a woman who was giving birth in her car. I was driving by and stopped to assist, but it turned out that Josie was perfectly capable of handling the situation on her own. I wasn't needed.'

'Oh, Josie, that sounds exciting, when did this happen?' asked Sarah, one of the midwives.

'Ages ago, before Christmas. It was nothing, really.'

'It wasn't nothing, Josie, you were a hero. The woman in question had a beautiful baby girl.' Charles smiled at her and she felt her cheeks pink up.

There was a chorus of aahs from the midwives and Charles grinned at Josie. She wondered if he intended on telling the assembled staff what happened next; the two days they'd spent together, including the night. But he turned away towards the door.

'Nice to meet you all. Doubtless, we'll get to know each other in time. Duty calls.'

He left and Josie felt as if her world had been rocked. Why hadn't he mentioned that he had taken a job at Leytonsfield? The card that he'd given her, which she still had somewhere, had clearly stated a London hospital. Had he mentioned changing jobs? She couldn't remember.

As Josie hurried down the ward to where the mother she was looking after was waiting to be induced, she pushed all thoughts of Charles Atkins from her mind. She had more important things than Dr Grumpy to occupy her thoughts.

Charles spent his first day in the maternity unit of Leytonsfield Hospital in surgery performing caesareans. There were many reasons why a woman couldn't give birth vaginally, and Charles felt they had all passed through theatre on his first day. There was a breech birth, and another baby was lying sideways and couldn't be moved. One mother had placenta previa with the placenta lying low in the uterus, covering the cervix. There was a woman with gestational diabetes and a heart condition, who, fortunately, was delivered of a bouncing baby boy with a lusty cry. All the babies were healthy, and the mothers exhausted but happy.

It had been a long, but rewarding, first day. Charles was on his way to his car when he saw Josie ahead of him.

'Josie! Wait.'

She turned and he hurried to join her as she stood next to her Mini, clutching her car keys.

'Hi. I'm glad I've caught you, I wanted to have a word.'

'Oh. What about?'

'I wanted to explain. You're probably wondering why I didn't mention that I was thinking of taking up a post here.' He looked at her enquiringly, but Josie's expression was blank.

'I'm sure you had your reasons. After all, we were total strangers so there was no earthly reason for you to tell me anything.'

'You sound angry and I don't blame you. It's just that I hadn't actually made my mind up at the time. It was only when you'd gone that I realised I had to make a decision and you had described Leytonsfield in such glowing terms that it made the decision a lot easier. It sounded such a friendly place.'

Charles watched Josie's face as he talked, trying to work out from her expression whether he was convincing her. It didn't look like it.

'If I had known that you were thinking of working here I could have been more helpful. As it is… welcome to Leytonsfield General maternity unit.'

'Thanks. There is one other thing.' Charles didn't know how Josie was going to take what he had to say next but felt it needed to be said so there could be no misunderstandings going forward.

Josie stood with her car keys in her hand, waiting for him to speak. He didn't want to upset her any more than he apparently already had, but this needed to be out in the open.

'I think it would be expedient if we didn't mention to anyone that we spent Christmas Day together. We don't want people to get the wrong impression. I realise the staff already know that we've met and there could be questions asked, but I'm sure we could keep the details to ourselves. What do you say?'

Josie glared at him unblinking. 'I take it you don't want me to announce to the whole unit that we had sex then?'

Charles laughed nervously. 'I know you're joking. Aren't you? Or have you already told them?'

'Of course I haven't told them.' Josie's voice was harsh and Charles realised he was making a hash of this conversation. 'It was just sex, it meant nothing. We were thrown together and had too much to drink.'

'Well, that's as may be but I don't regret a thing.' It was true. Charles had enjoyed making love to Josie, but for her, it was obviously just sex.

Josie sighed deeply and said, 'I think we should forget it ever happened. I'm sure we can work together and get on as colleagues. Nobody needs to know anything.'

She got into the car, shut the door, and wound the window down.

'I was hoping that we could be friends, Josie. We did get on quite well as I recall.'

Josie started the car engine, then said, 'Let's just leave it as work colleagues for now.'

'Okay, if that's what you want.'

Josie wound the window up and drove off. Charles stood watching her, wondering why she was angry with him. Was it the sex? Or simply the fact that he hadn't mentioned that Leytonsfield General was one of the hospitals he was considering?

As he walked to his car he resolved to repair their friendship. He would discover what he had done wrong and try to fix it. The thing that gave him confidence was the fact that Josie had been wearing the scarf he had given her for Christmas. That must be a good sign.

Josie drove home, trying not to think about Charles. But she was feeling too angry and the thoughts came thick and fast. The shock of seeing him stroll into the office as if he owned the place, then ingratiating himself with Helen and the midwives, coming across as all charm and twinkling blue eyes. Then telling everyone about the woman she had helped, playing down his role in the proceedings.

The thing that made her really mad was his insistence on keeping the truth from everyone. He was obviously ashamed that they had spent two days together in a cottage on the moors. But more than that, he was ashamed that they had sex. Well, she wasn't the one who initiated it, that would be Dr Grumpy. He kissed her.

Josie still felt the blow of rejection. He thought it would be expedient not to tell anyone. He didn't want people to get the wrong impression. Well, neither did she. She wasn't proud of the fact that she'd had a one-night stand with a virtual stranger. It wasn't the kind of thing she did. Josie believed in fidelity and loyalty and that sex should be reserved for someone special. If she'd been able to get back to Leytonsfield she wouldn't have been in that situation. And she'd drunk too much.

When Josie got home she sat on a kitchen chair and wondered what to do. She should have something to eat but was feeling a bit nauseous. She'd been stressed talking to Charles which must be the cause. Josie hated confrontation, but Mr Charles Atkins and his rejection of her had stressed her out. Maybe she should tell him exactly how she was really feeling; get it out of her system once and for all. They could still work together. In fact, if they cleared the air, both said their piece, then working together would be easier, wouldn't it?

Josie didn't want to work with him. She wished he'd gone to another hospital in another town. Why had he chosen Leytonsfield? It had to be just a coincidence, that's all. He would have made the same decision if she hadn't stopped to help Brenda. It was nothing to do with her really, she needed to get over herself, stop overthinking everything and get on with her life. Christmas was over, and they were halfway through January already. Time went so fast and Josie felt she was in danger of being left behind. She needed to take positive action and take steps to meet someone. Maybe she could try speed dating. Jay had done that once. Maybe she should talk to him about it.

But now, she was off to bed as she felt absolutely shattered.

After a glass of water and a quick wash, Josie got into bed. She'd shower in the morning. As soon as her head hit the pillow she was asleep.

Chapter Thirteen

The following day Josie realised the reason she had been feeling unwell with aching breasts and tiredness. It was because she had been getting her period. She suffered from heavy ones that lasted for a week and always felt wretched for at least three days. She took paracetamol and stuffed boxes of tampons in her handbag and soldiered on.

After a hectic morning, Josie escaped to the kitchen to eat her sandwiches. Low blood sugar could exacerbate low mood and she was determined not to let menstruation turn her into a snarling beast, so she would eat small amounts regularly during the day.

She made herself a mug of tea and thought about Charles. Her good intentions to be friendly hadn't been needed as she had hardly seen him. She'd been working on the post-natal ward and their paths had crossed only once as they hurried down the corridor in opposite directions. He had smiled but hadn't stopped to speak.

Josie had just taken a bite from her cheese and tomato sandwich when the kitchen door opened. Without turning around, she knew it was Charles. She could sense him hesitate in the doorway.

'Josie, sorry to interrupt your lunch, but I wanted to ask you something.'

Charles came into the kitchen and perched on a chair opposite her. She tried to swallow her food quickly.

'Of course,' she muttered, feeling a lump in her throat where the bread had got momentarily stuck as she had swallowed too large a mouthful.

'The thing is, I want to apologise for upsetting you. We haven't got off to a good start and I feel bad about that. All my fault.'

'Please, don't feel bad. I wasn't very polite to you and I should apologise too.'

Charles relaxed and he smiled. 'Would you allow me to buy you a drink? We never have the time to talk at work and I would love to chat as friends.'

Josie thought of the time they'd spent together in the cottage and the conversations they'd had, getting to know each other in a relaxed atmosphere. It wouldn't be like that, of course, as they would be in a pub probably but at least they could clear the air.

'Okay. Sounds good.'

'Brilliant. How about tonight? Can you recommend any good pubs?'

'The Old Oak's a nice one.' Near to the town centre and therefore within walking distance of her flat.

'Okay, tonight at seven? Shall I pick you up?'

'No, I'll meet you there.'

'Fine. See you tonight then.' Charles stood up and made his way to the door.

'Yes. See you tonight.'

When she was alone again, she smiled. Good staff relationships were vital to the smooth running of the unit. There was nothing worse than bad feeling between colleagues, it permeated everywhere and created bad energy. Josie was a believer in positive and negative energy. Some people, with bright and sunny dispositions, exuded positive energy as soon as they walked into a room. Others brought everyone down just by being there; they didn't even have to speak.

Charles had seemed to light up the staff room on his first day. The midwives were all smiling as they had gone about their day. Which was the opposite of her first impression of him when he seemed depressed and bad tempered. Of course, being alone at Christmas could have caused that.

Josie finished her sandwich and rinsed her mug. She felt bloated and tired as if she would be asleep in seconds if she shut her eyes. Well, she wouldn't shut her eyes, she'd get on with her job and stop being a wimp.

Josie decided to take advantage of an early finish and call into the shelter for domestic violence victims to see how Mandy was settling in.

Shelley opened the door when she knocked.

'Hi, Josie, come to see Mand?'

'Yes, how is she getting on?'

'Come and see for yourself.'

Shelley stepped to one side so Josie could enter the house. The hallway was long and narrow. It seemed dark and dingy at first, but Josie had been told by Hannah that this was deliberate. If any of the abusers tried to gain entry through the front door, they would have to get past the human shield that Hannah and other women who worked there formed.

Hannah was a large woman and so was her sister. They could be quite formidable and most of the abusing men were cowards and backed down when faced with strong women.

Josie knew the women would be gathered in the kitchen, at the back of the house, which was large, brightly painted and had a huge oak table in the centre with chairs around. Babies and toddlers crawled about the floor and there were toys everywhere, so visitors had to be careful where they put their feet.

Josie loved this kitchen, it embodied everything that was good about the shelter. The women helped each other, taking it in turns to cook and they were always brewing up for themselves, the others and visitors. They looked after each other's children. It was like a big family bonded by fear of their partners, but the women were learning to stand up for themselves and be independent.

Mandy sat at the kitchen table doing a jigsaw with one of the young children. Her hair was clean and shone with health and she looked happy.

'Hi, Mandy, how are you doing?'

'Hi. Doing fine thanks.'

'How are you settling in?'

'Great. The women are lovely, and Hannah and Shelley have been telling me about money I'll be entitled to. They've been helping me fill in the claim form for benefits.'

'Have you heard from the boyfriend?'

At the mention of her abuser, Mandy's smile slipped. She was obviously still scared of him.

'No. I haven't been out much.'

'I think you're doing the right thing. Stay inside as much as you can until the baby's born. You're safe here.'

'Yes, I will.'

'But don't forget your antenatal appointments, they're very important.'

'Right.'

Josie knew that the shelter would lend her some of the equipment Mandy would need for her baby until she was in a position to get her own. Shelley and Lexi were involved in fundraising for the shelter and Josie's father also supported the women as much as he could.

'Right. I'd better go. Glad you're okay, Mandy, and I'll see you later.'

'Thanks… for everything.'

'I haven't done much. It's this lovely lot who have.'

Josie looked at the women, some of whom she had helped to birth their babies. She felt a rush of affection for them. Childbirth was hard enough without having to live in fear of an abusive man.

'Yes, I know. They're great.'

Josie said goodbye and hurried to the Old Oak. She was going to be late if she didn't get a move on.

Charles bought a pint of bitter and settled down to wait for Josie.

The pub was a good choice on Josie's part. It wasn't as olde worlde as the George and Dragon but still had a peaceful atmosphere and an open fire. The locals had their personal tankards hanging from hooks over the bar. Charles had always thought it was a bit of affectation; they were stating their claim to stand in their usual spot at the bar as important customers. Perhaps he was getting old, but he wouldn't mind having a local where everyone knew him and took down the tankard with his name on it as soon as he walked through the door.

Charles liked Leytonsfield, or what he had seen of it so far. The people were friendly, and the pace of life was a lot slower than that of London where everyone rushed around with a frown on their face, not looking right or left, or acknowledging anyone else. At one time he had enjoyed the anonymity of the big city, but since Clarissa had left him, he admitted to feeling lonely on occasions.

Josie was late. It was nearly seven thirty, but Charles wasn't concerned. He knew Josie well enough to know that she was a person of her word. If she said she would do something, then she did it. And it was pleasant to sit and let his mind wander; he didn't often get the chance to do that.

Five minutes later, just as Charles was finishing his pint, Josie came in.

'Sorry I'm late, Charles. I was visiting a woman in the shelter for victims of domestic violence. She's pregnant and I wanted to see how she was settling in.'

'No problem, you're just in time, I was going to the bar. What would you like?'

'Half a bitter please.'

When Charles returned with the drinks, he took the seat next to Josie instead of the one opposite her. He felt surprisingly pleased to see her and hoped they could recapture the feeling of intimacy they had shared in the cottage. His thoughts turned to the sex and he pushed it from his mind before Josie asked him what he was grinning at.

'Cheers,' Charles held his glass up and Josie clinked hers against it.

'Cheers. So, what do you think of the Old Oak?'

'It's nice. Peaceful. Conducive to quiet conversation and gentle reflection.'

'You have the soul of a poet, Charles.'

Charles laughed and was pleased to see that Josie was smiling, her hazel eyes soft. She looked relaxed.

'Is this your local?'

Josie took a drink and looked thoughtful. 'Yes, it is I suppose. It's within walking distance of my flat and the place I tend to think of first if I'm meeting someone for a drink.'

'What's the flat like?'

'It's a Victorian villa converted into flats. I've got the top floor. There's a tiny balcony and I sometimes sit out there in summer. The view over Leytonsfield is impressive; I can almost see Manor Park.'

'Sounds nice. I need to start thinking of looking for a house. I'm in hospital accommodation at the moment. It's okay for now, but Megan's coming to stay in February, and I want something better to offer her.'

'Oh, that's great, Charles. I'm so pleased for you. Family is so important.'

'It'll give me the chance to really talk to her, find out how she feels about Todd. She keeps her thoughts to herself usually, so I'll have to be careful how I approach the subject. But I want a home here in Leytonsfield that she can come to whenever she wants.'

'Do Megan and Todd get on well?'

Charles wondered how much to tell Josie. She was a good listener, but it wouldn't be fair to burden her with his problems.

'I get the impression there is some tension. Megan always tells me her life is now fabulous—or wicked as she would say—but I wonder if that's the whole story. Clarissa and Todd are planning something big for Valentine's Day which is why they want to offload Megan.

They obviously want to be on their own without a child to look after.'

'Didn't you say Megan was sixteen? She's hardly a child anymore.'

'I suppose we still think of her as one. Anyway, I was going to ask you— say no if you don't want to do it, of course— but would you give me the benefit of your knowledge of Leytonsfield in finding the right property?'

'Of course I'll help you, Charles, it'll be a pleasure.'

'Are you free this weekend?'

'I'm off on Sunday if you are free then. My suggestion, to begin with, is just to drive around the town and outskirts to get a feel of the different areas and what's available.'

'Sounds good. Sunday it is then. Do you want another drink?'

'No, I'm feeling a bit tired, to be honest. Do you mind if we call it a night?'

'Not at all. I'll give you a lift home.'

As Charles dropped Josie off outside her flat, he felt pleased that they were friends again. She was a special lady, and he was growing fond of her. At least he had one friend in his new home town.

When Josie woke on Sunday morning she wished she could stay in bed and have a duvet day. It wasn't like her at all, she usually got out of bed as soon as she woke. But she dragged her body up feeling as if she weighed a ton. And the thought of breakfast made her gag. Perhaps a slice of dry toast and some fruit juice. There must be something going around; the usual winter bugs that laid everyone low in

January. One of the downsides to working in a hospital was picking up every bug going.

When she was dressed and had eaten her toast she felt a little better. Waiting for Charles to arrive, she mentally planned the route around Leytonsfield. First, she'd show him the houses in the south of the town, where her parents and older brothers lived.

Charles was on time and looked pleased to see her when she opened the door to him. He was dressed casually in jeans and a V-neck sweater over a white T-shirt with a suede jacket. Josie had also worn jeans and a sweater with the scarf he had given her for Christmas as it was soft and so pretty, and with its myriad colours, it matched anything.

'Hi, Charles.'

'Good morning, Josie. You look nice.'

'Thanks.'

Climbing into the four-wheel-drive Subaru brought back memories of the time she and Charles spent together. Now that she was home and back in her normal routine, she thought of those two days with affection.

They drove off with Josie giving Charles directions.

'What kind of house are you looking for?'

'I like space and would like one room as a study and a bedroom for Megan.'

'Three or four-bedroom detached?'

'Or a semi, with a nice garden to sit out in summer.'

'Right, then we'll drive around the streets and I'll show you where my family live.'

'Perfect.'

'Are you planning on visiting the estate agents today or is this just the recce?'

'I hadn't thought beyond looking around.'

'Okay. Recce it is then.'

Josie showed him the area that she imagined he'd like; detached houses with nice gardens and tree-lined streets. Then, just in case he had more money than she had assumed he had, the really expensive district on the outskirts of town. Mansions with acres of land, surrounded by fields and woods. Beautiful houses that sometimes couldn't be seen from the road as their driveways were so long. Houses like the one Caitlin had grown up in.

'Nice, but outside my price range. Andrew would like these houses.'

'Do you get on with your brother?'

'Not really. We tolerate each other. We called a truce when I hit thirty. I didn't have the time or energy to hate him anymore.'

'Right,' said Josie as if she understood. She didn't as she adored her brothers. In fact, when she fantasized about the perfect man, he had Riordan's intellect, Casey's physique, and Jay's personality. If she could meet a man like that, she'd be well happy.

Next, Josie mentioned the new builds; townhouses near enough to the hospital to get there quickly in emergencies but with plenty of space and privacy. Charles, however, wasn't impressed.

'Soulless. No character. Not for me.'

'So, what is for you?'

'I've been thinking that it's unlikely I'll find anything to buy before Megan arrives, so I'll rent somewhere just for the duration. She can't stay in the hospital accommodation.'

'Okay, how about a cottage? My twin bought one and it's lovely. Small, only two bedrooms but you could get a bigger one if you need more space.'

'Sounds perfect. Shall we do a drive-by?'

'Absolutely.'

Josie was enjoying herself. It was fun driving around and she was looking at Leytonsfield with new eyes. She was seeing it from the point of view of Charles. Someone who was looking for a place to live that would also be suitable for a teenage girl. It made her appreciate the diversity of the town; the old mill cottages, the new townhouses for the younger business people and the houses for families, close to schools.

Perhaps, if she ever found the stress and long days of working as a midwife too much, she could get a job as an estate agent. It wouldn't be a bad way to make a living, showing people around houses, helping them to find their perfect homes.

Then she thought of her women. Women like Mandy and Brenda, then all the others that she had helped give birth to healthy babies, and realised that midwifery was in her blood. Her mother and grandmother had been midwives. If she ever got around to having kids, they may be bitten by the midwifery bug as well. That would make her so proud.

'Do you fancy some lunch?' asked Charles.

'What a good idea. If you keep driving on this road out of Leytonsfield, there's a lovely pub about three miles away.'

'I'm on it,' said Charles and Josie though again how in harmony their thoughts often were.

Chapter Fourteen

On the last Friday of January, Jay and Caitlin organised a Beer and Chinese night. They were regular evenings where Jay's friends met for some down time. Fortunately, Jay's friends were Caitlin's as well; paramedics they worked closely with. Jay had also invited Emma who had been his housemate for a short while and looked after the place for him when he went travelling with Caitlin. And just happened to get married in Bali, without telling anyone except Caitlin's close friend, Sophie Simons. Josie had forgiven him for not telling her he was getting married, but she still felt hard done by. After all, she was his twin and that trumped close friends in her book.

Normally she looked forward to tucking into sweet and sour chicken and chow mein washed down by a couple of glasses of Pinot Grigio. But the thought of food was still making her gag. Josie was thinking seriously of going to the doctor. She still felt nauseous and tired out most of the time. Winter viruses could be debilitating and, if she did have a flu bug, she really shouldn't be working and putting her women at risk.

With eight people squashed into the small living room in the cottage, some had to sit on the floor or beanbags. Josie didn't feel well enough to rough it, so claimed a space on the couch before the others showed up. Paul had brought his girlfriend, Pandora, and they squashed together in an armchair, with Pandora practically sitting on Paul's knee. Pandora was pretty and shy, and the couple held hands for most of the evening.

Caitlin and Jay were also still loved up and, although they weren't stuck together like glue, they kissed every time they got near to each other and giggled and whispered together.

Emma, a pretty girl with red hair and freckles, made herself useful by pouring drinks and gathering together plates and cutlery. Sally, a paramedic in her forties sat next to Josie, and Matt, another paramedic and friend of Jay's sat on a beanbag nearby.

'So, how're you doing, Josie, not seen you for ages,' said Sal.

'I'm doing okay, thanks, how's yourself?'

'Fine. You're looking a bit pale, lass, are you sure you're okay?'

'Just tired, that's all. I'll be fine after I've eaten.'

'What're you drinking?' asked Sal peering suspiciously into her glass.

'Mineral water. Got a bit of an upset stomach.'

'Oh, that's a shame. You take care of yourself now.'

Later, Josie saw Sal and Jay with their heads together and, at one point, they both looked over at her. Perhaps it was a mistake coming here tonight. She wasn't hungry and definitely wasn't in a sociable mood. But she did want to talk to Jay, preferably when they were alone.

Josie got her chance after the food had been eaten and Paul, Pandora, Sal, and Matt had left. Jay came and sat next to her on the couch.

'Okay, I want the truth, what's the matter?' asked Jay.

'I'm just tired, Jay, that's all.'

'Are you sure? You hardly ate anything and you're not drinking wine.'

'Think I've got a bug or something.' Josie looked away as she always found it difficult to lie to Jay.

'Well in that case you need to go to the doctor. Go tomorrow, okay?'

'Okay.' Josie had already made up her mind to make an appointment with her GP.

'You have forgiven me, haven't you?'

'Of course. I admit I was a bit put out that I couldn't be part of your wedding, but I understand, really I do.'

'Good. Anyway, Caitlin and I have decided that we're going to have a party for all the family and friends that couldn't come to Bali.'

'That'd be all of us then,' said Josie teasing him.

'Yes, we thought about the Leytonsfield Hotel as a venue,' said Caitlin from the depth of the armchair.

'Great idea,' said Emma, 'Am I invited?'

'Of course,' said Jay and Caitlin together.

'Great. Sorry, but I think I need to go now, much as I hate to leave. Got tons of work to do over the weekend and I want an early start tomorrow.' Emma was at university training to be a nurse. 'I've stacked the dishwasher and left the kitchen clean and tidy.'

'Thanks for that, you're a star, Emma,' said Jay, walking to the front door with her.

Josie caught Caitlin staring at her. 'You do look tired, Josie, why don't you stay here tonight, and you can catch up with Jay in the morning as he's on a late shift. I'm on an early, unfortunately.'

'Thanks, I will.'

Three people had asked her what was wrong. Josie began to realise how ill she must look. A good night's sleep would do the trick. She hoped.

The next morning, Josie was still feeling unwell. She was also wondering why her usual heavy period of a fortnight ago, hadn't been usual or heavy. It fact it was what midwives called a "show" which was scant bleeding known as implantation bleeding when the fertilized egg attaches to the lining of the uterus.

She had other worrying symptoms of pregnancy too and couldn't get the thought out of her head. Surely she couldn't be as the last time she'd had sex was with Charles and the likelihood of getting pregnant after one sexual encounter was almost nil. But then so many women did fall pregnant after just one time. Especially if they were on the pill but hadn't taken it. She didn't have her pills with her in the cottage as she was expecting to be able to get home that day. And she definitely hadn't planned on sex. *Oh God, I'm pregnant!* No, she mustn't panic. It could be anything. She needed to take a test as it was the only way to put her mind at rest.

Jay was cooking breakfast when she finally dragged herself down the stairs.

'Hi, you okay?'

'No, not really.'

Jay was by her side instantly and had his arms around her, hugging her in his own special way. No one hugged as well as Jay.

'What's up?'

'I think I might be pregnant.'

'What! Really? I didn't know you were seeing anyone.'

'I'm not.' Josie started crying and Jay smoothed her hair down and laid his forehead on hers. A ritual they had when one of them needed comfort.

'Right. I'm confused now. Sit down, Sis, and tell me everything from the beginning while I stop these sausages from burning.'

'Don't make any for me, I can't eat.'

'Now you're scaring me. I'll make you some toast.'

'It all started on the day before Christmas Eve when I was coming back from Harriet's…' Josie told Jay the story of helping Brenda, being rescued by Charles from the ditch and staying until Boxing Day in a lovely cottage with a caring man who was a fabulous cook.

'You were taking a massive risk, staying with a complete stranger. Weren't you scared?'

'No, I was more scared of being lost on the moors in a blizzard which is what would have happened if I'd left the car. If Charles hadn't had the foresight to come and look for me, I wouldn't be here now.'

'It reminds me of the Stephen King story, Misery. You know, the one where the author was imprisoned by the nurse. She rescued him and then kept him tied to the bed.'

'Thanks for that, Jay. Anyway, Charles was the perfect gentleman.'

'So who got you pregnant?'

'I don't know if I am yet. I may be worrying about nothing. Forget I said anything.'

112

'I can't do that. You look awful and if you are pregnant, you'll need to start making plans. Anyway, finish your story. You were having Christmas dinner. Then what?'

'We had a lovely meal, drank too much whisky and… well, ended up having sex.'

'You had sex with a man you'd only known for two days? Did he coerce you?'

'No, of course not. It was amicable.'

'So neither of you could resist and you had a hot sex moment? Then what? Did you spend the night together? Are you going to see him again?'

Jay had made himself a sausage butty and took a large bite which at least stopped him asking so many questions.

'He's the maternity unit's new obstetrician and gynaecologist so I'll be working with him. We're friends now, nothing else.'

'But if you're pregnant, it's his baby?'

'Correct.' Josie took a bite of the toast Jay had made and fell silent. Jay was too busy eating to speak but he was thinking hard. She could always tell when Jay was deep in thought, he had a faraway look and a little frown between his eyebrows.

Then, in the silence, she heard Gran's voice. *No use sitting there worrying. Go and buy a test.*

Gran was right as she couldn't make plans unless she knew one way or another. If she wasn't pregnant then she could breathe a sigh of relief and get on with her life. If she was…

'What will this doctor say if you are pregnant with his baby?'

'That's the million-dollar question and the truth is, I haven't the foggiest idea.'

It was another week before Josie got around to buying a pregnancy testing kit.

As she sat on her bed waiting for the white stick to tell her whether or not she was going to be a mother, she tried to empty her mind. Positive thoughts only. Whatever the result was, she would face it and take things one step at a time.

It was no shock to Josie when the stick gave up its secrets and she found that she really was pregnant. All the speculation was over. She was going to have a baby. Charles's baby.

Josie burst into tears and sobbed into her pillow. It was not the right time. Charles was not the right man. He was a friend that was all. They would never be anything else but friends. Then she had a terrible thought. What would she do if Charles wanted her to have a termination? Would he? The man was an obstetrician. Well, she wasn't having one that was for sure.

Fortunately, it was her day off and she was desperate to talk to her mum. She sent a text first to make sure she was home, then got dressed and drove the short distance to her family home. She still thought of her parents' house as home even though she hadn't lived there for over ten years. Home wasn't a building, it was the people living there.

When she arrived, her mother took one look at her and enfolded her in a hug.

'Come in, darling, and tell me what's wrong.'

'I'm pregnant.' Josie hadn't meant to blurt it out like that, but her mother didn't seem fazed. Maybe she'd already guessed.

'Oh my love, come here.' Eloise hugged Josie again, for longer this time.

'Mum, I've been so stupid.'

'Sit down and I'll make some tea. I take it the father is the doctor you stayed with? Unless you've been seeing someone else and haven't told anyone.'

'No, it's Charles. It was once, Mum, just once. It's so bloody unfair.'

'Once is all it takes sweetheart.'

Josie watched her mother move around the kitchen, pouring boiling water into the old brown teapot, collecting mugs and a plate for biscuits. This was her domain, where she ruled supreme. Where she was happiest, feeding her family, looking after them, listening to their troubles and giving advice if asked. If advice wasn't called for, she listened with all the patience in the world, then hugged and kissed, bestowing her unconditional love.

Was that what it meant to be a mother? To be there for her family, always available, always willing. What about her? Eloise O'Connor was wife to a GP and mother to four children in the medical profession. And now there were wives and grandchildren to add to the family. Josie was reminded of a mother hen with a brood of chicks under her wings, protected from the world. Was there enough room for more chicks? Josie knew that her mother would find the room.

'I love you, Mum,' said Josie tearfully.

'And I love you, too.' Her mum sat at the kitchen table after placing a mug of tea in front of Josie and a plate of chocolate biscuits between them. She sipped her own tea and waited for Josie to talk.

'All I want is a good marriage, a supportive husband and kids. I want what you've got.'

'I'm very lucky, Josie. Not everyone will hit the jackpot on the first try.'

'What do you mean?' Josie took a chocolate biscuit and bit into it.

'Not everyone gets what they want in the way they want it. You've always yearned to be a mother and now you've got the chance. Being a single mother isn't the worst thing that could happen. Riordan was a single father and Lexi a single mother and they managed. You will too. You will always have the support and love of your family and, well... Charles could end up surprising you.'

Her mother poured them both another mug of tea.

'I don't know how to tell him. He's got his own problems you see. His wife has left him, and he hardly ever sees his teenage daughter.'

'You'll find a way. He deserves to know. And if he decides he doesn't want to be involved in the child's life, then at least you'll know where you stand.'

'I wish I was as wise as you are, Mum. You always know what to say.'

'I've always thought that honesty was the best policy. Don't keep the news from him for too long, love. You'll feel better when he knows and then you know what you're facing.'

'I'm scared but excited. You're right I have always wanted to be a mother and I've got a baby growing inside me. As a midwife I shouldn't find it hard to believe but, well... I do.'

'You'll make a great mother, Josie, and I'm excited too —another grandchild, how wonderful.'

'Thanks, Mum. For everything.'

Chapter Fifteen

Charles felt a mixture of emotions as he stood on the platform at Manchester Piccadilly train station waiting to meet Megan. He'd offered to drive to London to collect her, but Clarissa and Todd had both agreed that Megan was old enough now to catch a train on her own.

As he watched the passengers alight, he waited anxiously for Megan to appear. Then he spotted her. She wore a dark blue puffer jacket with a thick scarf and blue jeans with huge holes in the legs. Charles had never been fashion-conscious but couldn't understand paying the earth for designer jeans with holes in them.

Megan saw him and waved. He waved back and felt something shift deep inside at the sight of his daughter. He loved Megan so much and was depending on the next two weeks to help him grow closer to her.

'Hi, Dad,' she said.

'Hello, darling, how are you? How was the train journey?' He hugged her, relishing the smell of her coconut shampoo and the feel of her in his arms.

'I'm good, Dad, the journey was good.'

'Can I take that for you?' He stretched out his hand to take her suitcase on wheels, but she kept hold of it.

'No, I've got it.'

'Right, well, let's go then.'

Charles had parked his Jaguar in the nearby multistorey car park and there was a queue to get out. So far, Megan hadn't put her earbuds in to listen to music or checked the social media sites on her phone. Instead, she watched him as he manoeuvred the car out of the tight space and made for the exit.

'That'll be me soon.'

'What will be you?' Charles was puzzled. Had he missed something Megan had said to him?

'Driving. Todd's going to teach me to drive.'

'Not yet surely, you're not old enough.' The thought of Megan driving terrified him. She wasn't mature enough to handle a car.

'I can't drive until I'm seventeen, but I can, like, apply for my provisional licence now as I'm more than fifteen and nine months. I want to learn to drive as soon as I can, Dad.'

Charles couldn't look at Megan as he was concentrating on turning onto the motorway to take them to Leytonsfield.

'Why are you in such a hurry?'

'Because I want to be, like, independent. I need to be because...' She trailed off and stared out of the window.

'Because what, Megan?'

'Because I don't want to have to, you know, like, rely on other people. For anything. I want to be free to go where I want when I want.'

'I understand that. In fact, I was exactly the same at your age. But have lessons from a qualified instructor, not Todd, okay?'

'It's too expensive.' Charles was amazed. With all the money Todd and Clarissa had, driving lessons for Megan would be a drop in the ocean.

'Did you ask Todd?'

'Yeah, he said he'd loan me the money but I'd, like, have to pay it back.'

The miserly bastard wouldn't pay for driving lessons but forked out a small fortune on skiing over Christmas and New Year.

'I'll pay for them when the time comes. We'll talk about it again later, okay?'

'Thanks, Dad.'

They drove on in silence but still, Megan seemed to want to talk. She was growing up and Charles would have to get used to the fact. He didn't know whether he'd get to accept the amount of make-up she was wearing but wasn't going to mention it, especially as their time together had only just started.

'Did you have a good time over Christmas?'

'Yeah, it was cool. I love skiing. Made lots of friends. What about you?'

'Me, oh well, my Christmas was a trifle unconventional.' Charles wondered how much to tell Megan. She'd asked him so perhaps he'd give her an edited version.

'Why?' Megan settled back and put her feet up on the dashboard. He wanted to tell her not to do that but concentrated on the story he was going to relay instead.

'You know that I was spending Christmas in Uncle Andrew's cottage?'

'Yeah, all on your own. That's kinda sad, Dad.'

'Well, I wasn't alone as it turned out.'

'Oh, who were you with?'

'A midwife. It's a long story.'

'I wanna know. Is she your girlfriend?'

'No, not at all, although I do work with her, but didn't when I met her.'

'So, how did you guys meet?'

Charles told Megan the story of Josie helping Brenda to birth her baby. Then worrying when she decided to try to get home and finding her in a ditch. He told the story of tobogganing, making it as funny as he could so Megan was laughing by the end of the tale.

'That's so cool, and you work together now?'

'That's right.'

That's, like, a movie you know, the kind of thing they put on Netflix at Christmas. Why don't you take her out, you may end up together? You need someone, Dad, you can't be on your own, like, forever, especially now that Mum's got Todd. You need someone too.'

'Well it's good to know you approve of me being with someone, Megan, but that isn't likely to happen for a long time, if at all.'

'Why?'

What to tell her? She was a teenage girl on the cusp of becoming a woman and ripe for falling in love. He was a middle-aged man, trying to keep his life from falling apart. The last thing he needed at the moment was the complication of a relationship.

'It's not the right time, Megan.'

'When is the right time?'

'I'll let you know when it happens.'

Hopefully, that was the end of the conversation. Megan had grown bored and was now listening to music, her feet tapping on the dashboard and her head bobbing gently. She smiled occasionally as she checked texts and Facebook posts. She had changed a lot since Clarissa had left him for Todd.

Hopefully, she'd be okay, and they could move towards having a more adult father and daughter relationship.

Charles had made a special meal for Megan on her first night. Her favourite chicken korma with coconut pilau rice and hot chocolate fudge cake for dessert. Then, after he served it, she told him she didn't eat meat anymore, so he hastily put together a vegetable stir-fry, and put the chicken korma in the freezer.

'Thanks, Dad, it looks great.' Megan had hardly glanced at it.

Megan had gone straight up to her room when they had arrived at the rented house and unpacked her clothes. He hoped that she would say something about the house, as Charles had been happy to find the three bedroomed semi-detached for rent and wanted to show it off to her. It was in immaculate condition, freshly decorated with a new kitchen and bathroom and Charles couldn't help feeling pleased with himself for procuring the house at such short notice. She barely glanced at the things he showed her except to utter her favourite expression, "cool", periodically.

When she had come down from the bedroom she'd been allocated, she'd chattered nervously about how much better her life was now, because Todd was so rich, and she could have whatever she wanted. They were going skiing again next Christmas and to the Maldives in the summer holidays.

Charles listened patiently as Megan tried to act the grown-up young lady, but he wasn't fooled. She hardly ever looked him in the eye and seemed to have a surfeit of nervous energy. He knew something was wrong.

Now she sat at the kitchen table picking at the stir-fry but eating little of it. If she thought she was so grown up, then he would treat her accordingly.

'Would you like a glass of white wine, Megan?' It went against his instincts to offer wine to his underaged daughter, but he bet she drank it at home, and he didn't want to be the bad cop to Clarissa and Todd's good one.

'I'd love one, Dad, but I can't.' She looked up at him then with a look of fear and guilt as if she had said something she shouldn't.

'What do you mean, you can't? Don't your mother and Todd allow you to drink alcohol yet?'

'Yeah, they don't care what I do.'

Charles didn't like the sound of that. They should care what she did. Megan was only sixteen and needed the protection of both her parents and stepfather.

'So, why can't you drink wine? Don't you like it? You can have a soft drink if you prefer.' Charles would be relieved if Megan didn't like alcohol as, in his opinion, she was too young to drink.

To Charles's surprise and consternation, Megan suddenly burst into tears and sobbed loudly. He was at her side straight away and pulled her up off her chair and into his arms to hug her.

'I'm pregnant,' she sobbed, and Charles went cold. Pregnant? At sixteen? Every parent's nightmare. He suppressed his anger as best he could to offer her the comfort she desperately needed.

'Come and sit down. We should talk.'

He led her to the couch and they both sat, Megan still crying and Charles feeling sick. He was shocked to the core. It was something that happened to other people's kids, not his own.

'How far gone are you?'

'A couple of months.'

Charles held Megan and tried to soothe her, but she was inconsolable. She sobbed for about fifteen minutes and Charles handed her a tissue and waited for the storm to pass. Gradually she became calmer and her tears dried.

'Right. Now you can tell me everything.'

'Dad!'

'What do you mean "Dad", you're not old enough to have sex for goodness sake and I can't believe that your mother and Todd let this happen. What have they said about it?'

'Nothing,' Megan said quietly.

'Nothing! What do you mean nothing? Oh, I see, you haven't told them, have you?'

'No.'

'Why not?'

"Cos she'll kill me.'

'How do you know I won't?'

"Cos you're my dad and supposed to look after me.'

Charles would find it difficult to look after Megan when they lived in opposite parts of the country. But he was the one who'd left London, so he had no one but himself to blame. He'd never dreamed this would happen.

'Tell me about the baby's father.'

Megan sniffed and Charles handed her another tissue.

'Thanks. He's the son of a friend of Todd's. We've been out, like, a couple of times.'

'Only a couple of times?' Charles was suddenly reminded that he had enjoyed sex with Josie after knowing her for two days but pushed such thoughts from his mind. He was an adult and Megan wasn't.

'I like him, but I'm not in love. I just wanted to lose my virginity like all my friends have.'

'How old is he?'

'Sixteen.' They were both children.

'Didn't you use protection?'

'We didn't have any and he said he'd pull out before... you know.'

'And did he?' Charles was trying not to picture his daughter having sex with a child the same age. How could they have possibly known what they were doing? Was he being an old fuddy-duddy, oblivious to the fact that the world had moved on and kids of sixteen were sexually aware and streetwise nowadays in a way that his generation hadn't been?

'Not completely, but he said that, as it was my first time, nothing would happen.'

'And you believed him?' Charles tried to keep the scornful incredulity out of his voice. This boy had fed her a pack of lies and she'd believed everything he said. Megan may think she was mature but she was still a child in so many ways.

'Yes.' Megan put her head in her hands and started crying again. Charles was out of his depth and knew he would have to phone Clarissa. As Megan's mother, she would need to take care of this situation; he had no idea what to do or say.

This time, he waited until Megan had stopped crying. He was thinking hard of the next steps. Would she agree to stay with him until after the baby was born? Then he could monitor her pregnancy, even though he couldn't be her obstetrician. The first step, he knew, was telling Clarissa and Todd that Megan was pregnant. As she was so scared, he should do it.

'Megan, you need to tell your mum.'

'I can't, please, Dad, don't make me tell her.' Megan curled up into a ball on the couch and kept on sobbing.

'So, what happens when you begin to show? She'll guess and it'll be worse for you if she finds out then.

'She doesn't have to know yet. I don't know what I'm going to do.'

It occurred to Charles that he hadn't even asked Megan what her plans were. He'd just assumed that she'd be keeping the baby, but maybe she'd want a termination.

'So, if you decide to have a termination, you think you can keep the whole thing from your mum?'

'Maybe.' Megan's voice was small and watery. She sniffed and gasped as the tears came again.

'Okay. I think we should leave this for tonight. You're overwrought and tired. Why don't you have an early night, and we can talk about this tomorrow?'

'You promise you won't phone Mum?'

'I promise, but, Megan, whatever you decide to do, she has the right to know.'

Megan said nothing but stood up and made her way upstairs.

Chapter Sixteen

Josie had made up her mind to tell Charles that she was pregnant as soon as she could and hoped he was on duty that day. Not that she was looking forward to the conversation. She was dreading it. How was he going to react? It didn't bear thinking about.

Mandy Hughes was coming in for an antenatal appointment, and because Josie was her assigned midwife, she would be taking care of her right up until the birth. Mandy had missed out on many appointments due to the scumbag boyfriend not letting her come to the hospital, so she was going to receive extra special care in the last few months of her pregnancy.

When Josie had seen Mandy last, in the shelter, she had looked so much better than the day they had met. She had been clean and clothed appropriately for the weather. More than this, however, she had looked relaxed and happy, joining in the conversations around the kitchen table.

From Josie's point of view, Mandy was physically better as well. She was taking her folic acid supplements, was now eating healthily at the shelter and had been screened for HIV, and sexually transmitted diseases. Her scumbag boyfriend was a drug user and Mandy could have caught something from him. Fortunately, all the tests had been negative.

Josie was dismayed, therefore, to see the haunted look in Mandy's eyes as she came in, accompanied by Shelley. What had happened to change her demeanour?

'Hi, Mandy, how's things?' Josie asked.

'Okay,' said Mandy quietly.

'Are you still happy in the hostel?'

'Yes, thanks.'

Josie looked at Shelley who made movements with her head that looked as if she wanted to speak to Josie alone.

'I'll be back in a sec, Mandy, okay?'

'Sure.'

Shelley had moved down the corridor out of hearing range of the room Mandy was in. She beckoned Josie to join her.

'She's been getting texts from Tony, her boyfriend.'

'Really? Does he know where she's living?'

'No, thankfully, but he knows that this is where she'll come for antenatal treatment. You need to be really vigilant, Josie, as he'll be watching the maternity unit for a sight of Mandy.'

'Should we tell the police?'

Shelley frowned and shook her head. 'There wouldn't be any point until he actually turned up making trouble which, by the way, he probably will. He's not going to let it go.'

'How do you know?'

Shelley sighed. 'Because my boyfriend, Andrew, knows him and drinks in the same pub sometimes. He overheard a conversation between Tony and another man saying he was going to take the baby when he's born. He only wants a son and thinks because he wants it, it'll happen.'

'Does Mandy know?'

'Yes. He sent her a text saying he wanted custody of his son and she texted back saying it might be a girl and Tony replied, "It better not be". He'll blame Mandy if it's not the son he wants. Strange, as a while ago he was threatening to kick her in the stomach if she didn't have an abortion.'

Josie shuddered. 'I can't bear to think of him, and I've never even seen him. Poor Mandy. I'll have to tell Helen and alert the security officers to be on the lookout when Mandy comes for her appointments. Some of them I'll be able to do at the shelter, but when the baby's due, we'll have to have a permanent guard. He's not getting anywhere near Mandy, not if I have anything to do with it.'

Shelley smiled. 'Same here. I'm going to come to every appointment she has and be on the lookout for him. We won't let him win, don't worry.'

But Josie was worried. Tony sounded vile. Violent, abusive, and narcissistic. The worst kind of bully. But, like Shelley said, he'd never win. They wouldn't let him.

Josie watched Charles at the bar buying the drinks. He had texted her asking if she was available for a quick session in the Old Oak after work. She, of course, said yes. This was her opportunity to tell him about the baby.

'Mineral water,' said Charles putting the glass in front of Josie. Fortunately, he didn't ask why she didn't want any alcohol as she may have blurted the news out without having the time to lead into it gently.

'Thanks, Charles.'

'Cheers.' He drank deeply of his beer and then sighed. 'This will have to be a flying visit, I'm afraid, as I don't want Megan to be alone for too long. I shouldn't really have been working today, but we had an emergency and one of the other obstetricians was off sick.'

Josie realised with dismay that she had forgotten all about Megan's visit; her head was so full of Mandy and her abusive boyfriend.

'How is Megan?'

'Well, that's what I wanted to ask you about. She's pregnant.'

'What?!' Josie stared at Charles in disbelief. That was far from what she had expected him to say.

'Yes, that was my reaction too. She's sixteen and it was her first time. They didn't use protection, but it hadn't occurred to either of them that Megan may get pregnant. The boy is the same age.'

'Oh God, Charles, I don't know what to say.'

'That's disappointing. I was rather hoping you'd have some pearls of wisdom for me. Have any of the women you've helped been sixteen?'

'Yes, a few. Usually, by the time the birth comes around, the parents have got over the shock of finding their teenage daughter pregnant and are ready to be grandparents. I'm never had one who had no family support though. I'm not saying that Megan has no family support though, as she has you and your ex-wife. What does she say about it?'

'She doesn't know, and Megan has begged me not to tell her yet until she decides whether she is keeping the baby or not.'

'Oh, right. What do you feel about that?'

Charles sighed and stared into the middle distance. 'I

want what's best for Megan. She's a bright kid and I was hoping she'd go to university or college. She was talking about having driving lessons which, of course, she will be old enough to have in a year's time.'

Josie had put her own predicament to one side and was concentrating on what was best for Megan. After all, Charles trusted her enough to ask her advice. A midwife often grew close to the expectant mother and they were best placed to help.

'She could still go on to further education, couldn't she?'

'It'd be a lot harder with a child in tow. I can't see Clarissa and Todd taking over the childcare. They're too busy living the high life, jetting off to goodness knows where.'

'You sound angry. Do you blame your ex-wife?'

'Yes, I do blame her. Megan was in her care, hers, and Todd's. They should have been taking notice of what she was doing, who she was keeping company with. Instead, they seem to let her run free and do whatever she wants. Well, this is the consequence.'

Josie said nothing. She couldn't mention that she was pregnant now. For one thing, Charles had enough on his plate and for another, he seemed to be angry at the whole situation. She hated to think about how angry he'd get when he found out about *their* baby. No, she'd let the dust settle first; it would give her more time to make plans.

'Well,' Josie said finally, 'if you want my opinion, then you need to put your anger to one side and talk to Megan. Her wishes are paramount, and my advice would be to offer her your support and unconditional love and put aside your own feelings. And your ex-wife needs to be told as soon as possible.'

Charles drained his glass and looked at Josie. 'Sound

advice and exactly what I need to do. I'll go home now, make her a nice meal and we'll sit down to chat.'

'Good.'

'Thanks, Josie, oh wise woman.'

Josie shook her head and tried to smile. 'Not always so wise.'

'Well, you've helped me sort it out in my mind. I need to find out what Megan is really thinking and support her whatever she decides.'

'That sounds like a plan.'

'Can I walk you home?'

'No, Charles, you get home to Megan. I'll be fine. A bit of fresh air will do me good.'

'Right. Well, bye then and thanks for the advice.'

'You're welcome. Bye, Charles.'

As Josie walked slowly back to her flat, she wondered what the heck to do now. Charles needed to know about the baby, but this was obviously not the right time to tell him. She'd give it a week or so, then tell him. But it was a conversation she was not looking forward to having.

Charles told a subdued and tearful Megan that they were going to talk to her mum and Todd that night.

'I'll be by your side the whole time, but I'll only speak up if it's essential. It's up to you, Megan, to tell them, okay?'

'Okay.' Megan looked small and fragile and Charles wanted to take her in his arms and cuddle her like he had when she was younger. He didn't as she needed to face up to the pregnancy and start acting like the adult she believed she was. There'd be time for hugs, and tears wiped away, after the conversation.

Charles made macaroni cheese for their tea. It had always been one of Megan's favourite comfort dishes and he bet she would need all the comfort she could get before facing the anger of her mother. Charles didn't really care what Todd thought, this was a family matter, and he wasn't family. At least, as far as Charles was concerned he wasn't.

Once the meal was over and they'd stacked the dishwasher and cleared everything away, leaving the kitchen spotless, Charles powered up his laptop and rang Clarissa. Megan sat trembling beside him. His ex-wife's face came into view on the screen. She looked as if she was about to go out, with her face made-up and a sparkly necklace and matching earrings.

'Hi, this is a pleasant surprise. Are you having a good time, sweetie?' Clarissa asked, ignoring Charles altogether.

'Yes, thanks.' Megan's voice was quiet, and she sat huddled on the couch next to Charles who leaned forward with his elbows on his knees facing his laptop that he had placed on the coffee table.

'You don't sound very happy. Is something wrong?'

'Megan has something to tell you,' said Charles, then turned to Megan who looked as if she wanted to be anywhere but there. 'Go on, honey, just say it. It's the best way.'

'God, what are you two being so mysterious about? I'm intrigued.'

'Mum,' Megan said, her voice trembling, 'I'm pregnant.'

'What?! Are you serious? Is this a sick joke? You're pregnant?'

'Who's pregnant? What's going on?' Todd joined Clarissa, his face red and his voice booming with indignation. He looked as if he was in the process of getting dressed, his hair stuck up and his shirt undone.

Megan was crying hard and couldn't speak. Charles said nothing, waiting for the onslaught of questions. He listened to the conversation between his ex-wife and her new man.

'She says she's pregnant,' said Clarissa.

'Who's pregnant?'

'Megan, of course, who else?' Clarissa swept her hair off her face angrily and glared at the screen. Charles glared back but said nothing.

'Megan? You're pregnant? Are you kidding me?' Todd's voice was increasing in volume and Charles was determined not to join in a shouting match with him, so he said nothing. Megan was sobbing, so Charles reached over and took one of her hands, holding it between his, trying to transmit his support to her. Her sobbing decreased a little at his touch and she took a deep breath, obviously trying to get herself together.

'I'm sorry, Mum,' Megan said. Charles put his arm around her.

'You're sorry. You're sorry! What bloody good is that? I didn't even know you were having sex. Who's the father?' Clarissa and Todd were incensed, and Charles suspected it would take a while before they were calm enough to have an adult discussion.

'Jason,' Megan said quietly.

'Jason Osborne?'

'Yes.'

'Not Christian Osborne's son? What's this going to do for our business relations? We'll have to be really careful how we handle this, Clarissa. We don't want to alienate the Osbornes.'

'Todd, for goodness sake! This is about Megan, not your stupid business.'

'Oh, my business is stupid, is it? Not so stupid when it pays for your clothes, jewellery, holidays…'

'Todd, this is not the time.'

Trouble in paradise thought Charles with a sense of satisfaction. But he agreed with his ex-wife; Megan was the only one who mattered.

'Right, young lady,' said Todd drawing himself up and puffing out his chest, no doubt to show them all who was boss. 'Here's what's going to happen. You are coming home straight away and are grounded for the foreseeable future, at least until you've had the abortion. You are not leaving the house. Do you understand?'

Megan burst into a fresh bout of sobbing and Charles hugged her even closer to him.

'I don't think Megan has decided what she wants to do yet,' said Charles calmly.

'She's got no bloody choice. She's coming home even if I have to drive all the way to the north to collect her.'

Charles bristled at the way Todd described anywhere north of Watford Gap as "the north". He was also cross at the way the man had taken over the conversation while himself and Clarissa, Megan's parents and the only people who should have an opinion in Charles's view, were sitting mute and helpless. Well, he wasn't helpless, and it was about time he intervened for his daughter's sake.

'Right, that's enough. I'll tell you what we're going to do. Megan is staying with me, at least until she decides whether she is keeping the baby or not.'

Todd interrupted, 'She's having an abortion, that's what she's going to do. She's too young to be a mother and I'm not standing by and watching her ruin her life because of teenage hijinks.'

Clarissa, who'd been quiet long enough said, 'I agree with Charles. We need some time to think about this. We'll talk to you later.'

The screen froze then went blank as Clarissa terminated the call.

Charles and Megan sat in the sudden quiet of the room. Megan snuffled and crossed her arms, hugging herself. Charles lay back on the couch and put his hands on his head.

'Thanks, Dad, for sticking up for me.'

'I'll always be on your side, Megan, no matter what. This is your life and your future. If you want to keep the baby, then so be it.'

'How do I know if I can do it? Be a mother, I mean?'

'I wish I had something to say that would help. I only know that when I accompanied your mother to her first scan and saw you for the first time on that screen…' Charles stopped, feeling emotional suddenly, 'I knew that I would move heaven and earth for you. I loved you straight away and I will always love you no matter what happens.'

Megan cuddled up to Charles and he hugged her to him. They sat like that for ages, lost in their own private thoughts.

Chapter Seventeen

Three weeks later Josie still hadn't told Charles that she was pregnant. She'd had her eight weeks booking-in appointment and was due for her twelve-week ultrasound scan, to accurately assess her dates, in the middle of March.

Josie still couldn't get her head around the fact that she was pregnant.

All the family had gathered for Mother's Day Sunday lunch at her parents. It would be the perfect time to announce her pregnancy and be wrapped in O'Connor love. Of course, most of them, if not all, already knew. Her mother would have told her father who would have told Zoe as they worked at the same surgery. Zoe would have told Riordan. Josie had already told Lexi who she had grown to love very quickly when she married Casey and the two of them met regularly for drinks or girlie shopping trips. She'd also told Jay as he was her twin, and they had no secrets from each other.

So, the O'Connor grapevine would have been buzzing with the news. She was glad everyone knew as she wasn't proud of getting pregnant after one bout of energetic sex with an almost complete stranger.

The house smelled like a florist's when she walked through the door. Every surface was covered in vases of flowers and she had one of her own to add. There were orange roses, an assortment of spring flowers including freesia, blue hyacinth and daffodils, lilies, and Josie had brought a mixed bouquet with myriad flowers in shades of pink, purple, and white.

'How are you, darling?' her father greeted her.

'I'm fine, Dad, how are you?'

'I'll be better when I have a hug from my favourite daughter.' This was one of her dad's regular jokes as she was, of course, his only daughter.

'Hi, sweetie,' said Eloise joining them.

'Happy Mother's Day.' She handed over her flowers and her mum kissed her on the cheek.

'Thank you, darling, they're beautiful.'

They hugged and the kids jumped around them asking if they could join in. It wasn't long before a group hug was in progress in the middle of the kitchen.

At one time, various members of the family had offered to cook Sunday lunch for Eloise, but this idea was met with horror by the lady herself who knew her cooking was the best. Eloise had told them to buy her a nice bunch of flowers and she would cook the roast. All she really wanted was her family around her.

This year, Riordan and Tom had made cakes for Eloise and Zoe. One sat in the centre of the dining table on a cake stand so everybody could admire it. It was vanilla and had "Happy Mum's Day" in pink icing. The cake was a bit lopsided and the writing was squashed into one corner, but Tom was extremely proud of it. Zoe's cake was chocolate with chocolate buttons adorning the top. Tom had a photo of it on his phone and showed it to everyone to admire.

When they had all settled at the dining table, the toddlers Lucy and Abigail in their high chairs, and were tucking into beef and Yorkshire puddings as only Eloise could make, the questions started.

'Have you told him yet, this doctor?' asked Casey.

'When are we going to meet him?' asked Riordan.

'Are you having a baby, Auntie Josie?' asked Jade with a wide-eyed look of wonder.

'Yes, darling, I am. I haven't told him yet for a good reason and I was wondering if it would be okay to invite Charles and his daughter, Megan, to the party?'

'It's okay with me,' said Jay, 'is it okay with you, Caitlin?'

'Fine by me, the more the merrier.'

'So, what's this good reason, then?' asked Casey who was like a dog with a bone when he wanted information.

'The fact that his sixteen-year-old daughter is also pregnant, and the news has come as a bit of a shock as you can imagine. I don't think Charles could stand the stress of knowing he's going to be a father again and a grandfather one week apart.'

'Oh dear, that is bad timing,' said her mother.

'Why is everyone having babies?' asked Tom sounding disgruntled. He'd much prefer more dogs.

'I like babies,' said Jade spearing a whole roast potato and trying to shove it into her mouth.

'Jade, darling, let me cut that for you,' said Lexi.

'So, are we all set for the twentieth?' asked Jay.

'Looking forward to it, son,' said Dan.

Josie was also looking forward to the party that Jay and Caitlin were hosting in lieu of the wedding reception they didn't have. And if she could find the courage to tell Charles that she was pregnant, then all the better.

'You need to tell Charles about the baby before your scan as he'll want to be there,' said Casey. Her brother had missed the first four years of Jade's life and had strong feelings about the baby's father being part of the pregnancy. Casey had made up for it when Lexi was pregnant with Lucy as he went to every appointment and scan she had and was there when Lucy was born.

Josie wasn't sure that Charles would feel the same way. He had so much to contend with, after the news of Megan's pregnancy. His daughter would be his priority, it went without saying. But this child was his as well. Perhaps he would want to be there.

'Do you want me to be there, Josie, at the scan?' Eloise smiled tenderly and Josie smiled back.

'It's okay, Mum, I'm working that day, so I'll just take time out to have the scan and go back to work again.'

'What, with a full bladder?' asked Lexi.

'I'm a midwife, I don't get to use the facilities as regularly as I'd like. I'm used to working with a full bladder.

'Not as full as it will be when you have your scan, trust me,' said Lexi with a laugh.

'I'll be fine,' said Josie.

Josie realised she should have listened to Lexi. Never in her life had she been so desperate to pee; not even as a little girl in the infants class when she'd peed her pants as she'd been laughing so much at something her best friend had said. That was embarrassing but nothing compared to a grown-up woman wetting herself.

She lay, watching the screen, and as the sonographer moved the transducer device over her belly, Josie realised she was holding her breath.

'Is everything okay?' Josie couldn't help asking even though she knew she had to be patient and wait for the professional to do her thing.

After what seemed like an eternity, the sonographer, who Josie didn't know, smiled.

'Are you a twin, or do you have twins in your family?'

'I'm a twin,' answered Josie, her heart beating wildly. 'Am I having twins?'

'Yep, there they are.' She pointed at the screen at the two tiny people. 'Looks as if they're fraternal. They have their own placentas and membranes. We'll be able to tell their gender in the next scan.'

Josie was speechless and wished she'd taken her mother up on her offer to be with her at the scan. She wanted to cry, and laugh, but more than anything, she wanted to share the wonderful news with someone she loved.

'Congratulations,' said the sonographer.

'Thanks,' said Josie.

As she lay in a stupor, staring at the screen at her babies, a memory slid into her mind. She and Jay must have been about two and they were both trying to get onto Gran's knee, scrabbling and pushing each other to have the honoured place on the beloved knee. A place of warmth, security, stories, and the faint citrus aroma of Eau de Cologne 4711 which Gran always wore. She remembered Gran lifting both of them up and onto her lap. Then wrapping her arms around them and kissing one and then the other.

Thanks, Gran, Josie whispered knowing she had been sent that memory to let her know that all would be well.

The party was taking place in a large event room on the ground floor of the Leytonsfield Hotel. It was decorated with balloons and banners that proclaimed "Party Time", "Congratulations Jay and Caitlin", and "Happily Ever After", hung strategically on the walls.

Birthdays, anniversaries, wedding receptions and other get-togethers had been celebrated down the years at the Leytonsfield as it was the venue favoured by the O'Connor family. Jay and Josie had celebrated their twenty-first birthdays there and now Jay and Caitlin were celebrating their marriage. Where had those years gone?

Tables were piled high with food for the buffet and there was a free bar.

Josie spotted Jay and Caitlin's friends from the ambulance service; Paul and his girlfriend, Pandora, were standing with Matt and his partner, Ben. Sally stood with them, laughing at something someone said. Josie decided to say hello to them later and went to find Jay.

Josie had arrived early to help out with the meeting and greeting, and anything else that she could assist with. She was also keeping an eye out for Charles and Megan. Charles had seemed happy to accept the invitation to the party, saying that it would give him the chance to meet new people and get Megan out of the house for a while. He'd told her that, after the video call with Clarissa and Todd, she had seemed quiet and unnaturally subdued. Megan was an extrovert by nature, but she seemed to have shrunk into herself and Charles was wondering if she was having second thoughts about keeping her baby.

Josie offered to talk to her, and Charles readily agreed and thanked her. She had still not been able to bring herself to tell Charles about the twins but the later she left it the harder it would be.

Casey was at the bar with the drinks order and a tray to bring them back to the table the family had settled around. Caitlin and her best friend, Sophie Simons, were chatting in a corner and the kids were running around with other children, chasing each other, and weaving in and out of the tables. Nobody told them to stop or be careful, so they took advantage of the freedom to play a raucous game of their own devising. The DJ was setting up in another corner of the room.

Then Charles and Megan arrived, and Josie went to greet them.

'Hi, welcome. I'm so glad you could come.'

'Thanks for inviting us. This is Megan. Megan, this is Josie, the lady I spent Christmas with.'

'Hi,' said Megan. She was an attractive girl with eyes the same shade of blue as her father's, long blonde hair and she was dressed in a short, midnight blue dress. She looked younger than sixteen and seemed uncertain, staying close to Charles.

'Would you like to meet the rest of the family?'

'Love to.'

Josie led them to where her parents were.

'Mum, Dad, this is Charles and his daughter Megan.'

They all shook hands and turned as Casey walked over, carefully carrying a tray of assorted drinks.

'Right. Beer for Dad and Riordan, wine for you, Mum, and a soft drink for the pregnant lady.'

Charles stared at Josie in surprise, his look swiftly turning to anger. He obviously thought Casey meant Megan. Although Josie had told her family that Megan was pregnant, they knew they had been told in confidence and wouldn't mention it in front of Megan, realising how hard it must be for the sixteen-year-old to be amongst total strangers. The last thing she would want is people questioning her about her pregnancy.

Casey was still holding the lemonade she had ordered. 'Don't you want this drink, Josie?'

Charles's look changed from anger to bewilderment and then to growing realisation. Josie watched his face in dismay. This was not how she had wanted to give him the news of his twins.

'You're pregnant?' Charles asked, frowning at her. Josie nodded, unable to speak.

Casey said, 'Haven't you told him yet?'

'No, I hadn't, but he knows now. Thanks, Casey.'

Charles was rooted to the spot. He waited for someone to tell him what the hell was going on. Josie was pregnant and he hadn't realised she was in a relationship. Had she been seeing someone when they had spent Christmas together? He had fond memories of his time with Josie, but now they felt slightly tarnished. Josie hadn't seemed the type to two-time someone.

Fortunately, Eloise O'Connor took charge and put her arm around Megan. 'Why don't you join us, sweetheart, while your father and Josie have a quiet word. It shouldn't take long.'

Megan looked back at Charles and he nodded. Then she allowed herself to be led away and Casey was directed to return to the bar for a lemonade for Megan.

Josie had started walking out of the room and he followed. She left the hotel and headed around the side of the building where they were hidden from prying eyes and couldn't be overheard.

'I'm sorry, Charles, I've been meaning to tell you for ages, but you had Megan and her pregnancy to deal with and it just never seemed the right time.'

Charles was still in the dark. If Josie was pregnant that was wonderful news, but nothing to do with him.

'I didn't know you were seeing someone. Anyway, congratulations. I'm happy for you.'

Josie was looking at him as if one of them was mad and it wasn't her.

'I'm not seeing anyone, Charles. Christmas Day…'

'What?! You mean…'

'Yes. We are pregnant. You and me. And there's something else.'

Charles didn't want to hear any more. She was pregnant. After they had made love once. He thought of the irony of the comparison with Megan's situation. Megan. How was he going to tell his daughter?

'We're having twins, Charles.'

'Twins?'

'Yep. They tend to run in the family. I'm sorry you have to hear it like this, I wanted to break it to you gently, but my brother has a habit of putting his foot in it.'

Charles's instinct was to ask if this was a joke, but the look on Josie's face told him it wasn't. She looked embarrassed and kept her hands on her stomach as if protecting her babies. Charles felt as if he'd been picked up and plonked down in a parallel universe. A short time ago the worst thing he had to deal with was Clarissa leaving him.

'So, when were you planning on telling me?'

Josie looked uncomfortable and shivered. Even though it

was the third week in March, it was still quite chilly. She folded her arms and tried to smile.

'Soon. I was going to tell you soon. I wanted the dust to settle with Megan. I knew it'd be a shock—'

'That's the understatement of the year. I can't believe it. You should have told me before this, Josie.'

'I know I should. I haven't handled it very well, I'm afraid. But there it is. We're having twins.'

'So they must be due about a week after Megan gives birth.'

'The beginning of September.'

'That's going to be one hell of a week.'

Josie smiled, but he didn't feel like smiling back. This was a blow that he never saw coming and an unwanted one at that. It meant he was going to become a father and a grandfather in the same week.

'You told me you were on the pill.' Charles didn't want to blame Josie as he was just as responsible, but he was bewildered, and his head was spinning.

'I am… was, but I didn't have them with me as I thought I'd be back home that night. In the heat of the moment, I forgot…'

'You forgot?'

'Please don't look at me like that. Yes, I screwed up, I'm sorry but I didn't do it on purpose, I promise.'

'I can't believe you forgot.'

Josie gazed at him, then lifted her chin in defiance. 'I had a lot on my mind. These things happen.'

They were silent, gazing at each other. This wasn't the time for recriminations. Josie was right, these things did happen, but it was the last thing he had expected to hear.

'I need time to think and I have to find a way to tell Megan.'

'Yes, of course, I understand.'

'I think I should go home and take Megan with me. This is not going to be the easiest conversation I've ever had with my daughter. I'm sure you understand.'

Josie nodded but looked down. She was disappointed in his reaction to the news of the babies, but he couldn't help that, Megan came first, and she was going to be horrified after all the condemnation she had suffered concerning her own pregnancy. As her father, he should have behaved in a more mature fashion.

'Yes, of course, I understand. Let me know when you're ready to talk.'

Charles moved forward and took her hands. 'How do you feel about it, Josie?' He hadn't even considered it from her point of view, he was so worried about what Megan would think. But Josie must have been as shocked as he was to find she was carrying twins.

'Me? Surprised...' she gave a nervous laugh. 'It hasn't really sunk in, to be honest, Charles. I've always wanted to be a mother, but...'

'But not like this. I understand. Give me the chance to tell Megan, and then we'll talk. I'm here for you and will support you in any way I can.'

'Thanks. That means a lot.'

'I better go.'

He turned and walked back to the hotel.

Chapter Eighteen

When they arrived home, Megan slumped on the couch and glared at Charles.

'Why have you dragged me away from the party? It was so rude.'

'I'm sorry, darling, but we need to talk.'

'Couldn't it have waited?'

'No, I'm afraid it couldn't.'

Charles sat down on the couch next to his daughter and searched his brain desperately for the easiest way to tell her. But there wasn't an easy way, so he should just come out and say it.

Megan was watching him with a frown and her arms folded in a defensive posture. She was clearly not happy with him at the moment.

'Well? What have I missed the party for? I was looking forward to it. If I'm going to stay here for a while I, like, need to meet people.'

'Yes, I know, I'm sorry.'

The seconds ticked down as Charles searched for openings and discarded them. Megan gave a deep sigh that seemed to come from her boots.

'Dad! What?'

'Josie is pregnant. She's due the week after you are.'

Megan was quiet and her frown deepened. Her eyes searched the room as if she was trying to find the answer to the puzzle.

'And? I need to know that as a matter of urgency because…?' Megan looked at Charles waiting for him to supply the rest of the sentence, so he did.

'Because I'm the father.' Charles spoke quietly hoping a measured tone would lessen the impact. It didn't.

'OMG! You have got to be kidding me!' Megan jumped up and started pacing up and down. She had kicked her shoes off, and she strode around the room in bare feet, waving her arms around for emphasis. 'The woman you helped at Christmas, the one who was, like, stuck in the ditch?'

'Josie, yes.'

'The midwife who is supposed to be, like, the wise woman who knows everything about pregnancy and babies and all that? How did she get herself pregnant if she's so wise?'

'Megan, please sit down, you're making me dizzy. We need to discuss this calmly and sensibly.'

Megan kept walking around the room as if she had surplus energy that had to be dispelled by keeping on the move. Then she stopped and stared at him.

'Dad, you're a hypocrite. You're on my case for getting pregnant and blame Jason for not having condoms but… what about you? Did you use condoms, Dad?'

Charles squirmed at being interrogated by his teenage daughter about condom usage, but he knew she was right.

He was just as bad as Jason. Worse, in fact, because in his eyes, Jason and Megan were still kids. He was old enough and experienced enough to know better.

'It was a contraceptive pill malfunction.' Not strictly true but hopefully Megan wouldn't be as knowledgeable about the ins and outs of the pill. No such luck.

'So, the wise woman forgot to take her pill. What a cliché.'

In different circumstances, Charles would have found Megan's attempt to be grown up amusing, but there was nothing funny about the situation they both found themselves in.

Eventually, Megan stopped pacing and sat down on the couch.

'So, what are you going to, like, do about it?'

Charles, grateful that Megan had calmed down a bit and seemed ready to talk sensibly, sighed and leaned back onto the cushions.

'Well, of course, I'll support her all I can, but you are my priority, Megan.'

'But that's your child, you can't just walk away and leave Josie to it.'

'I have no intention of walking away. I'll offer any support I can, financial and otherwise, but you're my child and you come first. Anyway, there's something I haven't told you.'

'Something else? My God wasn't that enough?'

'Yes, more than enough. I wish this hadn't happened and especially now when all my care and attention should be given to you. I'm sorry, Megan, you have no idea how much.'

'Okay. What is it?' Megan looked at him as if she wouldn't be surprised by anything he had to tell her.

'Josie's having twins. She's a twin. Jay, the man who was hosting the party, with his wife, Caitlin, he's her twin brother.'

'I only met them briefly,' Megan said sadly.

'Well, don't worry about that. I have a feeling we'll be seeing a lot of the O'Connor family. We'll be related.'

'Cool. I always wanted a brother or sister. Now I might get both.'

When Charles and Megan had left the party, Josie joined her family.

'Sorry,' said Casey, 'me and my big mouth.'

'It's okay, I was struggling to find the right way to tell him. You may have done me a favour.'

'How did he take it?' asked Lexi.

'He was shocked but more worried about Megan than me, obviously, as she's his daughter. That's why he's taken her home. He wants to explain, although what he's going to say I've no idea.'

Eloise hugged her and said, 'There'll be plenty of time to discuss the practicalities. Let the poor man get used to the idea first.'

'I'm not sure I'm used to the idea yet. It's all come as a bit of a shock.'

There was a plate of food on the table that looked untouched, so Josie picked up a sausage roll and bit into it. She was over the nausea, thank goodness, and had got her appetite back.

'How do you feel about Charles?' asked Zoe, 'Do you think you'll stay friends to co-parent, or will there be wedding bells in the future?' Zoe's dark eyes flashed with amusement. Her sister-in-law was down to earth and could be relied on to ask straight questions.

'I hope we'll stay friends, but I doubt you'll be hearing wedding bells any time soon.'

'There must be something between the two of you. After all, you had sex,' Casey said.

'That's right, Casey, tell it like it is,' said Lexi punching him playfully on the arm.

Casey shrugged and gave her a "What did I say?" look.

They were watching Josie with varying expressions of love mixed with other emotions; amusement from her brothers, curiosity and concern from the women and just plain concern with an abundance of love from her parents.

Jay and Caitlin had moved nearer the DJ to request their favourite song. It looked as if Jay was going to speak. Thank goodness. Hopefully, her family would be distracted from her pregnancy and could concentrate on the happy couple.

Her wish came true when Jay blew into the microphone and prepared to make a speech. They all turned in that direction and Josie sighed with relief. It was inevitable that her family would want the details of her feelings for Charles and his for her. Bringing children into the world should not be undertaken lightly and yet, she and Megan were both pregnant, not because they had planned it that way, but because they had been careless. Nothing to be proud of.

Josie wished Charles and Megan had stayed at the party so he could have met her family properly and she could have talked to Megan and asked her if she needed any advice or guidance. After all, she may be pregnant herself, but she was still a midwife and her job was to help women plan the best labour for themselves.

Josie tried to concentrate on what Jay was saying.

'First, I want to thank you all for coming; it's great to see all my family and friends together in one place. And I need to apologise to you all for not inviting you to the wedding.' Jay looked at Caitlin who smiled her encouragement. 'The thing is, we decided to get married on the spur of the moment. I think the NHS would have collapsed if everyone here had taken annual leave at the same time to fly to Bali.'

There was a wave of laughter from the audience. Jay's got them in the palm of his hand, thought Josie. She felt a rush of love for her twin.

'Anyway, in my usual cack-handed fashion I managed to propose to my lovely Caitlin—'

'Did you go down on one knee?' Paul shouted and everyone laughed.

'I did, Paul, yeah. Got to do things right.'

'Well done,' shouted Paul and they all laughed again.

'We didn't want a long engagement and a beach wedding sounded wonderful. And it was.' Caitlin grabbed Jay's hand and they smiled at each other as only people in love could. 'Anyway, you all know the rest.'

Josie watched as the love poured from their eyes as they gazed at each other. She felt tearful suddenly and closed her eyes, taking deep breaths to stop herself from crying.

'The other thing I wanted to say was thank you to my wonderful family for welcoming Caitlin into the O'Connor clan and making her feel loved and welcome.'

Caitlin grabbed the microphone and said, 'I second that. Thank you, everyone.' She pushed the microphone back at Jay and everyone laughed again. Caitlin held on to Jay's arm and he continued his speech.

'Last but not least, I want to thank my lovely wife for agreeing to spend the rest of her life with me and for making me the happiest man on earth.'

There was an eruption of cheers and applause that seemed to go on for a long time. Josie gave in to her tears and wiped her face with a tissue that someone, she thought it was Riordan, had shoved into her hand.

Her beloved brother was now a married man. For so long it had been Josie and Jay, now it was Jay and Caitlin. And soon, there'd be two more O'Connors to welcome into the family. How she wished that she also had a loving partner, a significant other, that she could say made her the happiest woman on earth. Co-parenting with a friend could be as good as it ever got for her. She didn't want to think about that. She was still young and like her mother had told her, people don't always hit the jackpot at the first try.

Putting her own problems aside and raising her glass of lemonade, Josie toasted the happy couple.

'To Jay and Caitlin.'

Chapter Nineteen

When Charles got up the following morning, Megan was already out of bed and talking to Clarissa via video call. She looked up from Charles's laptop as he came into the kitchen and he noticed she had make-up on and was wearing the same outfit she had worn when she travelled up from London.

'Good morning,' he said.

'Dad, I'm going back to stay with Mum and Todd. Mum'll explain.'

Megan got up so he could take her place. He did, feeling a lead weight in his heart.

'What's going on Clarissa?'

'I'll tell you what's going on, Charles. You are behaving like a teenager, getting a woman you don't even know pregnant. What the hell did you think you were doing? You're supposed to set a good example to Megan and yet you show her that it's okay to sleep around and it doesn't matter if the woman gets pregnant. How could you be so irresponsible?'

Charles listened to his ex-wife's tirade, hating the bitterness and patronising attitude but knowing that he deserved it. He wondered if Clarissa knew *the baby* was twins, but then decided it didn't matter as it was none of her damned business. He wasn't going to tell her.

But he really didn't want Megan to go. She would be cared for during her pregnancy with him and he was scared that Todd would try to talk her into having a termination. Charles knew that she wanted the baby, and he would do everything in his power to make sure that happened.

'Clarissa, I really don't think it's necessary for her to leave yet. We've hardly had any time together and she can be looked after in the maternity unit I work in. In fact, I think she should stay with me until the baby's born.'

'No.' Clarissa's voice was clipped as if she wasn't even prepared to talk about it.

'What do you mean "no"? Aren't you even prepared to discuss it?'

'Ask your daughter what she wants. Go on, ask her.'

He turned his attention to Megan who was leaning against the kitchen counter, biting her bottom lip, and avoiding his gaze.

'Megan? Do you want to leave and go back to London?' She nodded without speaking. 'Why? We were going to have some quality time together. I'm sorry about the party but there'll be other opportunities to meet people.'

'Dad… I'm sorry but, I want to go home.'

'But why?' Charles was bewildered. He desperately wanted her to stay so they could repair their broken relationship.

'She wants to come home, Charles, because she hates your double standards. You should be a role model for your daughter, but it turns out you're no better than Jason. We're driving up today to collect her. I have to go as Todd's anxious to make a start.'

'Are you going to stay the night? I have enough room.' The last thing he wanted was Clarissa and Todd staying in his house, but the journey from London to Leytonsfield was the best part of an eight hour round trip.

'No, we don't want to stay. We want to get Megan home with us as soon as we can. Where we can look after her properly.'

'I'm looking after her properly,' Charles said, ready to be affronted by Clarissa's superior attitude. He glanced at Megan and saw that she had tears in her eyes. He melted. He'd done this, upset his daughter. She had enough to cope with dealing with her unexpected pregnancy. He wouldn't make life any harder for her than it already was by fighting Clarissa and Todd. Especially if it was what Megan wanted as well.

His daughter was nearly an adult and he needed to start listening to her and taking more notice of what she chose for her own life.

'Okay, if it's what Megan wants.'

'Fine. See you later.' The video call ended abruptly, and Charles closed the laptop.

'So, we've got a few hours before they arrive. Is there anything, in particular, you want to do?' Megan shook her head and wouldn't look at him. 'Megan, talk to me, please. I know I've messed up, but it's happened, and I'm trying to deal with it the best way I can.'

'But you're not dealing with it, are you? You're letting Josie take care of everything. At least Jason is, like, support-ive. He wants to be a father to the baby. You haven't even seen the scan of the twins, have you?'

Charles didn't know what to say. He *hadn't* seen the scan

of the twins, hadn't even considered that Josie would have had the scan by now, which is how she knew she was having twins. He'd given little thought to Josie's pregnancy and what she'd be going through. As an obstetrician, he should know better. As the babies' father, he was a disgrace. He felt his life was spiralling out of control and he didn't know what to do about it.

'Okay, Megan, you're right. About everything. I need your advice. It's one thing helping women give birth and looking after them before and after labour, but it's a different thing being a father. It's sixteen years since I watched you come into the world, and I'm out of touch. You're my daughter, and I love you more than life itself, but you're also a young woman who is about to experience probably the most wonderful thing to happen to her. To give birth. I need you to help me here. What should I do?'

At his words, Megan's attitude changed. She smiled, stood up straighter and took his hand, leading him to the living room where they both sat on the couch together.

'Okay, Dad, this is all new to me, but this is what I think. Josie needs to know that you're going to be there for her whenever she needs you. That's, like, really important. Not just for money but to take an interest in what Josie's going through. If she wants to talk about the babies, especially the things she's scared about, then you have to listen. Don't give her advice if she doesn't want it, just listen to her.'

Charles nodded and waited for more pearls of wisdom from his sixteen-year-old daughter. She was a wise woman in training, and he couldn't be more proud of her than he was at that moment. He decided he rather liked the role reversal.

After his lecture, he made them both breakfast and then

they watched a movie together and a short time later, the doorbell rang. Clarissa and Todd stood on the step.

'Is she ready?' asked Todd abruptly.

'She is,' answered Charles. He felt calmer than he had a few hours previously. They had made a few tentative steps towards being a loving father and daughter again. He was determined that he wouldn't mess it up this time.

'Goodbye, darling, and don't forget, you can come back whenever you want, just ring me.'

He hugged Megan to him and felt an ache deep inside that he was losing her again so soon.

'I will. Take care of Josie.' Megan hugged him tighter and he hated to let her go.

'Definitely.'

'Right, come on then, if you've finished, we've got a long journey back.' Todd was jittery, obviously eager to get home. Charles didn't blame him. He never drove to London if he could help it, and always took the train so he could read the papers and get some work done.

'Bye, darling.' Charles waved her off and shut the front door.

Charles missed Megan as soon as she'd gone. The house was too quiet, and he had nothing to distract him from his thoughts. He went over in his mind everything Megan had said, realising that she was absolutely right. He was guilty of double standards and knew he had to make it up to Josie. He'd been cold and distant when she told him about the twins, instead of embracing her and promising her he would be there for her. He needed to ask her forgiveness and try to convince her that she could rely on him.

Charles had been given a second chance at being a father. The first time, with Megan, he had been working long hours and missed so much of her development. This time, with the twins, he would do a better job, if Josie let him play his part.

Now, as a consultant, he worked fewer hours, so had more time to devote to being a father. How much richer his life would be, though, if he had someone to share things with. He was sick of being alone with his miserable thoughts. This house was too big for one person. It needed a family here for it to become a home. He thought of Josie living here with the twins and Megan with her child. Families came in all shapes and sizes these days. They could be a family, with the three children growing up together. How much love and laughter would be in that home?

The following day Charles went back to work. There was no point taking annual leave without Megan and he had nothing else to do but rattle around on his own feeling sorry for himself.

Charles found Josie in the kitchen at lunchtime, trying to grab her sandwiches from the fridge and make a cup of coffee at the same time.

'Here, let me get that.' He made two coffees while Josie tucked into her sandwiches.

'What are you doing here?' she asked, 'I thought you were with Megan.'

'She's gone home to London. I'm afraid she's rather ashamed of me at the moment and so am I to be honest.'

'Was she upset about the twins?'

'She was angry at my double standards and ashamed of me for neglecting you and not giving you the support you deserve. And she's right. I'd like to make amends if I may. Would you allow me to buy you dinner?'

Josie was smiling as she ate. 'Yes, I certainly would. Where are we going?'

'Well, I've heard good things of Rocco's and I love Italian food if you do.'

'Rocco's is a good choice and I love Italian food too.'

'Great. How about Saturday?'

'Yep, I'm on an early so that would work.'

'Shall I pick you up at seven?'

'Seven it is.'

'Wonderful.' Charles drained his coffee and rinsed the mug. Josie watched him with a tentative smile playing around the corners of her mouth. 'Oh, and could you bring the scan? I haven't seen it yet.'

'You want to see your children?'

'Yes, I do. Very much. Better go. See you Saturday.'

'Look forward to it.' Josie was grinning widely, and Charles felt his spirits lift.

'Me too.'

Chapter Twenty

Josie had made an effort with her appearance, discarding the jeans, sweatshirt and boots, which was her attire of choice when she was off-duty, and wearing a little black dress with heels. She also used more make-up, especially around her eyes, and was pleased with the look she'd achieved. Attractive but not too sexy. She and Charles were only supposed to be friends now, after all; a thought that caused a frisson of loss deep within before she told herself to stop being so stupid.

Her middle was starting to develop a tiny bulge and Josie realised it was time to think seriously of the babies as a reality and not just a strange dream that she felt she would soon wake up from. She was going to be a mother and needed to start facing that fact.

First of all, she needed maternity clothes. It was such a shame that Megan had returned to London as they could have had fun shopping together. It was too early to start thinking of prams, cots, and nappies, but that time would soon be upon her too.

Josie brushed her hair until it shone. She wore it pinned up when she was nursing as it was more hygienic and practical, so when she was in her own clothes rather than her uniform, she wore her hair down. She added silver drop earrings and a silver necklace that her parents had given her for her last birthday, and she was ready.

At precisely seven, the doorbell rang. Charles had arrived, punctual as always. She slipped on a warm jacket and, after locking her flat, ran lightly down the stairs to the front door.

'Hello,' said Charles, 'you look lovely.'

'Thanks.' Josie nearly said, "so do you" as Charles had made an effort too. He wore black trousers and a smart blue shirt with a dark blue jacket. No tie, he wore the shirt with the top button undone. Josie breathed in the spicy, woodsy aroma of his aftershave, or cologne appreciatively.

'Right,' Charles said cheerfully, 'shall we go then?'

'Yep, let's go.'

Josie had hoped Charles would have offered her his arm to take, but he didn't, instead, turning away and walking ahead to open the gate for her to go through first.

'Thanks.'

'You're welcome.'

Josie hoped they wouldn't spend the evening being polite and distant with each other. This was the nearest thing she'd had to a date for ages. Longer than she cared to remember. She hoped they could return to the easy friendship they'd enjoyed in the cottage. She had fond memories of the few days they'd spent together.

They spoke little in the short journey to the town centre and parked in the community car park before strolling to Rocco's.

When they entered the restaurant they were met with

the aromas of garlic and spicy food cooking. Josie's stomach rumbled and she realised how hungry she was.

A waiter showed them to a table and offered Charles the wine list and handed them a menu each.

'What would you like to drink, Josie?' Charles asked.

'I'll just have mineral water, please.'

'Just two mineral waters then,' Charles said, handing the wine list back.

'Of course, sir.' He left and Charles opened his menu.

'What do you fancy?' he asked.

You thought Josie. Charles was looking smart and extremely fanciable, and Josie was feeling horny, which she knew was a side effect of the pregnancy. All those hormones. She also knew, however, that it was not advisable to have sex when carrying twins. So she needed to ignore her body's clamouring for that kind of attention and feed it instead.

'Just curious but, why are you drinking mineral water?' asked Josie.

'Because you are. I'm being supportive by not having wine. I want to share in this pregnancy, Josie, as much as I can, and going without the things you have to go without is one way to do that.'

Josie grinned, 'That's very noble, Charles, but it's really not necessary. I appreciate the gesture, but I won't hold you to it. Is it only when you're with me, or are you going to have a sneaky pint in the Old Oak now and again?'

'I'll get back to you on that,' Charles said, grinning, before returning to studying the menu.

Josie laughed. 'I think I'll just have garlic bread for a starter and Spaghetti Carbonara,' she said.

'I'll have garlic bread too and Tuscan chicken.'

The waiter brought their mineral waters and, after taking their orders, disappeared again.

Charles leaned forward and raised his glass. 'Cheers, to us and the twins.'

Josie clinked her glass against his and said, 'Cheers.' She took the scan out of her handbag and handed it to Charles. 'Our twins,' she said with a catch in her voice.

Charles picked the scan up and studied it. 'Wow,' he said. 'I've seen literally hundreds of these things, but I never really looked at one until now. Our babies.' He didn't say any more but, misty eyed, he continued to stare at the scan.

'What about Megan's scan? You must have seen that.'

'Yes, I must, but I honestly don't remember. Everything was a bit of a blur in those days. All I remember is being permanently exhausted and wondering how on earth I was going to be a father. It's different now. I know I've made mistakes, but I'm determined to get it right with the twins.'

'I believe in you, Charles. Megan has turned out fine, despite what you think about your part in her upbringing. Everything will be okay. You worry too much, you know that?'

Charles laughed. 'So, how have you been, Josie? Has the nausea gone now?'

Josie wondered if he was asking as a professional, a friend, or something else?

'Thankfully, yes it's gone. I can eat almost normally again, no cravings yet.'

Charles nodded. 'Good.'

Josie wondered if she should mention her desire for sex, then decided against it. There was nothing they could do about it anyway.

'How's Megan getting on with her pregnancy?'

'She seems to be coping well. I just wish she hadn't gone back to London. I could have kept a close eye on her here. I'm sensing she isn't as comfortable with Todd and Clarissa as she tries to make out. The poor kid doesn't feel she belongs anywhere now.'

'That's a shame, we all need a feeling of belonging. It helps to ground us.'

The waiter brought the garlic bread and they thanked him and tucked in. It was delicious and Josie had to stop herself from consuming it too fast. Heartburn was a side effect of pregnancy, and she wanted to avoid it at all costs.

'I'm thinking of looking for a house to buy,' said Charles, 'and wonder if you would be so kind as to act as estate agent again.'

'I'd be delighted.'

'I was thinking that, if I had my own home—nothing wrong with the rented house but it isn't mine if you know what I mean—then Megan might be more amenable to moving to Leytonsfield permanently. Now she's sixteen she can legally decide who she wants to live with.'

'She'd be missing out on all the skiing holidays though, won't that bother her?'

'I think her priorities have changed since she became pregnant.'

'I can relate to that,' said Josie. 'In fact, I've been thinking the same thing. As I live on the top floor of a converted house with no lift, I'm going to struggle to get up two flights of stairs when I am near my time, and after, trying to get a pram up there would be a nightmare. I may have to go back to live with my parents for a while and look for a more practical place to buy.'

Charles was quiet as if deep in thought.

The waiter cleared away the starter plates and replaced them with the main course. Josie didn't wait for permission, she got stuck in. Charles asked for two more mineral waters.

'I have a proposition for you,' Charles said as he looked at his plate.

'Oh. What proposition?'

'My daughter showed me that I need to face up to my responsibilities as far as the twins are concerned. Not just financially, but in other ways. I want to be part of the babies' lives, to be there for their first smile, first word, when they start to sit up, crawl and walk. I missed out on so much of Megan's babyhood as I was a twenty-six-year-old doctor working around the clock. I regret how much I missed. I want it to be different with the twins.'

Josie was touched by the things Charles was saying, but she still didn't know what the proposition was.

'Charles, I am happy to accept your part in bringing up the twins and, of course, you can see them whenever you like.'

'Thanks. But... I want to be a hands-on dad, not a part-time father. Josie, would you consider living with me? And hopefully Megan and her baby? Or... if you want things done properly, we could get married if you like?'

Josie stared at Charles, at his eager expression and his gorgeous blue eyes. As proposals go it wasn't up there with the most romantic of them. *Beggars can't be choosers.* Gran was awake. And she was right. Josie wasn't in a position to be choosy, and she would be well fed as Charles was a fabulous cook. On the other hand, she wanted real love, not an arrangement that suited them both just because she was pregnant. Charles was trying so hard to do the right thing and she was reluctant to bring him back down to earth, but she had no choice.

'Charles, I'm sorry, I appreciate everything you're saying, but I would rather be alone as a single mother than be in a loveless marriage.'

Chapter Twenty-One

How could he have been so utterly stupid? To ask Josie to marry him and the way he did it, almost as an afterthought. No wonder she'd knocked him back. What would she think of him now?

But still, Charles felt rejected. She could have let him down easily, told him she'd think about it. But no, that "loveless marriage" rang in his head like a reproach. He should have told her that it wouldn't be loveless. Charles's feelings for Josie had grown over the weeks that they had worked together. He had tremendous respect for Josie as a professional and a wise woman. But making love in the cottage had ignited a spark inside him and it could easily become a raging fire if circumstances were different. He wanted her again. If he was brutally honest, he'd never stopped wanting her. She was gorgeous and they'd been compatible.

Now, however, carrying twins, sex was out of the question. If things were different, he'd have tried to reignite the spark. But now, he realised that it wasn't what she wanted.

She'd never even given his proposition a chance. Not even considered it.

The meal had been pleasant and could have led to the two of them growing closer, confiding in each other about the way they were feeling about the twins. But Charles had been hurt, and when he felt that way he retreated into himself and sent out "leave me alone" signals.

They had left soon after and Josie didn't invite Charles in for a coffee. He wouldn't have accepted anyway.

Now, he was sitting in an empty house, alone, and wondering whether to resurrect his relationship with the whisky bottle. But even getting drunk didn't appeal anymore. He had a job to do and couldn't afford to make mistakes. Women depended on him to make correct diagnoses of conditions of pregnancy before they went too far and cost the lives of the women and their babies. He was a surgeon who performed caesareans and needed a steady hand and a clear head. Getting drunk was never the answer.

Charles went to bed thinking over everything that had happened since Christmas. The two most important women in his life were now out of his reach. Megan was back in London and Josie... he didn't know what to think about Josie. The mother of his unborn twins and a woman he was growing to love. But she didn't love him, that was obvious. If she had she never would have described his proposition as a "loveless marriage".

Charles realised that he had to withdraw and give Josie the space she so obviously wanted. A life without him in it.

Josie had been enjoying the meal at Rocco's until she ruined it. She was too outspoken, said it like it was. It was one thing being truthful, quite another bludgeoning someone over the head with it. She should have been gentler. Charles was more sensitive than he appeared.

They had not had the chance to talk since that night, and Josie had the feeling Charles was avoiding her. If they passed each other in the corridor, the canteen or anywhere else in the maternity unit, she smiled but Charles merely nodded and hurried on. On the one occasion, she had been in theatre when he was performing a caesarean, they hardly spoke. The fact she'd hurt Charles made Josie feel sad and guilty.

It was a hectic morning and Mandy Hughes was due for a scan and assessment. Shelley would accompany her but still, Josie was nervous. What if the scumbag boyfriend decided that today was the day he'd muscle his way into Mandy's life again? What if she decided to go back to him? Would she be that stupid? But women under the influence of abusive men didn't always act rationally. They were too scared and thought only of surviving.

When Mandy's appointment time came round, Josie alerted security to be in the maternity unit and ready to act if necessary.

Shelley and Mandy arrived.

'Hi, you two, how's it going?'

'Good, how's yourself?' asked Shelley.

Mandy just smiled shyly but she looked clean, well fed, and more relaxed than usual. That was a good sign.

Josie did all the usual checks, including taking her blood pressure and measuring her fundal height, the distance from the pelvis to the top of the uterus. This was to make sure Mandy was gaining weight and the baby was growing consistently.

'Is there anything you want to ask, Mandy, or talk to me about?'

'Some of the women in the shelter have been telling me about their pregnancies. I know it's going to hurt, but... I can have gas and air, or an epidural, can't I?'

'Of course. You can write your preferences in your birth plan. But you can always change your mind nearer the time. And there are relaxation techniques you can try. The more relaxed you are, the easier it will be to cope with the pain.'

'Okay.' Mandy smiled and Josie thought that Mandy would probably be the only person who was relaxed. Josie was terrified of the scumbag boyfriend turning up and hurting Mandy, the baby, or even the midwives. She wished there was some way she could get the police to lock him up, but as he hadn't committed a crime—yet—there was nothing anyone could do. Just make sure the security men were around and looking tough that day.

'Has Andrew heard anything more from the scumbag?' asked Josie when she was alone with Shelley.

'No, he hasn't seen him. I've asked Andrew to keep a special lookout for Tony as the more information we have the better armed we'll be.'

'Do you really think Mandy's in danger?' Josie watched Shelley's expression harden as she thought about her answer.

'Yes, I'm afraid I do. He's an evil bastard.'

That told Josie everything she needed to know.

Josie was relieved when she waved Mandy and Shelley off and felt herself physically relax. As if poor Mandy didn't have enough to worry about with bringing new life into the world, but she also had the threatening behaviour of a psychopath to deal with. Well, she would be protected. No one was going to hurt Mandy or her baby. Josie would make sure of that.

———————

On Easter Sunday, Mandy's labour started. Josie had requested she be on duty over the Easter weekend as she had predicted Mandy's baby would be born then.

Shelley was with her as her birth partner and was fascinated by everything that went on.

'That could be me one day if I can persuade Andrew,' Shelley said.

And it would be her too, thought Josie, except she might have to have an elective caesarean. She put thoughts of the twins out of her mind and concentrated on Mandy. She had alerted security and asked them to be in the maternity unit over the weekend and had also told Charles who had looked thoughtful and nodded.

'Thank you for telling me. I'm on call, so I'll be around.'

'Thanks, Charles, I appreciate that. Listen, I'm sorry about the way I just blurted out—'

'It's okay, Josie, I should never have asked. It was my fault entirely.'

'No, really, it wasn't. It was a lovely thought.'

'I need to be in theatre. See you later.'

'Bye.' Josie watched him striding down the corridor feeling a deep sense of loss.

Mandy was trying to get comfortable and failing. Her stress levels were increasing, so Josie suggested the birthing pool.

'I don't want to give birth in water. She might drown.'

'You don't need to. We can get you out before you give birth. It's a way of relaxing. The warm water can be soothing and because you're buoyant you can move around easily.'

'Sounds good,' said Shelley.

'Okay, I'll try it.'

Everything was going well, and Josie had just started to relax and believe that Mandy would have a good labour when she heard a commotion outside. A man's voice was raised, angry and aggressive, shouting for Mandy.

'Oh God, it's him. Please don't let him in.' Mandy started to scramble out of the birth pool, dripping water everywhere and crying. All the good work they'd done relaxing Mandy and supporting her had disappeared in an instant. The girl was terrified, and Josie saw red.

'Right,' she said. Game on, she thought.

Shelley was behind her. 'Don't go out there, phone the police. Josie, be careful, he's dangerous.'

'So am I,' Josie said through clenched teeth, 'Stay with Mandy, Shell, I'll deal with this.'

He was standing at the nurses' station and shouting in the face of one of the midwives who was trying to reason with him. When he caught sight of Josie he walked towards her.

'Mandy doesn't want to see you and you're trespassing, so I suggest you leave immediately.' Josie's voice didn't shake, in fact, she sounded quite calm, even though part of her was quaking at the thought of confrontation with this man.

'Ah, so she's in there, is she. Well, get out of my fuckin' way and let me get to her. That's my son in there and I'm taking him.'

Josie stood her ground and stared at the scumbag boyfriend. He wasn't as big, or tall, as she'd expected. In fact, he was a pathetic specimen of a man with badly inked tattoos and bad teeth. He looked as if he was under the influence of drugs, as his gaze was unsteady, and the pupils of his eyes were pinpoints. What a lovely girl like Mandy had seen in this disgusting creature, Josie couldn't comprehend.

'Well, don't just fuckin' stand there, get the fuck outta me way.'

'Mandy doesn't want to see you, in fact, she wants nothing more to do with you, and if you attempt to go into that room, you'll have to go through me first, and I am not in the mood to deal with a dickhead like you.'

Josie was feeling surprisingly calm as she stood her ground. She sensed there were other members of staff behind her but where were the security guards? She'd have to stall until they turned up. One thing was sure, Josie wasn't about to let this poor excuse for a human being anywhere near Mandy.

'I'm taking me son and no one, not a stuck up bitch like you or anyone fuckin' else is going to stop me.'

'You don't have a son.'

'Course I have. It's my baby.'

'Be that as it may, you haven't got a son.' Josie watched as his expression, gormless to start with, grew more uncomprehending. Was he so thick he didn't understand what she was telling him?

'I'm taking him so get outta the fuckin' way.'

Just then Josie spotted the security guards walking swiftly down the corridor towards them. At last.

Then, Josie's worst nightmare happened. The scumbag pulled a knife from his jacket and waved it in Josie's face. She stepped back and he stepped forward.

'Not so brave now are you, bitch?'

It happened so quickly that Josie didn't have the time to

react. Charles appeared from nowhere, or that was how it seemed, and grabbed scumbag around the face from behind with one hand, while his other hand grabbed the wrist of scumbag's knife-holding hand and twisted it behind his back. The knife fell to the ground with a clatter. Charles put his foot behind the man's knees and brought him to the floor in one swift movement. Then the security guards were there and held him down, shouting, kicking, and screaming.

Josie, who had been holding her breath, turned to Charles. 'That was—'

'Are you alright?' They spoke together, then smiled sheepishly at each other.

'Where did you learn to do that?' Josie's voice was full of admiration.

'I did self-defence at university. It comes in handy.'

'I'll say. Well done. Anyway, I need to get back to Mandy. Has someone phoned the police?'

'Yes, I did,' said one of the midwives.

'Do you need any help? With Mandy?' asked Charles.

'Not at the moment, thanks. I'll let you know.'

'Maybe we can talk—later?'

Josie nodded. 'Yes, I think we should.'

When Josie returned to the labour room, Mandy was back in the birthing pool. She looked up anxiously and Josie smiled her reassurance.

'I thought this was the best place for her,' said Shelley.

'Well done, yes it is. Your ex was carrying a knife, so the police have been called. The security guards are holding him until they arrive.'

Mandy started to cry, and Shelley put her arms around her shoulders. Josie noticed that Shelley was nearly as wet as Mandy was. She was taking her role as birth partner seriously.

The sound of sirens approaching grew louder until they stopped.

'The police are here,' said Josie.

Despite the fear that Mandy had felt and the disruption to her peaceful labour, several hours later she gave birth to a beautiful girl who was perfect. She only needed gas and air in the end. A good result thought Josie.

'Wow,' said Shelley as Josie laid the baby on Mandy for skin to skin contact. 'That's amazing. No wonder you wanted to be a midwife. What a way to spend your working life.'

'Midwives are always needed if you're thinking of training.'

'Me? I could never do that. I'm not clever enough.'

'Rubbish. Of course you are.'

Shelley blushed and Josie cleaned up the room for the next mother.

'What are you going to call her?' asked Josie.

'I'm going to call her Whitney,' said Mandy.

'Lovely,' Josie responded. She watched mother and baby together. Mandy was oblivious of everything going on around her, and only had eyes for her baby. But there was something Josie needed to discuss with her.

'Mandy, the police are going to arrest your ex as he was carrying a knife and threatening us with it. This is the time to come forward and tell them about his abuse of you. All the threats and the fear he put you through. Not to mention the physical violence.'

Mandy was listening carefully and nodding at the things Josie was saying.

'I know. I'm going to tell them. I want him locked up and away from me and Whitney. I'm ready now.'

Chapter Twenty-Two

When Charles arrived home he was exhausted. He'd been on call all over the Easter weekend so far, but had the following day, Easter Monday, off to recover. He'd been busy in theatre and had then gone over to the labour ward to see a patient when he'd heard the shouting and remembered what Josie had said about Mandy's abuser.

Enraged on seeing the man holding a knife in front of Josie's face, he had acted on instinct. Fortunately, he'd remembered how to disarm an attacker from behind and, although it wasn't a textbook move, it was effective. Josie was impressed anyway.

That thought left a warm fuzzy feeling in his stomach. He had done little to impress her so far, apart from his cooking skills, and it was a good feeling to be thought of as a hero, even if only briefly.

Charles wondered if he deserved a whisky. He'd finished his on-call duties so there was nothing stopping him from having a drink. Nothing, that is, except the promise he'd made to Josie that he wouldn't drink because she couldn't. He decided to have a coffee instead.

An hour later, he was glad he had made that decision. Megan rang him.

'Dad, can I come and stay with you?'

'Megan, I can hardly hear you there's so much background noise. Where are you?'

'I'm at Euston station. The train leaves in ten minutes. Can you come and pick me up?'

'Yes, of course, darling. Just sit tight at Piccadilly and I'll find you.'

'Thanks, Dad.'

Charles smiled. Megan was coming home. For her home was with him and he would fight Clarissa and Todd if need be. He didn't know what the problem was this time, but whatever it was, Megan was going to stay with him at least until her baby was born. Hopefully forever.

It was late by the time he had collected Megan from Manchester and brought her back home to Leytonsfield, so, the following day, they both had a well-deserved lie-in.

They ate a leisurely breakfast and Charles was reading the Sunday paper, which he hadn't had the chance to read the day before, when Clarissa phoned for a video call.

Clarissa didn't waste time on polite chit-chat, she came straight to the point.

'What's going on, Megan? We came home from the party to find your note and you gone!'

'I've decided to stay with Dad. I couldn't tell you because you weren't there.'

'We were only at a party, darling, we would have been home soon and could have discussed it then.'

'A party that lasted all weekend.'

'But it was in London, we weren't far away.'

'I think we should concentrate on the future instead of playing the blame game,' Charles said.

'No one's playing anything, Charles, and I'd appreciate it if you'd kindly stay out of it. This is between Megan and I.'

Charles said nothing even though words sprang from his brain to his mouth too readily for his liking. Insulting words full of reproach for Megan being left alone for so long in her condition. But they weren't kids exchanging insults and Megan would hate the thought of her parents fighting over her like two dogs with a bone.

'Mum, I've made my mind up. You and Todd weren't there much of the time and I was lonely and, like, bored. Dad looks after me.'

'Oh, so you've given up work then, have you, Charles? My recollection is being left alone with a new baby to fend for myself while you worked all day, every day. Who's going to look after Megan while you're at work?'

It was a fair question and one he hadn't given a lot of thought to. 'I'll reduce my hours.' It was the best answer he could give having been put on the spot.

'Well, I do hope the NHS won't collapse with the shock.' Clarissa's voice was bitter, and her sarcasm made him wince.

'You and Todd don't have to worry about the NHS, do you, seeing as you're both private patients?'

As soon as he had spoken Charles realised he had said the wrong thing as Clarissa came back with a counterargument. 'Yes, thanks for reminding me. That's another thing.

We want Megan to be seen privately and to give birth in a private hospital. We discussed it, didn't we, darling?'

'Yes.' Megan's voice was small, and Charles put his arm around her.

'If that's really what Megan wants, she can be seen privately here. I'll arrange it. Now, I think we should say goodbye and let Megan get some rest.'

'Well, I think Todd and I should drive up this afternoon to collect you. I'm not happy about this, Megan, not a bit happy.'

'Mum, I've made my mind up. I'm staying here, at least until I've had the baby. Then... we'll see.'

Charles said nothing as his daughter was managing fine on her own. She had matured a lot since she had found out she was pregnant. He was proud of her.

'What about Jason? You can't just shut him out. If you stay up there, he'll never see his child.'

Megan sighed. 'Mum, Jason doesn't care. We talked. He's, like, not ready to be a father. That's what he said. He just wants to hang out with his mates and play football. I tried to tell him what was going to happen, and he was like, whatever. He doesn't get it. I need to be with people who understand. Dad, and Josie.'

Charles was surprised Megan had mentioned Josie. Surprised but pleased.

'Well, I'm not happy about any of it. You're my daughter and you need your mother at a time like this.'

Clarissa and Todd had been given the chance to look after Megan, but they'd failed. Charles still couldn't believe they'd left her all weekend to go to a party for goodness' sake. It must have been some party. Perhaps his ex-wife and her new squeeze had become swingers. He'd heard all about these parties that the rich and famous went to.

Charles hid a smile. He couldn't imagine those two swinging from the chandeliers.

'Right. I think that's enough. We'll talk later, okay?' said Charles.

'I haven't finished talking to my daughter if you don't mind.'

'I think Megan's had enough, for now, Clarissa. We'll talk later.'

'I want to talk to my daughter alone, without you hanging around.'

'Later,' Charles said firmly.

'Bye, Mum,' Megan said, and Charles ended the call.

'Want to watch a film?' Charles asked when Megan got up and stretched.

'Maybe later, Dad. I think I'll go and have a sleep. I'm tired.'

'Okay, sweetheart.'

Megan went upstairs and Charles went back to reading the paper. She was back where she belonged and that was all he cared about. That and a healthy delivery. He would have liked to ask Josie to be her midwife, but the twins were due only a week away from Megan's due date, so that was out of the question.

However, now that Megan had mentioned Josie as someone she trusted to help her with her pregnancy, Charles was more hopeful that Josie might agree to move in with them.

Josie was desperate to talk to Jay. She'd hardly seen him since he and Caitlin had come back from Bali and she needed his wisdom and advice. It would be good, too, to get a man's opinion of the situation.

Ever since Charles had performed his heroic act and disarmed scumbag, Josie hadn't been able to get him out of her mind. He'd been incredibly brave; some might say foolhardy. Josie thought he was a hero.

Charles Atkins was a good man. Kind, gentle, sensitive but also manly, sexy, and competent. He was a good obstetrician, appearing to have an instinct for when to intervene in a woman's labour and when to let nature take its course. He seemed to understand women which was a useful skill in a profession dealing exclusively with pregnant ones.

Josie's pregnancy seemed to be going well. Hopefully, the twins would be born with a minimum of fuss and medical intervention. But she needed to think about where she was going to live when they were born. Her parents', where she would be looked after and wrapped in cotton wool, or with Charles and Megan, where she would be part of a new little family.

The thought of her twins and Megan's baby growing up together was appealing. She could help Megan, and Charles could help both of them. But was it the right thing to do? She really didn't know which is why she needed to talk to Jay.

Fortunately, Jay had the same day off Josie did. Caitlin was working a late shift, so Josie visited her twin, bringing wine and chocolates which she wouldn't be sharing. The weight was piling on her and she doubted she'd ever get rid of it completely.

'Hi, Josie, how's things? Thanks for these.'

'Hi, Jay, I miss you, I haven't seen you for ages.'

They hugged, then Josie kissed Jay on the cheek and

both of them went into the kitchen. Josie to sit at the table and Jay to make tea.

'Okay, what's the news? How many months are you now?' Jay asked.

'Sixteen weeks. I'm due another scan in three weeks.'

'Everything going well?'

'Yep. Touch wood.' Josie touched the kitchen table for luck.

'Good. Are you going to go back home when the twins are born? You can't manage in your flat. Pity you didn't buy the bottom floor then you'd have had no problems. It's got a garden as well.'

'Good thinking, Bro, pity it wasn't for sale at the time. Anyway, I didn't have my crystal ball with me and couldn't have foreseen being pregnant with twins.'

Jay put a mug of tea in front of Josie and rattled the box of biscuits.

'Oh, go on, if you insist. Have you got any chocolate ones?' Josie had never had any willpower where biscuits were concerned.

'Of course. Do you need to ask?'

When they were settled with tea and biscuits, Josie sighed.

'I need to ask your opinion on something.'

'Fire away,' said Jay, eating a Jaffa cake.

'Charles has asked me to move in with him and Megan. He thinks we could be a little family together.'

Jay nodded. 'Makes sense. How well do you get on with Megan?'

'I've only met her once and that was at your party. I never even got the chance to speak to her properly.'

'Right. I remember. Well, you need to find out how well you two are going to get on before committing yourself.

She's a teenage girl and might resent another woman trying to muscle in on what she perceives as her territory.'

Josie took a Bourbon cream and bit into it thoughtfully. 'I was wondering that myself. She was living with her mother and her new boyfriend, but now she's back with her dad. Maybe she just wants Charles to herself. I don't know how she feels about the twins. It's a really difficult situation.'

'More tea?' Jay asked as he poured another mug from the large brown teapot, a replica of the one their parents had.

'Thanks,' Josie said.

'I know you're going to laugh at this, but... it can be hard for the man in this situation, you know.'

'By situation, I take it you mean a woman being pregnant?'

'Correct. After the man's played his part—'

'By which you mean ejaculated.'

'Do you have to be so clinical?'

'Yep,' Josie said with a smile. 'Sorry, go on.'

'Well, afterwards, he feels a bit... surplus to requirements. He has nothing to do with the pregnancy apart from look after the woman.'

'Which so many men do so well,' Josie said sarcastically.

'Okay, I know men can be... um...'

'Dicks?' offered Josie.

'Not all men, be fair.'

'No, you're right. Men either carry on as normal which means spending every hour they can down the pub with their mates, or they are overprotective, flapping around like a mother hen and annoying the woman they're supposed to be helping.'

'What I'm trying to say,' said Jay, grinning, 'is that the

man is not in charge, the woman is. So make the most of it while you can.'

'So, you think I should move in with Charles and Megan?'

'I think you should get to know Megan first and see how she feels. If she's happy, then, yes, move in and be a family.'

'What about love? I upset Charles by saying I would rather be a single mother than be in a loveless marriage.'

'I can understand why. It seems to me he's trying to do the best for you and his daughter. The poor bloke could find himself caught between a rock and a hard place if Megan doesn't want you to move in with them.'

'It would make life easier for Charles if we got on and all lived under the same roof.'

'Exactly. When the babies are born, you could review the situation.'

'That's very practical, but not romantic. Tell me something… you loved Caitlin while she was engaged to be married to someone else. How did you cope? Surely there must have been times when you thought you'd never be together.'

'There were. When Caitlin moved back home with her mother, Paul encouraged me to go speed dating. I met Emma.'

'And did you think she might be a substitute for Caitlin?'

Jay shook his head, then put his hand over his mouth to prevent biscuit crumbs escaping. 'Never. There never could have been a substitute for Caitlin. I only went speed dating to shut Paul up. I never stopped loving Caitlin. Never will.'

'That's the kind of love I want. Unconditional.'

'Love can grow in the right environment. Give the man a chance.'

Josie sighed. 'I don't want to get it wrong. Do you think

it's too big a risk? Should I play safe and go and live with Mum and Dad?'

'Remember what happened to Riordan. Once he moved back home with Tom, he got used to them babysitting. If it wasn't for Zoe, he'd probably still be there. And our parents aren't getting any younger. And then, of course, you're having twins. Double trouble.' Jay grinned and Josie grinned back. She remembered the mischief the two of them had got up to when they were little.

They fell silent, both crunching on biscuits as they thought about their childhood.

'You're right. I'll take her shopping for maternity clothes and find out how she feels about me moving in. If she's not happy, then I'll have to move in with Mum and Dad.'

'Sorted,' said Jay.

'Thanks, Jay,' said Josie. 'Any more tea?'

Chapter Twenty-Three

Charles had invited Josie to dinner with the express purpose of his two girls, as he thought of Josie and Megan, meeting and getting to know each other. He was delighted when Josie accepted the invitation.

Josie turned up with bunches of daffodils and a box of chocolates. Despite being a week behind Megan in her pregnancy, she was already bigger and had put on a lot of weight.

'Right, you two, I'll leave you to chat while I perform miracles in the kitchen.'

'Don't turn any more water into wine, Dad, I think we have enough,' said Megan.

'Ha, ha, funny girl,' Charles said, secretly glad of her cheekiness and sense of humour. She was obviously relaxed and happy, which was good to see. Josie, however, looked tired and strained.

He heard them chatting together, but he couldn't hear what they were saying, just the ebb and flow of their voices;

Megan's slightly higher than Josie's soft contralto. Then he heard his daughter laugh and smiled. They would be okay.

He was cooking spicy mushroom and broccoli noodles with less spice than he would usually use. Then a millionaire's cheesecake, as he knew how much they both loved chocolate. They were drinking mineral water and would have a latte or cappuccino to end the meal.

When they were sitting around the dining table, Charles proposed a toast, and they lifted their glasses.

'To the three of us and the three yet to join us.'

They clinked their glasses together and Charles grinned. This is what he had dreamed of and here they all were together, eating good food and enjoying each other's company.

'Umm, this is good, Charles,' said Josie.

'Yeah, it's cool, Dad,' said Megan.

'Thank you. Glad you're enjoying it.'

They ate in silence for a while, Charles enjoying the relaxed atmosphere around his dining table.

'You said you were going to look for a house to buy,' Josie said. 'Have you started looking yet, as I'm available to help anytime you want?'

'I've had no time, and I'm wondering if we should wait until the babies are born. I don't want to tire you, Josie, especially as you're still working full-time. Have you decided yet when you're going to stop working?'

'I'm not sure. I was going to go on to the recommended time of twenty-eight weeks but that's eleven weeks away and I'm feeling rather tired now. I think I should stop working before then.'

'What are your other symptoms?' Charles was concerned about Josie and wanted to encourage her to finish work now, move in with him and Megan and take it easy. But he knew how independent Josie was; she would do things in her own time.

'Weight gain, swollen ankles and tiredness mainly. But they're all normal symptoms so I'm not worried.'

Charles frowned. 'What about your BP and urinalysis?'

'Eh, Dad, gross...' said Megan, 'Do you have to talk medical at the dinner table?'

'It's not gross, Megan, it's the way doctors determine that everything is going the way it should.'

'They were normal at my last appointment, so stop worrying, Charles.'

'You're doing a physical job so it's not surprising you're ankles are swelling. You need to rest and put your feet up—literally.'

'What would I do all day? And being in the maternity unit for work, I'd be in the best place if something did go wrong, wouldn't I?'

'Not if you were in the middle of delivering a baby. Think about finishing sooner rather than later, that's all I'm saying.'

'Okay, I'll think about it.'

'Right, who's for millionaire's cheesecake?'

'Me please,' said Megan.

'Lovely,' said Josie.

When Charles had cut the cheesecake and given his girls a slice each, and one for himself, the conversation turned to Mandy and Charles's heroic effort to disarm her abuser.

'My dad, a hero—who'd have thought,' said Megan.

'He was a hero,' said Josie, 'I was there and can vouch for that.' Josie smiled at Charles and he winked at her.

'Have you seen her since the baby was born?' Charles asked.

'No. Her care is now in the hands of a health visitor, but

I did ring Shelley. The maximum sentence he could receive for threatening violence with an offensive weapon is four years. He's got previous so he will serve a sentence. Mandy's told the police all about his physical and mental abuse towards her, but that's a separate charge. Hopefully, with the two charges, he'll go down for a long time.'

'Let's hope so, and then Mandy can get on with her life,' said Charles.

'Absolutely. Mandy's changed since Whitney was born, according to Shelley, she's determined that no other women will suffer as she did. She's become a lot stronger with the support of the shelter staff and the friends she's made.'

Megan had been quiet, listening to the conversation. Charles realised that it wasn't always necessary to join in a conversation to be part of it. To listen is sometimes enough. Megan was still so young, and Charles's instinct was to protect her from the unpleasantness in life, but that wasn't always the best thing. She was an intelligent young woman and would be immersed in it through her own experiences and with social media. A parent couldn't protect their child from all negativity, no matter how much he may want to.

'What about the father of your baby?' Josie asked Megan, 'Is he going to be involved in bringing him or her up?'

'At the moment, he's like, not interested,' said Megan slowly, 'but I'm hoping he'll change his mind when he gets used to the idea.'

Josie said, 'He may feel differently when the baby's born. At the moment, he's got nothing to attach his feelings to. The baby is just an idea, not a reality. That'll change, I'm sure. It must be hard, you're both so young.'

'We did Shakespeare in English and Juliet was only about fourteen. Romeo was, like, way older.'

'And look what happened to those two,' said Charles.

'Sixteen isn't that young, you know,' said Megan.

'It seems young to me,' said Charles.

'That's because you're, like, dead old.'

'Well, thank you for that, daughter. Who's for a coffee?'

'Latte please,' said Megan.

'Same, thanks. Do you want any help?' asked Josie.

'No, you two get to know each other. I'll be fine.'

As Charles pottered around in the kitchen, making coffee, and stacking the dishwasher, he felt happy that the meal had gone well, and Josie and Megan seem to be getting on nicely. It wasn't the right time to discuss Josie moving in with them; there'd be plenty of time for that.

When they were sipping their coffee and relaxing on the couch and armchairs, Josie sighed, and Charles looked over at her. She looked exhausted and, for the first time, he felt a twinge of unease.

'When's your next antenatal appointment, Josie?'

'Eighth of May. I'll have another scan on the seventeenth.'

'Is it okay if I come with you?'

Josie beamed. 'I thought you'd never ask. Of course it's okay.'

Charles felt guilty that he hadn't attended any of Josie's appointments, but he hadn't been entirely sure that she'd want him there. Now he wished he'd asked her before.

'Great. Thank you.'

'You're most welcome.' Josie was smiling and Charles felt the familiar warmth stir deep inside him whenever he saw her smile. Her eyes were bright, even though she had dark bags under them, and her smile was genuine.

'Dad, I need clothes, I'm running out of things to wear.'

'I've heard that before. I take it you mean maternity clothes?'

'Yeah, big pants with elasticated waists. Really, like, fashionable but I can't wear my skinny jeans anymore.'

'I've got the same problem,' said Josie. 'I need maternity clothes too. Or maybe I'll just go to the nearest outdoor shop and buy a tent.'

They all laughed, and Charles wondered how his life had changed for the better so quickly. He basked in the joy of his two girls relaxing and getting on well. The future looked good for the three of them.

'Why don't we all go shopping and we'll get the clothes you need and the paraphernalia for the babies.' Charles hated shopping but would make the effort for his girls. Fortunately, Josie came to his rescue.

'I've got a better idea. Why don't I take Megan to Manchester and we'll have a girly day together. I'm sure you have better things to do with your time, Charles, than to follow us around, bored out of your mind. We'll buy clothes and order the cots and other stuff to be delivered here.'

'Yeah, Dad,' said Megan, 'Me and Josie can manage.'

'Okay, if you're sure.'

'We are, aren't we?' Josie asked Megan.

'Totally,' said his daughter.

Chapter Twenty-Four

Josie drove steadily and carefully down the motorway to Manchester. She had precious cargo in the car; two women and three unborn babies.

Megan sat in the passenger seat, humming to herself and watching the scenery flow past. Josie was glad she had this opportunity to get to know Megan better as she hadn't decided yet whether she would move in with Charles when she gave up work. On the one hand, it made perfect sense as the three of them got on well together and Megan seemed fine with her being part of the family. On the other hand, it was a big commitment, and it would be awful if it didn't work out and she had to split the family up. She had to make sure she made the right decision.

There was a lot she wanted to ask Megan about. How did she feel about becoming a mother? What were her feelings towards Jason? Was she scared at the thought of giving birth? Instead of just blurting things out as she usually did, she would tread carefully, talk of ordinary things such as clothes, had she chosen names for the baby? That kind of thing.

'You can listen to music if you want,' said Josie.

'No, that's okay, I'd rather talk to you.'

'Good. I do hope we're going to be friends, Megan. Do you miss London?' A lame question, but at least it might break the ice.

'Not as much as I thought I would. When Mum and Todd got together we moved to a different neighbourhood and I had to switch schools. I left all my friends behind.'

'Oh really? That must have been tough.'

'Yeah, it was, but now I'm pregnant I don't, like, have anything in common with the girls in my new school, so I don't really miss them. I went for a drink with some of them last time I was there and all they talked about was boys and clothes. I was so bored.'

'Yes, I can imagine. Will you go back to school when the baby's born?'

'No. I might go to college, but I don't know what I want to do.'

'There's no hurry. You've got plenty of time to decide once the baby is a bit older and settled into a routine.'

'Yeah, that's what I thought. I'm still young enough to have a career.'

'Of course you are.'

Josie turned off the motorway and headed for Manchester city centre. She would park in the centre, so they didn't have to walk far. She was feeling tired already and the day had only just started.

Two hours later they headed for the nearest Starbucks. Josie was desperate to sit down and rest, and even Megan, who, Josie had learned, could shop for England, was tiring. They must have shopped in every large store that sold maternity clothes, and then some more expensive boutique shops for the prettier clothes that they could wear for social occasions. Josie didn't think she'd bother with the social occasions as all she wanted to do was lie down and sleep.

'What are you having?' Josie asked Megan who was sorting through carrier bags of things, having another look at what she had bought.

'A latte and a piece of carrot cake, please.'

'Okay, coming up.'

Josie waited in line, wondering what to have. She was feeling slightly sick and a bit dizzy but knew that it could be due to low blood sugar as she hadn't eaten since breakfast. Even then, she'd only had a piece of toast and a cup of tea. It was difficult to eat when nausea struck, but Josie knew that the nausea could be a result of not eating properly. It was a vicious circle that she had to break if she was going to be well enough to drive them home.

Finally, she got to the front of the queue and bought two lattes and two pieces of cake. As she waited for the coffee to be made, she took the plates of the cake back to the table. Megan was on her phone and hardly glanced up. Josie felt a flash of annoyance that quickly dissipated. Megan was still a teenager, she couldn't be expected to know that Josie was only just holding it together. She wasn't going to tell her either as she didn't want to scare her. This was supposed to be a pleasant shopping trip where they got to know each other and bought maternity clothes. It would be awful if Josie collapsed and Megan had to look after her.

'Latte,' said Josie as cheerfully as she could as she put the coffee on the table and sank gratefully into her chair.

'Thanks. Are you okay?'

'Me? Fine? Why do you ask?'

'You look a bit pale.'

'Oh, I probably need a bit of sun. Been non-stop working since Christmas.'

'You need a holiday,' said Megan.

'I do, that's for sure.' Josie smiled and drank some of her latte. 'Mmm, this is good. How's the cake?'

'It's good,' said Megan who had already eaten half hers. Maybe they should have ordered more healthy food, but this was only to keep them going until they got home. And it was carrot cake so had one of their five a day in it.

Josie was already planning on what she would have for dinner. Pizza maybe as she wouldn't be in any state to try cooking something. Maybe Charles would ask her to stay for dinner. The thought made her smile and she realised the coffee and cake was doing its job and she was feeling better already.

It was pleasant to sit in the coffee shop, people-watching and listening to the familiar hissing and gurgling of the coffee machine, and the staff calling people's names when their coffee was ready. Josie wondered what people thought of her and Megan. A young girl and an older woman, both obviously pregnant. Not that it mattered what people thought, but she was curious. Then she realised that no one was taking any notice of them. An old lady had smiled as she walked past, but that was the sum total of attention they had received.

What would it be like if she did live with Charles and Megan? The three of them out for a walk in the park, pushing two prams, one containing twins. She remembered the twin pram that she and Jay had when they were babies. Theirs was one where they sat next to each other, instead of in line. Mum had chosen well with that one as they would probably have fought to be the one in front. Although they adored each other, they had always been competitive.

Josie had put her hands on her belly without realising what she was doing and, when she looked up, Megan was smiling at her.

'You okay?' she asked.

Josie smiled back. 'Yes, I'm fine. Just thinking about the pram that Jay and I had as babies. I'll need to get one for these two.' She stroked her stomach protectively.

'Can't imagine having twins,' said Megan, 'one's enough.'

'I've been meaning to ask,' said Josie. 'What did you think when your dad told you about the twins? It must have been a shock.'

Megan looked thoughtful as if she wasn't sure how to answer.

'Well… to be honest, I was angry at the beginning as people were, like, getting on my case for not taking precautions. Then my own father goes and does the same thing.'

'It was my fault, not your father's. You mustn't blame him.'

'Oh, I'm well over it now. People make mistakes. Shit happens. My dad is going to be a dad again and I'm cool with it now. I like the idea of them all growing up together.'

'Don't you think it's a bit weird though? Your dad being a father again and a grandfather within a week of each other?'

'Yeah, but nice weird, you know? It makes us different from everyone else. I like that. I don't want to be the same as other people. That's so boring.'

Josie was warming to Megan more as the day went on. She was a special person. Not only was she Charles's daughter, but she was also becoming a friend, someone Josie could share baby stories with, and they could help each other in practical ways.

'You have your scan on the tenth and mine is a week later. Then we'll know their genders. Have you thought of any names yet?'

'Yeah. Grace for a girl and Elliott for a boy.'

'Lovely. You're a lot more organised than I am.'

'Have you thought of names?'

'No. I think I'll wait until I know the sex.'

'Josie? Are you going to move in with us?'

'How do you feel about it?'

'I want you to move in. Then I'll have someone who knows what I'm going through.'

'That's a good point. I'm still thinking about it, but you'll be the first to know what I decide. Okay?'

'Okay. Can we go now?'

'Good idea.'

As they gathered up all the carrier bags and made their slow, steady way to the car, Josie felt relieved that Megan was on board with the idea of her moving in. Now all she had to do was sort out her feelings for Charles. *Well, that'll be easy peasy.* Gran's voice in her head made her smile. It was obvious who Josie had inherited her sarcasm from.

Chapter Twenty-Five

Charles watched anxiously as the sonographer put gel on Megan's exposed belly, after tucking tissue paper around her clothing to protect it.

Megan looked nervous, so Charles took her hand and held it tightly. He smiled at her to reassure her that everything would be fine.

In the car, Megan had been firing questions at him concerning the scan. What were they looking for? What if something's wrong? And the last thing she had said, 'I'm scared, Dad,' which had shaken him to the core. There were so many things that could go wrong, but this was no time for him to list them, Megan needed his love and support so he told her that it would all be fine.

Now, watching the sonographer, a middle-aged woman called Patricia, silently move the handheld probe over his daughter, he prayed to a god he wasn't sure he believed in to keep mother and baby safe. He silently promised all kinds of things if only this baby was okay.

It was quiet in the dimly lit room so Patricia could

concentrate on all the checks she needed to make. Megan was tense, and Charles wished he could do or say something to reassure her, so he kept hold of her hand, trying to convey his loving support to Megan and her unborn child.

'I'm just trying to get a clear picture for you and to find out whether it's a boy or girl.'

'Right,' said Megan with a trembling voice. She looked at Charles with a question in her eyes, so he nodded and smiled. His face was starting to ache with holding the smile in place. Smiling wasn't his default expression.

When they heard the baby's heart beating, Megan looked ecstatic at the sound.

'Right, there we are,' said Patricia. 'There's her head, spine, hands and feet.'

'Oh,' said Megan as the picture cleared and the baby was there for them to see. 'It's a girl and she's sucking her thumb.'

'They do that,' said Patricia.

'Is she okay?' asked Megan.

'From what I can see, she's fine and dandy, developing as expected.'

'Dad?' Megan turned to Charles, but he couldn't see for the tears that were threatening to roll down his cheeks.

'She's beautiful.' His voice was husky and he wished he could let go and cry, but Megan needed him to be strong, not a blubbing wreck.

'Oh, Dad, it's okay, she's good.' Megan, bless her, was trying to reassure him.

'It's wonderful. You're wonderful.'

Charles got himself together, wiped his face where the tears had escaped, and tried to return to the professional he was. But at that moment, he was just an ordinary father and grandfather looking after his daughter and seeing his grand-daughter for the first time.

'Thanks, Dad. Is it over now? My bladder is fit to burst.'

A week later Charles was back in the same small room with Josie. Patricia was, once again, the sonographer and she smiled when she saw Charles.

'Couldn't keep away, eh? Hi, Josie, hop up onto the couch.'

'Hi, Patricia. Sorry, can't hop at the moment.'

Charles smiled but said nothing as he helped Josie scramble up onto the couch and settle herself for the scan. Even though she was a week behind Megan in her pregnancy, she was much bigger. She was also, worryingly, quite swollen in places such as her ankles and feet. She was wearing loose-fitting sandals and a maternity dress. She looked flushed and uncomfortable.

Charles knew that there was a greater risk of complications with twins, but they were having non-identical twins who each had their own placenta and membrane, so the risk was lower than if the babies were identical.

Still, he would need to keep an eye on her and keep on at her to stop working. It must be hard to do her job feeling the way she must. She needed to be at home where she could relax and sleep as much as she needed to.

'Okay, there they are. I can only see one baby clearly enough to tell you her sex.'

'I think you just did,' said Josie. 'One's a girl but you can't tell what the other is?'

'That's about it, Josie.'

Josie looked over at Charles. 'So, if the other's a girl too, how are you going to feel in an all-girl household?'

'God help me,' he said, even though the prospect wasn't an unpleasant one. He just wanted healthy babies and mothers. All his concern at that moment was for Josie, who appeared to be struggling but refusing to admit it. He was worried but knew that he needed to choose his words carefully as Josie was as independent as they come and wasn't the kind of person to ask for help.

As he assisted her down from the couch, he put his arm around her and hugged her. Josie slipped her arm around his waist and rested her head on his shoulder.

'I'm so tired,' she said.

'Come on then, let's get you home.'

The three of them sat in the lounge and Josie rested her head back and closed her eyes. She had been spending more time at Charles and Megan's lately and was starting to think of it as her second home. She felt safe and looked after. Charles was right about her finishing work, she was finding it increasingly hard to move quickly and bend down to attend to a woman in labour. The thing she feared the most was not being able to respond to an emergency situation as swiftly and efficiently as she needed to.

It was still May, although the end of the month, but she felt hot and sticky all the time. As soon as she'd had a cooling shower and dried off, she was sweating again. Heaven knew what she'd be like if they had a hot summer.

Charles was wonderful, making her drinks and cold compresses for her forehead. He had even bought a small fan so she could have cooling air on her face all the time.

Megan didn't seem to be suffering from the same symptoms. Maybe it was because she was younger, or simply that she was carrying one baby and not two.

Charles had made banana milkshakes for herself and Megan and a coffee for himself.

'Right, Josie. I'm concerned about you and think you should give up work. When you go back, hand your notice in and if you're not feeling well enough to work your notice, go to the doctor for a sick note. Okay?'

'Okay.'

'What… no arguments?' Charles looked surprised but pleased.

'No arguments, Charles. I've been thinking the same. The twins come first, and I need to be well for them. But I'll go on maternity leave rather than quitting as I don't know how I'm going to feel about going back to work afterwards.'

'Cool, we can hang out together,' said Megan.

'I'll enjoy that,' said Josie. Now the decision had been made, she felt the tension lift. It was the most sensible course of action.

'Have you given any more thought to moving in with us?' Charles looked hopeful as did Megan. They were both lovely people and Josie couldn't think of any reason why she shouldn't live with them. Except for the thought that she and Charles weren't madly in love and lusting after each other every second of the day. But, the way she was feeling, she appreciated Charles's sweet, tender caring attention more than the prospect of a quick session between the sheets anyway. She thought of the way he had held her after the scan and how much she appreciated being able to lean on him for that short time, loving his strength and support.

'Yes, I think I would like to move in with you, if you are

both sure that it's what you want. It'll be a big change for all of us.'

'Yay!' said Megan.

'We're up for the challenge, aren't we, Megan?' said Charles.

'Yeah.'

'Right, how about a celebratory salad. I think you two need some healthy food inside you.'

'Sounds good,' said Josie.

When Charles was in the kitchen banging around with pots and pans, and whistling tunelessly, Josie came in and stood nearby so Megan couldn't hear their conversation.

'Charles, are you sure it's okay for me to live here? It'll be a lot more work with me and the twins. You know how useless I am in the kitchen.'

To her surprise, Charles wrapped his arms around her as best he could and held her gently. 'There is nothing I want more than for us to be together. Not just for Megan's sake and not even because of the twins. My feelings for you are real, Josie. In fact, I think I'm falling in love with you. I haven't said anything before now because we've all had so much to think about, I didn't want to put any pressure on you.'

'I… I'm not sure what to say.'

'You don't need to say anything. If you don't feel the same way, that's alright. I wasn't expecting any declarations of love in return. Just know that I want the best for you, and I think being here with us is the best.'

'I appreciate your honesty, Charles. I wish I could say it back to you, but my feelings are confused at the moment. It's all happened so quickly.'

Charles kissed her on the forehead. 'It's fine. I just want

you to know that I'm committed to us and that I'm here for you. Now go and put your feet up.'

He kissed her gently and she wandered back into the living room. Megan had gone upstairs, so she sat alone and thought about Charles loving her. What did she think about it? It was a compliment and typically Charles. He'd told her in such a matter of fact manner. She couldn't imagine him getting down on one knee with a rose in his teeth, that wasn't Charles's way at all. But she believed him when he said his feelings were real. He must have been thinking about it for a while.

Josie thought back to the cottage at Christmas and how they had enjoyed the time they spent together. And the love-making which was sweet and sexy all at the same time.

Josie had never been in love. She had experienced crushes on boys at school and boy bands. There had been a few relationships in her twenties, but nothing that shook her world and she had hardly missed them when they broke up. Charles was the first man to have told her he loved her. Did she love him? She definitely had feelings for him. She was incredibly fond of him, grateful for his support when she'd told him she was pregnant. She had been fully expecting to bear the brunt of being a parent on her own.

Physically, the attraction was there. She wondered if they would share a bed.

Josie yawned and closed her eyes. How lovely it would be to let someone else make all the decisions and let her sleep until the babies were due. Someone she could lean on. Charles…

Chapter Twenty-Six

It was the beginning of June and Josie's twenty-three-week scan.

'Your blood pressure is a bit high, Josie, have you thought about giving up work?'

'How high?' Josie knew her midwife, Letitia, well as she had worked with her loads of times. She trusted her judgement and if her blood pressure was high, that was a cause for concern.

'One hundred and fifty over a hundred.'

'Urinalysis?'

'There's no sign of protein and the rest of it's fine. Are you getting any exercise?'

'Not much, but this oedema holds me back.' She glanced down at her swollen ankles which were getting worse.

'What about headaches, visual disturbances or any other signs of pre-eclampsia?'

'No to all that. I am tired all the time though.'

'I could have you admitted and monitored closely, but you do have an expert on hand in Charles.'

'Does everyone know about us?'

'Oh aye, but you know how fast gossip circulates in this place. I'd give some thought to finishing work and putting your feet up. Try to ease the swelling in your ankles and feet.'

'Yes, I'll do that.'

'Do you promise?'

'Pinky promise?' Josie held out her pinky finger and Letitia hooked hers around it and laughed.

'Right. You have to do it now.'

Josie was true to her word and told her line manager that she was stopping work but only intending to take maternity leave as she might come back to work after the twins were born. She also went to her GP and got a sick note for two weeks. Hopefully, she'd feel better after a rest and be able to work the last two weeks. She didn't want to miss her leaving party, even though it would just be a quick glass of orange in the staff room at lunchtime. If they even got a lunch break.

Josie knew she'd miss her colleagues and the mothers and babies, but she had to put the twins first.

She thought about Charles a lot and wondered why she couldn't return the compliment and tell him she loved him too. Was it because she didn't love him and never would? Or was it because she'd never been in love and didn't know what it felt like? Or… *it's because you're a fool and don't know a good thing when you see it.* Josie grinned, thanks for that, Gran.

Josie had no idea why she'd thought she'd be bored if

she wasn't working, her two weeks off sick were spent sleeping, watching TV with Megan, drinking lots of water and then going back to bed again. She stayed with Charles and Megan as she was finding it increasingly hard to climb the stairs to her flat.

It was June and the weather was bright and sunny. Josie tried sitting in the garden, but even in the shade under an umbrella, she was too hot and was forced back inside to sit in the living room with her fan on full blast. Megan stayed outside in the garden with sunscreen and large sunglasses.

The two of them were getting on well together. Charles was still working full-time and Megan kept her entertained with stories about her first attempt at skiing and snowboarding, and Josie told Megan about Charles on the toboggan.

Jay rang her, inviting her to their next Beer and Chinese night, but Josie declined as she didn't feel up to socialising, or eating too much, which she always did at these get-togethers.

'You're okay, aren't you, Josie?'

'If by okay you mean as large as a house with swollen ankles and feet, moving like someone auditioning for a part in *The Walking Dead*, then, yes, I'm okay.'

'That doesn't sound good. How's your blood pressure?'

The problem of having medics in the family is that they always knew the right questions to ask and it was difficult to fob them off.

'It's a bit high, but nothing to worry about.'

'How high?' Jay wasn't going to let it go so she may as well tell him the full story.

'One hundred and fifty over a hundred but before you ask, no protein, headaches or flashing lights.'

'Maybe you should be in hospital.'

'Jay, I'm not taking up a precious NHS bed for nothing.

I'm okay, just having twins. I have so much respect for our mum if she went through this to have us. No wonder we're her favourite kids.'

Jay laughed. It was a running joke in the family that the twins were favourites even though Riordan always retorted that they stopped after having the two of them, which meant they couldn't bear to have any more like the dynamic duo. It was too big a risk. Casey always kept silent during their arguments and smiled knowingly. It was obvious he thought he was the favourite.

'Does Charles know?' Jay was still thinking about her blood pressure, obviously. Josie couldn't resist teasing him.

'Charles knows quite a lot of things, specifically how to cook which is a bonus as neither Megan nor I can boil an egg.'

'Does he know about the hypertension, Josie, and don't change the subject?'

'He's at the hospital. I'll tell him when he gets home.'

'Right. Things going well between the two of you?'

'Good. He told me he loved me.'

'That good, eh? And I hope you told him you loved him.'

'No, as I don't know how I feel at the moment.'

'Do you want me to come over? I've got some time before Caitlin comes home.'

'No, it's okay. I've got Megan to keep me company, but we'll get together soon.' Josie looked around as she sensed someone in the doorway. It was Megan and by her expression, it looked as if she had heard the conversation.

'Okay.'

'Speak soon, love you.'

Josie had ended the call without waiting to hear Jay say it back. Megan came into the room and collapsed in the comfiest armchair. She sat with her legs crossed and her arms crossed too. She looked like a tiny Buddha with her small bump and her yoga position.

'You heard that.' It was a statement, not a question and Josie wished she'd been more discreet.

'Yeah. Dad loves you but you don't love him.'

'No, that isn't what I said. I don't know how I feel. Your dad is lovely, kind and supportive and I'm grateful for everything he's done for me.'

'You had sex though. Do you always have sex with men you don't have feelings for?'

'No, do you?' Josie felt a spear of anger that she was being questioned by a sixteen-year-old who got pregnant the first time she had sex. But then she looked at Megan's face and felt awful for snapping at her.

'Sorry,' said Josie.

'I didn't mean to be rude,' said Megan.

They both spoke at the same time, looked at each other and laughed.

'It's complicated, Megan. I've never been in love before and I don't know what I'm supposed to feel. Would it make sense if I said I wanted to be in love with him, but I just don't know if I am?'

'Kinda. I don't love Jason, but I like him a lot. I've never been in love before either.'

'We're a right pair, aren't we?' said Josie. 'Heaven help our babies.'

They both burst into giggles at the same time. Once they had started, they couldn't stop, and tears of mirth streamed down their faces. When one tried to stop, the other laughed harder, until they were both close to hysteria.

The living room door opened, and Charles came in.

'What the f... flippin' heck is going on with you two?'

'We're practising laughter yoga,' said Josie. 'You have to sit like Megan and laugh until you wet yourself.'

'Oh no, I need a wee now,' said Megan which set them off laughing harder.

'Me too,' said Josie who didn't think she was going to make it to the bathroom.

'Good grief. I'm going for a shower,' said Charles.

'I think your dad would benefit from laughter yoga,' said Josie.

'No,' said Megan, serious now, 'He just needs you to tell him you love him.'

Chapter Twenty-Seven

Over a weekend in the middle of June, Josie left her flat and moved in with Charles and Megan officially. The two fat ladies, as Jay called them, supervised the move while willing helpers did all the heavy lifting.

Josie and Caitlin stayed in the flat and packed her clothes, make-up, and toiletries, important documents that she kept in a concertina file and personal keepsakes that she kept in a box with a kitten on the lid.

Charles, Jay, and Casey moved suitcases, boxes of books and other treasures, running effortlessly up and down the stairs to a van that Charles had hired for the weekend. Josie knew they were being macho and trying to outdo each other in the fitness stakes and felt affection for all three of them as well as thinking how stupid they were to rush about in the heat. June was turning out to be one of the hottest on record.

Josie intended to keep the flat and rent it out for the time being so all the furniture and the few items she had bought for the kitchen were staying. Some of the kitchen appliances had never been used. Charles had said he didn't need anything, so she was leaving them for the tenant when they rented out the flat.

When they'd finished and Josie locked the flat for the last time, she got in the front of the van with Charles; Caitlin, Casey and Jay were in Casey's car.

'How are you feeling now?' asked Charles.

'Not brilliant,' Josie said, not wanting to moan but knowing how much could go wrong in a pregnancy. She knew that Charles had to be on the alert in case she needed help suddenly.

'I'm worried about you, Josie.'

'I'm getting a bit worried myself, Charles. But what can I do except rest, eat properly and keep going to my appointments?'

'I think you should be admitted and have a thorough examination with more blood tests. Your next scan isn't until the tenth of July. You need to be seen earlier and to ask to see whichever obstetrician is on duty.'

'Okay, I will.'

'Promise?'

'Pinky promise.' That was two pinky promises Josie had to fulfil. Maybe Charles was right as she was getting concerned about the way she was feeling and a short spell in hospital may sort it out. She didn't want anything to harm these babies; the further her pregnancy went on, the more love she felt for them. They were her precious children, and they deserved the best start in life.

When they got back to the flat, Megan was doling out beer and fruitcake. Casey was scarcely out of breath, Jay's T-shirt was soaked with sweat, and Charles had appeared to have forgotten about competing with the men and was helping Josie to sit down and elevate her feet.

'Now, don't move, okay,' said Charles.

Josie was so grateful to all of them for helping her. She realised how little she could do as she was so big now and her body felt as if it didn't belong to her. It was almost as if she was wearing a fat suit that was weighing her down and her real body, the one that had always functioned perfectly well for her, was hidden inside somewhere.

Megan handed her a glass of water which was the only thing she wanted to drink. Even the thought of lemonade made her feel nauseous.

'Thanks, honey. Well, I'm here.'

'I'm glad,' Megan whispered.

'So am I,' Charles added, 'you need looking after. We're going to keep an eye on you from now on.'

'What's up?' Casey asked.

'Nothing for you to worry about.' For all his confident demeanour, Casey was a worrier. He was also a fixer and tried to solve every problem he came across.

'Josie has symptoms of pre-eclampsia and I think she should be admitted.'

'Right, we'll take her then. Do you need to phone the ward?' Casey was on his feet and ready for action.

'Have you met my brother?' she asked Charles, 'He thinks he's a superhero and can solve all the problems of the world.'

'Stuff the world, it's you we're worried about.' Casey looked at her with such tenderness that Josie felt like crying.

'I'll ring tomorrow for an earlier appointment. Okay?'

'Well, just see that you do. And I'm going to check so no excuses.' Casey sat down again and drank his beer, but he kept glancing at her and then away.

It was pleasant to sit quietly with her feet up and listen to the O'Connors and her new family chatting amongst themselves. It was good to see how well Casey and Charles got on. Jay was charming Megan who kept giggling at things he said, and Caitlin sat next to Josie on the couch holding her hand for some reason.

When it was time for them to go, Caitlin held her for a long time and whispered, 'Take care of yourself, we all love you so much.'

After all the hugs and kisses, Josie felt quite emotional. When they had left, Josie let the tears that had been threatening run down her face. This was ridiculous, she wasn't a crier normally. Was it hormones? Where had her strength gone? She felt helpless, physically, and emotionally. This wouldn't do, she needed to pull herself together and keep it together for the sake of the twins.

Josie was disappointed that she hadn't been invited to share Charles's bed, even though she was so restless at night that she would probably drive him mad. So, she took over the spare bedroom and made it as personal as she could. She'd been sleeping in that room for weeks now but thinking of herself as a guest. Now she had to think that it was her room, at least until the twins were born. She might put some of her pictures up if Charles didn't object.

As she lay in bed that night, she was so tired she thought she'd fall asleep straight away. But instead, she lay listening to the sounds of the house settling down.

Josie got out of bed and walked slowly down the stairs to the kitchen.

Megan had gone to bed, but Charles was still up,

reading the papers that he never got the time to read during the day. Josie sat opposite him at the kitchen table.

'Josie, are you okay? Nothing wrong is there?'

'No, I just thought I'd come and talk to you as I couldn't sleep. Or I'll just sit here if you want to read.'

'No, I don't want to read. Nothing worth reading about anyway. I'd rather talk to you. Do you want anything? Milky drink to help you sleep?'

'No thanks, I'm fine. I just wanted to thank you for letting me move in.'

Charles reached across the kitchen table and took her hand. He held it and gazed at her, his blue eyes like lasers.

'I should be thanking you, I've wanted this for ages. When you told me about the babies, I was shocked at first, but then delighted. It seemed the answer to a prayer.'

'How so?'

'When we met at Christmas, I was at my lowest. My wife had left me, my daughter was becoming a stranger and even work didn't satisfy me the way it once had. I was lethargic, bored with life and with myself. Then I met you and things changed.'

'What things?'

'You were so full of joy. The way you sang to the Christmas carols reminded me of when life was good and full of hope. Then that toboggan… I don't think I'd enjoyed myself so much for years. You made me realise that life is worth living. The little things can mean so much. I began to feel positive again.'

'So… coming to Leytonsfield was a deliberate move? Because I was here?'

'Yes. I couldn't get you out of my mind and wanted to see you again.'

'Let me get this straight, you moved all the way from

London to Cheshire, leaving behind everything familiar, just to see *me* again?'

Charles grinned sheepishly. 'Ah… guilty as charged. Also, I needed a fresh start and Leytonsfield seemed like a good choice.'

'If you hadn't met me, would you have moved here?'

'No, probably not. But you are here and now we're living together. It could turn out to be the best move I've ever made. Megan loves you as I do. No pressure, Josie, but it's all up to you now.'

'No pressure.'

Charles lifted her hand to his lips and kissed her knuckles. A shiver travelled from the top of her head to her swollen feet. Erogenous zones started to wake up and shameless thoughts invaded her mind. Just wait until I'm not pregnant, she thought.

'Seriously,' he said. 'I'm just glad you're here and we're going to be parents. Whatever happens in the future, we'll deal with it together. I don't want you to feel rushed to make any decisions about us. We're going to have our hands full with three babies.'

'That's for sure.'

'Let's just get the babies born first and then think about the future later.'

'Sounds good to me,' said Josie.

'And phone the ward tomorrow and get an appointment. Tell them how worried you are.'

'I will, Charles, I've fielded those type of calls and if a mother is concerned we never refuse to see her.'

'Good. Right. Let's go to bed.'

Josie leaned forward and whispered, 'Are you propositioning me, Mr Atkins?'

Charles kissed her gently on the lips and said, 'I wish.'

He kissed her again, with exquisite tenderness and with a longing that Josie matched. 'But you just wait until the twins are here.'

'I'll look forward to that,' Josie whispered.

'Not as much as I will,' Charles said.

Chapter Twenty-Eight

Josie was true to her word and phoned the hospital the following morning. They told her to come in. She packed an overnight bag just in case they admitted her.

Jean, the midwife, looked her over, frowned, and nodded as Josie explained how unwell she felt.

'You're worried about pre-eclampsia I take it?'

'I am and so's Charles.'

'You're right to be worried, it's a serious condition as you know. I've asked Mr Taylor to pop down and examine you. If he thinks it's necessary, we'll admit you.'

'Thanks, Jean.'

'He won't be long, pet.'

Josie smiled at Jean. She had been in her position so many times, using reassuring words to put the mother at her ease. And now the roles were reversed. She was the worried mother who needed kindness. She felt calmer in the maternity unit. Everyone did their best here and the treatment the mothers received was second to none.

'Ah, Josie,' said Mr Taylor as he strode through the door. 'I hear you're not feeling too good.'

Josie went through it all again and the obstetrician listened and nodded occasionally.

'Right. You've told me enough to convince me that you need to be admitted and scrutinised.' Dr Taylor smiled at her and Josie smiled back. The thought of being scrutinised by a medical team was meant to reassure her and strangely enough, it did. She depended on them entirely for the safe delivery of the twins.

When Josie was settled on the ward she phoned Charles. She left a message on his voicemail as he was in theatre, then she phoned her mother, Jay, and Casey. Once she'd spread the word, she lay back against the pillows with a romantic novel to await events.

She must have fallen asleep as, when she woke, Charles was sitting by her bedside, wearing scrubs, and looking worried. He also looked deliciously sexy, with tousled hair and the hint of a five o'clock shadow. Josie had always fancied an attractive man wearing scrubs. *You've chosen the right profession then.* Yes, Gran, thanks for your input.

'Hi, darling, how are you feeling?'

'The same, but at least I'm in the right place now. I'm going to rest up and do exactly as I'm told.'

Charles grinned and Josie expected him to say "that'd be a first" or something similar, but he didn't.

'I'm glad to hear that,' said Charles.

'How are you?'

'Tired but glad you're getting the treatment you need. Have you told your family?'

'Yes, no doubt there'll be an O'Connor invasion later on today.'

'I need to go, but I'll be back later.'

'Megan's on her own.' This was something that had bothered her. Megan was now twenty-five weeks pregnant and was fine and healthy, but Charles didn't want to leave her on her own for long periods.

'I'll try and get back for a while before I come to see you. Don't worry about anything, it's all being taken care of. You just rest and get your blood pressure down.'

'Okay.'

Josie was right about the O'Connors. Jay, Caitlin, and Lexi called in after their shifts, Riordan and Casey turned up at different times and stayed for about five minutes before dashing off again and her parents visited in the evening.

The following morning Zoe came to see her before morning surgery. She smiled and chatted normally but the look in her eyes told Josie a different story. Zoe had lost a baby and she, more than any of them, would know how worried Josie was.

'How are you feeling?'

Josie smiled at the standard question. If she had a pound for every time someone had asked her that, she'd be a rich woman.

'I'm feeling a lot better, thanks, and my blood pressure is starting to come down now. There's talk of discharging me tomorrow.'

'That's great, Josie, but look after yourself, won't you? At the first sign of any of the symptoms of pre-eclampsia, you must come back, straight away. I know you, as a midwife, think I'm preaching to the choir, but medical people are good at the maxim, "do as I say, not as I do" and have a tendency to neglect their own care. I've seen it so many times.'

'I know. It's okay, Zoe, I appreciate what you're saying. I'm not working now and just sit around chatting to Megan. I don't lift a finger, I promise.'

Zoe grinned. 'So, how are things with Charles?'

'Things are good. Charles is very attentive and seems happy at the prospect of three babies in the house. Most men I know wouldn't be. Megan seems okay with me being there. I think I made the right choice moving in with them.'

'Good. I'm glad to hear it. Anyway, better be off or I'll miss the beginning of surgery. Take care of yourself, Josie.'

Zoe hugged her warmly and kissed her on the cheek.

When she'd gone Josie lay still and thought about how awful it must have been for Zoe to lose a baby like that. Some women would never come back from that. But now she had Riordan, Tom and Abigail and was happy and fulfilled.

Josie drifted off to sleep, her thoughts, as always, with the twins. She and Charles had better start thinking of names soon.

Josie was bored. She had been back home for a few days now and it was hot in the house and even hotter outside in the garden where Megan spent most of her time, her tan slowly building so she now looked as if she had just come back from a holiday in the Bahamas.

On her third day out of hospital, Josie decided to visit her mother. She needed some TLC and had questions for her.

'Do you want to come with me?' she asked Megan.

'Ah, not this time, thanks. Maybe next time?'

'Okay.' Perhaps Megan needed to be on her own for a short while. The two of them were spending a lot of time in each other's company. No matter how well you got on with someone, you couldn't be with them around the clock. Charles was still working crazy hours and hadn't had the chance to decrease them yet, there was just too much work in the maternity unit. And less work for him meant more work for the other obstetricians.

Josie drove carefully to her parents' house. She wouldn't risk longer journeys, but just within Leytonsfield itself, she felt safe to drive.

It was another scorcher. The end of June with July and August set to be hot too according to the weather forecasts. Trust her to be pregnant during one of the best summers on record. Pregnant with twins and hot weather was not a good combination.

Her mum had ice-cold home-made lemonade waiting for her, and her favourite biscuits. She hugged her tightly, neither of them wanting to let go. Josie knew how worried everyone in the family was which made her feel more anxious herself. Childbirth was supposed to be a natural process and Megan seemed to be sailing through her pregnancy with no problems whatsoever. But Megan was sixteen and having one baby. Josie was thirty and having twins. And, as she knew from being a midwife, no two pregnancies were the same.

'Hello, darling, how're you feeling now?'

'I feel better than I did before my stay on the maternity ward, but my ankles are still swollen.' Josie raised one foot to show her mother.

'Right, let's sit in the living room and you can put your feet up.'

'Okay.'

Once Josie was settled with both feet elevated and food and drink to hand, Eloise sat down and studied her only daughter.

'Come on then, spill the beans. How are you really?'

'To be honest I'm worried. So many things can go wrong. I've put on nearly two stone and my legs are swelling. They're so uncomfortable. What was your pregnancy like with us, Mum?'

Eloise smiled. 'Well, don't forget it was my third pregnancy, so it was easier for me. I knew what to expect and doubled it.'

'Did you have any symptoms?'

'Fortunately, no. Only the expected ones. I was tired and rested as much as I could. But your symptoms, Josie, are different. You had high blood pressure and the water retention hasn't decreased much, has it?'

Josie looked at her hands which looked swollen to her, her fingers like uncooked sausages.

'No. The bed rest helped, and my blood pressure did come down. Charles takes it every day now. He's been marvellous.'

'Has he really thought about what life will be like with three newborn babies in the house? I'm sure he has the best of intentions, but I wish you'd come and stay with us. We could look after you, darling.'

'Yes, I know and sometimes I'm tempted. But these babies are all his. Two children and a grandchild. He's been so supportive and sweet, it'd break his heart if I moved out now. I don't think he's considering all the hard work, he's walking on air at the moment and seems delighted at the prospect of having three newborns to look after.'

'He's quite a special man by the sound of it. What are

your feeling towards Charles now? You were a bit ambivalent last time we spoke.'

Josie rested her head back and thought about how to answer. 'My feelings have changed but not in a wildly passionate way. I'm still attracted to him and, if he wasn't in my life, I'd miss him desperately. I think I do love him but not in the way I thought I'd fall in love.'

'And what way was that?' Eloise poured more lemonade for Josie and handed her the glass.

'Thanks. In the pulse racing, girly bits twitching kind of way.'

Eloise laughed out loud at that.

'The type of things you find in romantic novels you mean?'

'Exactly. I suppose you're going to tell me that those feelings aren't real?'

'Oh, they're real alright, but they don't last. You and Charles seemed to have skipped the feelings you just described and gone straight to the deeper kind of love. Respect and strong feelings of friendship can lead to a much greater and lasting love. That's the real kind.'

'Was that how it was with you and Dad?'

Her mother smiled and the love she felt for Dan O'Connor was radiating from her eyes. It was obvious how true those feelings were.

'I love your father as much today as I did at the beginning with the racing pulse and all the rest. Having babies and bringing them up to be the adults that you all are now, has only deepened that love. You and Charles are just beginning your relationship. You've got a long way to go and it won't all be plain sailing, but I have a good feeling about you two.'

'Thanks, Mum. I needed to hear that.'

Chapter Twenty-Nine

July was hotter than June. Josie lay around on the couch, trying to drink as much water as she could and feeling fatter and more uncomfortable with each day that passed. Despite her inactivity, she felt unwell and was still worried about her symptoms.

Megan, meanwhile, was looking like a poster girl for a healthy, happy pregnancy. Her skin glowed, her hair shone, she smiled all the time and looked good in the maternity dresses bought on their shopping trip. From the back, you could hardly tell she was pregnant as she had a neat little bump and didn't appear to have put on much weight anywhere else.

Jason came up to Cheshire to see Megan on a weekend and the two of them disappeared for hours at a time. Megan showed him around and he seemed impressed with Leytonsfield. Josie was pleased to see that he was showing an interest in his child as he had taken a copy of the baby's scan home with him.

Charles was working long hours but had promised to take time off when the babies were due.

By the third week in July, Josie was starting to feel extremely unwell. She was admitted with increasing symptoms of pre-eclampsia. At her last appointment, she'd had protein in her urine, her blood pressure was creeping up again and the swelling was worse than ever. This time she was in the high dependency unit to be treated for her symptoms. It was confirmed that she was suffering from pre-eclampsia. This time it was serious.

'You'll be in until the babies are born,' said the obstetrician who admitted her. 'Complete bed rest.'

Josie knew this was the correct procedure, but she was still only thirty weeks and would have to be in hospital, in bed, for a long time. Her heart sank. This wasn't how she'd envisaged pregnancy. Josie had thought she would feel like an earth goddess, strong, powerful, and confident in her own body. Instead, she was bloated, sick, and scared.

Josie hated to admit to those close to her how scared she was. The twins now meant everything to her. She loved them and didn't think she could cope with losing them. And with pre-eclampsia, if it wasn't controlled, that was a real possibility.

When Charles came to visit her, she could see by his expression that he was as worried as she was.

'You must stay in bed, Josie, and do everything you're advised to do.'

'I will.' Before this moment she would have accused Charles of being patronising. She was a midwife for goodness' sake, she knew all about pre-eclampsia. But she didn't. She had no idea it would feel like this. She wasn't being strong and confident, ready to face any problems as Josie the midwife would have been. She was Josie the mother who was terrified for her unborn children. It was a scary, lonely place to be. Of course, she'd do anything people told her to do if it meant her babies would be safe.

As usual, the family came to see her as much as possible, trying to fit visits around their busy schedules. Her father looked at her with so much love in his eyes that she burst into tears and he held her and rocked her as he used to do when she was a little girl. He soothed her with gentle words and slowly her tears dried.

'Dad, I'm scared.' Josie whispered.

'I know, my love, but stay calm. I know it's easy for me to say that, but it will help. Remember your training. What would you tell a mother in your care in this situation?'

'I'd tell her the same thing while worrying that the only cure for this condition is for the baby to be born. I'm still only thirty weeks, Dad, it's too early.' Josie could feel her voice rising with the tension she was feeling. She took deep breaths to calm herself down.

'That's it, deep breaths in and slowly out again. You know the drill. You're a strong woman, Josie, and you're doing everything right. Get the symptoms under control and stay in the HDU until you're further on with the pregnancy. Yes, the babies may have to be born a bit earlier, but they'll be fine.'

Josie wanted to ask her dad to promise that everything would be okay, but she wasn't a child any more, she knew that there were no guarantees in this situation. She tried to smile for her dad's sake. She loved him so much and needed his strength and support now more than she ever had in her life.

'Come and see me again, Dad, when you can.'

'I will, my darling girl. We all love you and are thinking of you.'

'Have you spoken to Charles?'

'Yes. He's a good man and I'm glad you two are together. He'll look after you. That's all I've ever wanted for you four—to be in a loving relationship as your mum and I have been.'

They hugged and then her father kissed her before taking his leave. He seemed reluctant to go and Josie wished he could stay longer. Eventually, he said goodbye. He turned back twice to blow her kisses which made her smile. Maybe it would all be okay.

———

Despite Josie's best intentions, her symptoms didn't get any better and two weeks later, the thing that everyone dreaded happened.

Josie sat up to alter the position of her pillows and she felt as if someone had hit her over the head with a brick. A sharp, blinding pain that started at the top of her head, caused her to cry out in agony. Immediately, midwives were at her side. Then she saw flashing lights and her vision blurred.

Josie closed her eyes and she heard someone say, 'Get the on-call.'

Josie had never felt pain like it but could still think clearly enough to know that she and the babies were in grave danger. As she lay still she only had one thought that she was too ill to articulate. *Please save my babies.*

———

Charles got the call as he was finishing an antenatal clinic. He rushed to the HDU to find Carl Taylor, the obstetrician looking after Josie, telling her that they were going to do an emergency caesarean.

'I want to be there,' Charles said without preamble. His heart was beating out of his chest. This was the thing he'd been dreading. At thirty-two weeks the babies stood a good chance of surviving but they would be small, on the border of being very preterm and moderately preterm.

'Charles, I'm not sure that's a good idea. You're too involved—'

'Of course I'm involved, they're my children and Josie is the woman I love.'

'Exactly. Why don't you leave it to me?'

'There's no time to argue about this. Let me rephrase it. I'm going to be there. Okay?'

Carl sighed. 'Yes, I'd be the same. Right. Let's go and scrub up.'

Carl had known that Charles meant he wanted to be on the team performing the caesarean, not just there as the father of the babies. He was grateful, in that moment, for the understanding between medical professionals that allowed him to be part of the twins delivery.

Half an hour later, Josie was in theatre, fully prepped and ready.

Charles had kissed her and told her not to worry, but she looked scared and the only thing that would change that now was the birth of the twins.

Despite his anxiety, Charles couldn't help but be impressed with how fast and efficiently Carl worked and ten minutes later, both twins were born and on their way to the special care baby unit. A boy and a girl.

Carl stitched Josie up after the placentas had been delivered and Charles stayed with her until she was ready to return to the HDU.

He kissed Josie and told her the babies were being looked after and she would see them soon. Josie was in tears and Charles felt like crying himself. She had been through so much with a difficult pregnancy and now two premature babies to worry about. But Charles had faith in the staff of this hospital. Everyone went the extra mile for their patients and gave exemplary care.

As Josie was taken back to the HDU, Charles promised her he would come up to see her once he'd seen the twins.

Charles made two phone calls: one to Eloise O'Connor asking her to tell the rest of the family and one to Megan.

'Hi, darling. How are you?'

'Fine, Dad. What's wrong? Is Josie okay?'

'We had to do an emergency caesarean, and the babies are in the special care baby unit as they're so young. They need help with their feeding and need to be monitored. I'm going up to see them now.'

'What did she have?'

'A boy and a girl.'

'Cool. I think that's what she wanted but she didn't say that.'

'Are you sure you're okay?'

'Fine. Give Josie my love.'

'I will. I'll see you later.'

Once he'd finished his call, Charles rushed to the special care baby unit to see his children. His and Josie's twins were here, they were in the world, fighting to hold on to their slim grasp on life.

Charles fought back the tears before he went into the unit. He had to be the strong one for both his twins and Josie's sake. They were depending on him. He wouldn't let them down. He had broad shoulders and he would need them for the next few months until three of the five people who meant the world to him were home and safe.

Chapter Thirty

Charles had seen premature babies before. He had delivered them for countless women over the course of his career. But nothing had prepared him for how he would feel when he saw the twins, his own children, for the first time.

They looked so incredibly tiny, with minute hands and undeveloped fingernails. They were, however, breathing on their own and only needed help with feeding, so they both had a nasogastric tube in situ. The boy looked like a full-term baby, just smaller and more delicate. The little girl looked as if she was a bit behind her brother in development, but she was still able to breathe without artificial aid.

Charles wanted to pick them up and hold them as he had with Megan when she was born. Instead, he gazed at them for ages, trying to memorise every detail of their tiny bodies. Then he remembered his phone and took photos to show to Josie.

'Hi, Charles, gorgeous aren't they?'

The midwife who had been in theatre and who had brought them to SCBU came up to him smiling broadly.

'Yes, they are.' Charles's voice was croaky with emotion and the midwife squeezed his arm.

'They're going to be fine, you know. We just need to fatten them up a bit. Is Josie going to express milk for them?'

'I'll have to come back to you on that one,' Charles said. His head was spinning, and he couldn't think straight. Everything had happened so quickly. They hadn't even decided on names for the babies.

'No worries, I'll leave you with the twins.' The midwife strolled off before Charles had the chance to answer.

His attention returned to the twins. As he gazed at his offspring the rest of the world melted away. Nothing else mattered at that moment but the two tiny babies lying side by side in the incubator. They looked perfect, but Charles knew they weren't out of danger yet. They were susceptible to hypothermia so had to be kept warm, also low blood sugar, so they had an intravenous drip with dextrose to help them grow.

Charles had no idea how long they would have to stay in the SCBU, but they were in the best place for twenty-four-hour care. Now he must tear himself away from his little ones and go back to the HDU to see how Josie was.

Josie was groggy but awake when he returned to the unit. She held out her arms to him straight away, so he sat on the edge of the bed and enfolded her in a gentle but firm hug.

'How are you, my darling?' he asked quietly.

'The babies,' was all she could say through her tears.

Charles wiped her tears away with his thumb, then kissed her softly on the lips.

'They're fine. They're together in an incubator, breathing on their own but needing a bit of observation. They'll be fine.'

'Really?' Josie asked gazing at him with eyes still full of tears. She looked pale and ill, and Charles's heart went out to her. This wasn't how women should experience their first pregnancy, in pain from an operation, not able to even see their babies, let alone hold them, kiss them, and breathe in that unique newborn smell.

'Yes, really.' Then Charles remembered the pictures. He took his phone out and showed her.

'Oh, they're beautiful. How tiny they are. Are you sure they're okay?'

'I give you my word,' said Charles, wondering if he was tempting fate by promising too much. But he couldn't bear to see Josie so upset after everything she'd been through.

'Our babies,' Josie whispered as she stared at the screen.

'Our, as yet unnamed babies. We really should think of what we are going to call them now that they're here.'

'Can I see them?'

'Are you feeling up to it? You've only just come back from theatre.'

'Yes. I want to see them. Now. Please.' Josie was determined and when that happened she usually got her way. Charles was pleased to see something of her old fighting spirit was still there, despite her being so ill.

'Okay. I'll fetch a wheelchair and square it with Zara.' He said it casually but knew what a brick wall the senior midwife on the HDU could be when she disagreed with something. He'd have to sweet talk her round. Charles smiled. As if that would ever happen. Zara was old school and ran her unit with a fist of iron.

As it was, Zara was on her lunch break and a sweet

young staff nurse was on duty. She nodded when Charles told her that he was taking Josie to see her babies and asked to see the photos. She cooed over them, then Charles whipped Josie off the unit before Zara came back from lunch.

Josie was exhausted, sore from the stitches, red eyed from crying and needed a shower and to wash her tangled rat-tails that passed for hair. But, despite all that, as soon as she saw the twins, she forgot her ailments, forgot everything that had gone before and felt a gushing of love like a burst water pipe and smiled as Charles wheeled her as close to the incubator as he could.

'Oh, you little darlings… Charles, look at them. They are perfect. So tiny and so perfect.' The boy wore a little blue hand-knitted hat and the girl a pink one. She watched as their little chests moved up and down. Their hands were touching, and she was so glad they had each other for comfort.

'Yes,' came the gruff reply next to her. She didn't turn around as she didn't want to embarrass him. He was obviously as overcome with emotion as she was. Josie suspected they'd both feel that way for a while.

She longed to hold them, touch their velvet soft skin, and kiss them. Tears rolled down her cheeks, but she made no attempt to brush them away. They deserved her tears. She was their mother, but she hadn't given them the best start in life. They should still be in her womb, warm and protected in their secure world. Instead, because of her high blood pressure, they had been cut away from her and dragged into the world, then left to fend for themselves.

Well, that was an exaggeration as they were being looked after around the clock and couldn't be receiving better care. But Josie felt guilty as if it was all her fault. It wasn't how she had planned to have her family. *The best laid plans of mice and men...* Gran. Quoting Robbie Burns. Just what she needed at that moment. *What do you think of the twins, Gran?* Josie waited for a reply and in her mind, she heard her gran's voice. *They're lovely, dear.*

'Yes, they are.'

Charles put his hand on her shoulder. 'What did you say, Josie?'

Josie, who hadn't realised she'd spoken aloud, said, 'The babies are perfect.'

'Yes.' Charles sighed. 'I should take you back now before Zara finds you gone.'

'No, not yet. I want to stay a bit longer.'

'You need your rest, Josie, and I don't need a bollocking from Zara, the day's been stressful enough.'

Josie turned her head to look at Charles. She had been so full of her own problems that she had failed to see how tired he looked. He had bags under his eyes and a five o'clock shadow.

'You look as bad as I feel.'

'Thank you, darling.' Charles kissed her on the cheek.

'Did you phone Mum?'

'Yes, and I've told Megan.'

'Thanks. I need a shower, I smell like something left at the bottom of a wheely bin.'

'Not surprising with everything you've been through,' said Charles solemnly.

'What! You're supposed to say I smell as sweet as a rose.'

'A decayed rose maybe.' Charles grinned and Josie allowed herself to smile.

Then the emotion of the day overtook her, and she felt the tears fall again. This time she couldn't control her sobbing. She put her hands over her face and shook with the wave of mixed feelings that were surging through her. Utter relief that the babies had been born safely and she hadn't lost them, worry that things could still go wrong, and they weren't out of the woods yet, and elation that she had two beautiful babies and a gorgeous man at her side. What had she done to deserve such riches?

Charles put his arm around her and held her as well as he could considering she was still in the wheelchair. She had planned to get up and walk when they had arrived at the incubator but found she was physically unable to stand. So she stayed in the chair, feeling helpless and tearful.

'Right, I'm taking you back. You need to rest, Josie, and get your strength back. And you need to get your blood pressure down or they'll never let you go home.'

'I need a shower,' she said stubbornly. Josie was so tired she couldn't think beyond the need to be clean.

'I think a bed bath is the best you're going to get today, my love. So what if you smell? You need rest before anything else.'

'If you say so.'

As it was, she got her shower and her hair washed, so felt a hundred times better for her visitors.

Charles and Megan came back in the evening and Dan and Eloise O'Connor. The rest of the family decided to visit a few at a time, so as not to tire Josie out. Charles sent the photos to all the O'Connors and got congratulatory comments back from them all.

When everyone had left and the HDU settled down for the night, Josie closed her eyes and fell asleep almost the instant her head touched the pillow.

Chapter Thirty-One

When she awoke the following day, Josie felt as if she had been hit by a bus. She ached all over, still had a headache, and felt slightly sick. But the memory of her twins made her smile, and she couldn't wait to get back down to the special care baby unit to see them. She was a mother and she wanted to start enjoying her new role without all these bothersome symptoms to worry about.

Josie threw back the covers and swung her legs over the side, pulling herself up slowly so as not to cause more pain where the stitches were. She slowly slid her feet to the floor, feeling around for her slippers. She was in pain but determined to overcome it.

'Where do you think you're going?' Zara's booming voice made her shiver. 'Get back in that bed, Josie O'Connor, or I'll put you in a straitjacket.' Her expression was serious but her eyes with dancing with mirth. Zara was a formidable woman at nearly six feet tall, with jet black hair and dark eyes. You crossed her at your peril. Despite this, Josie had a lot of respect for her.

'Morning, Zara, I'm going to see my babies.' And you can't stop me, she wanted to add but didn't want to aggravate the woman any further.

'You are not. Do you want to set yourself back? You're recovering from pre-eclampsia and a caesarean, you need to get better before you go running around the ward.'

'I wasn't going to run, Zara, honest. I'll walk slowly.'

But it was futile, Zara and another midwife helped Josie back to bed with instructions to stay put. Zara hung around, straightening the bed covers and looking as if she had more to say to Josie.

'You look better than you did yesterday.'

'Thanks.' She must have looked a sight, so it was hardly a compliment.

'Listen. I'm sure it won't be long before one or more of your extensive family descend on us and they can take you in a wheelchair to see your babies. But you need to put yourself first. Your blood pressure is still too high, and we can't let you go home until it's down. You've been very ill, and you need to take things slowly.'

'Yes, I know you're right. And I want to thank you for your care. I don't know where I'd be without it.'

'You'll be having more blood taken for platelet counts and to check liver and kidney function. And we're still looking for protein in your wee, so you're not in the clear yet.'

'I know. You're right. I'll behave, I promise.' Josie just wanted to be well enough to look after her babies but understood the sense of what Zara was saying. She was recovering from a caesarean with all the physical and emotional implications. Her breasts were tender, and she was still in extreme discomfort.

'Good. Right. We'll get you some breakfast, you need to keep your strength up.'

'Thanks, Zara.'

But the senior midwife had already started walking away. Josie put her head back on the pillows and closed her eyes.

The first visitor was Casey, who rushed in, kissed her, told her the babies were beautiful, then rushed down to Accident and Emergency to start his shift.

Her older brother, Riordan, stayed slightly longer but kept looking at his watch and muttering about a multi-disciplinary team meeting he had to attend. He kissed her on the forehead, told her he loved her and that he'd be back when he could, then strode purposefully out of the unit.

Josie breathed a sigh of relief when her mum appeared, smiling broadly, and carrying a basket that, hopefully, would contain some of her home-made food.

'Hello, darling, you're looking better. How are you feeling?'

'Well, I'm suffering from fatigue, sore tits and discomfort everywhere. So, I've been told by Zara to stay in bed until my lovely mum arrives and then I can go and see the babies. So, let's go.'

Eloise needed no further encouragement and ten minutes later, they were watching the twins sleeping. The girl was cuddling up to her big brother which nearly caused Josie to dissolve into floods of tears, but she managed to hold it together. She'd cried enough. It was time for her to toughen up and get on with things. She had to believe that soon, she and the twins would be home where they belonged, with Charles and Megan. *Good girl.* Gran? Josie had a picture in her mind of her gran in a rocking chair knitting. Tiny white bootees. Did they knit in heaven?

'Mum?'

'Yes, darling.' Eloise dragged her gaze away from the tiny babies and looked at Josie.

'Did Gran knit? I don't remember her doing so.'

'Gran? Why do you ask?'

'I... I just want to know.' Josie had never told anyone that she heard her gran's voice in her head. To Josie, it was perfectly normal as she had heard her periodically ever since the old lady had died. But others might think she was losing it and Zara would get the chance to use the strait-jacket after all.

'Yes, she did as a matter of fact. And crochet. She was quite the accomplished needlewoman. Why?'

'I think I should learn to knit. Then I can make things for the babies.'

'What a lovely idea. I'll teach you if you like. Maybe we could teach Jade as well. She's good with her hands. The little love was very excited about the twins and was longing to come and visit, and most put out when I told her she'd have to wait as she was too young.'

'I can imagine.' Jade was a strong-willed little girl. Being Casey's daughter Josie could see where she got it from.

'Still, I think it's a good thing they don't allow young children. Too much equipment around to put them in danger,' said Eloise.

'And put the patients in danger. I can imagine Jade wanting to push all the buttons, to see what they do.'

It was good to laugh with her mum. They stayed for a

while longer, watching the babies who were just lying there, but were still fascinating to their doting mother and grand-mother. Josie was mesmerised by every movement, twitch, and waving arm. They still had their eyes closed and Josie longed for the day when she could watch as they opened them in surprise and started interacting with her. There were so many milestones ahead for them but for now, she would be happy to simply cuddle them.

'They remind me of you and Jay when you were born, although you were bigger of course being full term.'

'Oh. In what way?'

'Just the way they are together. You were close like that, had to be touching or to be able to see the other one. You hated being separated.'

Still do, thought Josie, remembering how she felt at not being invited to Bali to see Jay and Caitlin tie the knot.

'I just hope I'm half as good a mother as you are. I'm worried I'll get it wrong and the twins will suffer because of my ignorance.'

Her mother put her arm around her and hugged her. 'You, my love, are the child of a long line of strong women and mothers. I felt exactly the same as you, terrified of not giving you enough to eat, or too much. I worried when I took you out in the pram that it was too hot, or too cold. But you both thrived, despite me and my worries. And by the time you were Abigail and Lucy's age, you were in the garden eating soil and digging up worms like every other toddler. Kids are tougher than you think.'

'I didn't eat soil, did I?'

Her mother laughed and tapped her nose. 'Not telling. It was a long time ago.'

'I bet it was Jay. It was Jay, wasn't it?'

'Come on, sweetheart, let's get you back to bed before the dragon in charge starts breathing fire.'

'Bye, babies,' said Josie as her mum wheeled her away from the incubator. She really must talk to Charles about names. They couldn't keep calling them girl twin and boy twin.

Chapter Thirty-Two

Gradually Josie's blood pressure returned to normal, her excision healed cleanly and she spent all day every day, down in SCBU talking to her offspring. The first time she was allowed kangaroo care was a real step forward for Josie. She felt like a real mother at last as she held the two tiny people to her bare skin and kissed their soft heads. She cried, even though she told herself not to. It was an extremely emotional moment.

The babies grew and became stronger until they could breastfeed. That was her second emotional moment. Josie changed their nappies and washed them which was hard as they were still attached to wires and monitors.

Josie the midwife had gone on holiday, and Josie the mother had taken her place. The staff treated her the same way they treated the other mothers, explaining exactly what they were doing and why. Even Charles admitted to feeling disconnected from being an obstetrician and related more to being a father again.

They had a long discussion one visiting time when it was

just the two of them. Charles held her hand and gazed at her as if she was an earth goddess after all.

'Names, Josie, we need to name our kids.'

Half an hour later they had the babies' names. It had taken a lot less time and discussion than Josie thought it would. It seemed she and Charles agreed on names as well as other things.

'So, we have Bethany Eloise and Benjamin Charles.' Charles seemed pleased that she wanted to name their son after him and had no problem with Bethany having Eloise as her second name.

'What about your parents? Will they be bothered that we haven't named the twins after one or both?'

'Not in the slightest,' said Charles dryly. 'They are indifferent to me and my life and always have been. Andrew is the favourite son; I've always been a constant source of disappointment to them. Oh, I'm sure they'll come and visit one day and make the right noises, but they're not hands-on grandparents.'

'Does Megan get on with them?'

'She hardly knows them.' Charles sat back in the visitor's chair and stretched his legs out as best he could in the cramped space around the bed. 'Clarissa hated my mother, and the feeling was reciprocated. They clashed every time they were in the same room. It became almost funny in the end. At least I thought it was. When things weren't going well between us, which was a lot of the time, especially towards the end, they were like two hens pecking at each other.'

'What about your father?'

'He disappeared behind his paper and pretended he couldn't hear them. He never got involved.'

'You've never really talked much about your marriage. You don't mind me asking about it, do you?'

'Not at all.'

'So... how did you meet?' Josie settled herself more comfortably in the bed and listened intently to Charles.

'At medical school. A party. Clarissa was quite stunning when she was younger. She spent a fortune on her hair, make-up, and clothes. I asked her to dance thinking she'd say no as I knew I was punching above my weight, but against all the odds she said yes. I learned later that she was trying to make her ex-boyfriend jealous by dancing with me. It didn't work so when I asked her out she said yes to that as well. No idea why, she didn't fancy me. But I was smitten by then. I wasn't experienced with women, didn't have much time for a social life, and having a gorgeous woman going out with me gave my ego a heck of a boost.'

Josie thought she should feel jealous at Charles calling Clarissa gorgeous. Nobody had ever called her that, except a man in a bar who was so drunk he could hardly see straight, and called, "Hello, gorgeous" as she walked past. She wasn't completely sure he was talking to her anyway.

'So... how long after that did you fall in love?'

'I fell for her straight away, but I'm not sure it was real love. I was flattered and she probably thought that I could keep her in the style to which she was accustomed once I became a qualified doctor. Unfortunately for her, I wasn't interested in private practice and only had an NHS salary.'

'And that wasn't enough for her?' Consultant salaries weren't to be sneezed at.

'Nothing about me was enough for her as it turned out. I didn't earn enough, worked long hours and I was a hopeless father in her view. As far as the last one's concerned, I think she was probably right. I feel bad about it, but Megan and I are sound now.'

'I'm sorry.' Josie didn't know what else to say. Poor Charles. *There's two sides to every argument.* Thanks, Gran. She was right, of course, Clarissa would probably tell a completely different story.

'Well I'm not sorry,' Charles said, 'If I hadn't met Clarissa I wouldn't have Megan and her baby. Whatever was between myself and my ex-wife is lost in the mists of time as far as I'm concerned. The only people I care about are my daughter, my grandchild, and you and the twins. The rest of the world can go to hell.'

'What about my family? I know you haven't had much to do with them yet, but… you like them, don't you?'

Charles leaned forward and took her hands in his. He looked down at her fingers, then kissed the backs of her hands, sending shivers down her spine. At least she still had her libido. Thank goodness. Josie wondered if she would ever get back the sexual hunger she had felt early on in her pregnancy.

'Josie, I love you, I also love everything about you which includes your family. I realise I don't know them all that well, but your father has offered to take me for a drink in the Dog and Partridge and I think I'll take him up on that offer before you and the twins come home. Is that alright with you?'

'I'm thrilled. Of course it's alright.'

'Good. Right. I'm going to leave you now, so you can get your well-earned rest. I'll see you tomorrow, sweetheart.'

He kissed her on the lips, and she wanted to whisper, "I love you". Josie was conscious of the fact that Charles told her he loved her frequently, but she hadn't said it back yet.

As she watched him walk away, turning and waving as

he got to the door, she knew that her life would be empty without him. She wanted to be with him forever, not just because of the twins. She needed him to walk beside her into the future. Next time, she would tell him she loved him.

Dan O'Connor lifted his pint and said, 'Here's to you, Josie, Bethany and Benjamin. Oh, and Megan and her unborn child too of course.'

'Cheers, thanks.' Charles drank deeply from the pint of bitter which was the first alcohol he'd drunk since he had agreed to stop drinking to support Josie. Although, technically, Josie couldn't drink yet as she was breastfeeding and didn't want the twins to be affected.

'Abstinence makes the heart grow fonder,' said Dan with a twinkle in his blue eyes.

'Yes, it's nice to be able to drink again.' Charles thought of the other thing he was abstaining from. He'd only made love to Josie once and wanted to repeat the experience, when she was ready, of course. He wanted her desperately, loved her completely and couldn't wait for her homecoming.

'This is the O'Connor local,' said Dan.

'Nice pub.'

'We come here for serious conversations as well as a quick half.'

'Right.' Was that Dan O'Connor's way of saying he wanted to have a serious conversation with him?

'I just thought it would be good to get to know each other a bit better, seeing as you're now part of the family.'

'Okay. Thanks for that. And thanks for thinking of me as part of your family. I know what an honour that is.'

Dan chuckled. 'Well, I'm not sure about it being an honour, but we're not a bad bunch when you get to know us.'

'You're a close family, loving and looking out for each other. That means a lot.'

Dan nodded. 'Yes, we are all that. And we're available to help you and Josie if there's anything you need, especially when the babies are home. Having twins isn't easy, but it's so rewarding to watch them grow and interact with each other.'

'Thanks, Dan, I appreciate that. I feel I have a lot of ground to make up.'

'In what way?' Dan wasn't being nosy, he was just caring and making sure things were okay for his only daughter. Charles would feel exactly the same if he was talking to Megan's partner.

'I should have looked after Josie when she first realised she was pregnant. I was so obsessed with Megan being pregnant that I didn't pay Josie close enough attention.'

'You couldn't have known she was going to get pre-eclampsia. It wasn't your fault she became so ill.'

'I should have been looking out for the signs. I dismissed her increasing weight and the oedema around her legs and ankles as part of normal pregnancy. It was staring me in the face, and I ignored it. As soon as she told me it was twins, I should have been looking out for it. I can't help it, Dan, I do blame myself.'

'Well, following your logic, we were all to blame for not realising. We're all medics in one way or another and no one spotted the signs. I really think you should stop beating yourself up about it. Josie and the twins have survived and are going home soon. Did you say next week?'

'Yes. Next Friday.'

'If I were you, I'd forget what's gone before and enjoy having them home. And your daughter and her little one. Count your blessings, don't curse over what you see as the negative. Nothing you can do about it now anyway. Worrying never changed anything, especially regretful worrying.'

Charles knew Dan was right. Josie and the babies were doing well, and he had Megan to obsess about if he needed something to keep him awake at night. Not that he planned on staying awake. When Josie came home she would move into his bed and the babies would have a makeshift nursery until they were in a position to go house hunting. There was a lot to look forward to and his blessings were mounting.

'Another pint, Dan?' Charles asked getting to his feet.

'Yes, go on, why not. Another quick one.'

Charles smiled realising how lucky he was to have the O'Connors adopt him into their family.

'Thanks,' Charles said.

'Whatever for?'

'Everything.'

Chapter Thirty-Three

They were home. Josie and the twins had left the hospital and were back in the rented house. Megan had Bethany on her knee and Josie was cuddling Benjamin.

'Good practice for you,' Josie said to Megan.

'They're so tiny.' Megan held the baby as if she would break and gazed at her in wonder.

'Because they were only thirty-two weeks when they were born, they're still only thirty-six weeks, but they've been putting on weight and are developing well,' Josie said.

'Right, who's for a hot drink?' asked Eloise who had moved in to help out. She had already changed the beds and loaded the washing machine. Charles had gone into the hospital for a couple of hours, promising to be back as soon as he could.

Josie would be glad of her mother's help in the weeks to come, but she knew she couldn't stay forever and eventually the twins would be left in the care of herself and Charles. She was nervous and excited at the prospect of being a mother at last. She hadn't felt like a mother in the hospital, more like just another patient.

Josie had experienced being on the other side of the counter and hoped that her experience would make her more sympathetic to the frightened mothers that came into the maternity unit, completely dependent on the staff there to ensure they took home healthy babies. She had first-hand knowledge of how easily things could go wrong and vowed she would never take anything for granted again.

———

'Megan, I want you to do me a massive favour.'

'What, Dad?' Megan asked, trying to get comfortable on the couch. She was getting bigger now as she got closer to her delivery date, and everything was an effort. She was nearly at her time, but everyone assured her first babies were always late, so she knew she may have to wait another couple of weeks.

'Tomorrow, could you leave Josie and me alone? Have an early night or something. And could you look out for the twins in the evening? I don't want us to be disturbed. I know it's a lot to ask. Would you mind?'

'No, but why? Oh, I know... you're going to propose?'

'Shhh,' Charles put his fingers to his lips with a grin.

'You are, aren't you?'

'I plan to make a romantic meal while she's taking the twins to her parents. I've had to let Eloise in on the plan, so she doesn't ask her to stay for dinner. Then, yes, I'm going to propose.'

'Cool. Yeah, I'll keep out of the way.'

'Thanks, sweetheart. Do you think she'll say yes? I'm really nervous.'

'Course she will. She'd be stupid not to.'

Charles kissed Megan on top of her head. 'You're an angel.'

Five weeks after coming home, Josie was just starting to feel that she was on top of being the mother of twins, thanks to her lovely mum and her advice. The best was to get them both on a schedule, so they slept, fed, and "played" at the same time. She was lucky to have Megan on hand to help with the feeding, and gradually things got easier.

Charles was still working long hours, but from the following week, he was going to cut down his hours considerably and help with the twins. He had no intention of leaving everything up to Josie and Megan.

She had resumed driving and Charles had fixed baby seats in the back of the Mini. He was muttering about getting a bigger, more substantial car for her to drive, but Josie loved her Mini and didn't want to swap it.

The twins seemed to find car travel relaxing as they were both sound asleep when Josie arrived at her parents' house. Her mum came out to help lift the baby seats out of the car.

'How are you, darling?'

'I feel a lot better now. I'm getting stronger and the scar's healing. I need to think of ways to get rid of this weight though.'

'Well, take your time about that, won't you. Don't overdo it.'

'No, I won't. Walking to start with. I'll push the twins around the village.'

'Good idea.'

It was nearly September, Josie's favourite month. Lots of walks in the park in autumn. That would help to get her weight down.

Josie and Eloise spent a relaxing, enjoyable afternoon, talking babies. Josie never tired of hearing all the stories of herself and Jay when they were little, and Eloise never tired of talking about them. Josie was reluctant to move and hoped that her mum would invite her to stay for dinner, but surprisingly she didn't, and Josie reluctantly loaded the twins back in the Mini for the journey home.

'Right, I'll be off then.'

'Drive safely, darling, and take care. See you soon.'

When Josie arrived home, she took the twins out of the car and brought them back inside.

Charles was in the kitchen and there was a delicious aroma floating around. But she got the surprise of her life when she looked into the dining room and saw the table laid for two with a single red rose in a vase and an ice bucket with a bottle of champagne in it.

'Expecting someone?' she asked.

'Yes,' said Charles. 'I'm entertaining a very special lady tonight, so only the best will do.'

'Do I need to get changed?'

'No, you're perfect just as you are.'

'Right. Where's Megan?'

'She's upstairs and she's happy to have the twins while we eat.'

'That's kind of her. I'll take them up and have a quick wash.'

'Okay. Dinner in thirty minutes.'

Josie took the twins upstairs and changed their nappies quickly, putting them into their sleepsuits. Megan came in while she was doing that and helped put them to bed.

'Thanks for this, Megan. Do you know what your dad's up to?'

Megan turned away and said, 'Just wants to do something nice for you I think.'

'Right. Better get changed then. I smell of baby sick.'

———————

When Josie returned downstairs, having changed into a pair of black trousers with elasticated waist and a pretty blouse in broderie anglaise, Charles was dishing out the meal. It was duck again with mashed potato and caramelised onion but instead of the chestnuts, he was serving it with cabbage and orange sauce.

'This looks and smells delicious,' said Josie. 'Memories of last Christmas.'

'We've come a long way since then,' said Charles pouring the champagne.

'Cheers.' Charles lifted his glass and Josie clinked hers against his.

'Cheers.'

'How's your mum?'

'She's fine. Sends her love.'

They talked of mundane things as they ate the duck. Josie knew there was something behind this meal and the obvious thing sprang to mind. Was he going to propose? Even though she'd never actually told him she loved him? Charles seemed a bit jittery and not at all his usual relaxed self when he produced a meal. He kept glancing at her and looking away.

After the meal had been eaten with a small bowl of fruit salad to follow, Josie was trying to lose weight, after all, she looked at Charles and he held her gaze this time.

'What now?' she asked quietly.

Charles stood up, took something out of his pocket and dropped to one knee.

'Josie, I love you so much and I would be honoured and delighted if you would marry me.'

Josie felt tears at the back of her eyes and took the little box he held out like an offering.

A beautiful silver solitaire diamond engagement ring sat in the box lined with burgundy material. It shone in the light and Josie was overwhelmed. It must have cost Charles a fortune.

'Do you like it?'

'I love it, Charles, it's beautiful.'

'Try it on. It may need adjusting.'

Josie slipped the ring easily onto her finger where it sat snugly, the diamond catching the light. Aware that Charles was still on one knee, she realised she should put the poor man out of his misery.

She knelt down in front of him and put her arms out. 'Of course I'll marry you, I love you too, so much, even though I've never told you.'

They got up and hugged properly. Then Charles kissed her, gently at first, then more passionately and she kissed him back with all the love she could convey.

Josie felt her girly bits twitch and smiled. She still felt the need for sex, even though Charles had been a gentleman and told her that it was her decision when they made love. Josie wanted him now but was conscious of Megan upstairs looking after the twins. Maybe they'd have time for a quickie if they didn't make too much noise.

Then the moment was shattered as they heard Megan cry out. Immediately, Charles ran up the stairs.

'What's happened?' Josie shouted.

'Megan's waters have broken, I'm taking her to hospital.'

Josie the midwife wanted to interfere and ask questions about contractions and how often they were coming, but she kept quiet and let Charles the obstetrician take over and drive his daughter to the maternity unit.

'Let me know, when you can,' she said as Charles guided the frightened Megan to his car.

Then she was alone in the house. But she wasn't really alone as the twins were sleeping peacefully upstairs. She went to the nursery and gazed at them for a while. She didn't think she'd ever get bored with looking at her children. In a short space of time, they had become the centre of her universe. With Charles, of course.

The engagement ring sparkled, and she studied it. Silver. Charles had remembered that she wasn't fond of gold and preferred silver jewellery. Josie didn't know what the future had in store for them, but she felt that, with Charles by her side, she could weather any storm.

Josie went back downstairs to await a phone call from Charles. But it could be hours yet, so she made herself useful by clearing the kitchen, then tidying the living room. Then one twin woke and started crying. She thought it might be Benjamin. Then the other started, so she prepared the bottles and went back upstairs to feed them.

At three o'clock in the morning, her mobile rang. She'd been in bed for hours and was sleeping soundly. At first, she couldn't work out why it was ringing or who could possibly be disturbing her at this hour. Then she remembered.

'Charles.'

'Hi, darling. Megan's had the baby. She's going to call her Grace. Mother and baby doing well. I'll be home soon.'

'Thank goodness. Give her my love.'

'I will. I love you.'

'I love you too.'

Chapter Thirty-Four

A week after Megan and Grace came home, Clarissa and Todd, with Jason trailing behind them, came to visit and see the baby.

The house looked as if a crowd of baby elephants had been partying there. There were bottles, teats and dummies on every available surface, baby clothes strewn around the place, towels, face cloths, nappy rash cream, a baby thermometer and wipes on the coffee table, along with mugs containing cold coffee or tea, and teddies.

It looked as if all the items needed for the babies had been put in the living room, near to hand for the three adults, who looked happy if slightly dazed by the invasion of the three tiny people.

'Would you like a drink? Coffee or tea?' asked Charles, trying to be as polite as he could. The last thing he wanted at the moment was to play host to his ex-wife and the successful businessman she'd taken up with. Todd, as usual, looked immaculate. He wore a shirt and trousers, with a sports jacket and stood in the middle of the living room because every chair and the couch was full of stuff.

Charles was conscious that he hadn't showered since the day before and he could hardly remember when he had combed his hair last. He must look a fright.

'Not for me, thanks,' said Todd.

'No. Thank you,' Clarissa said.

'Can I have tea, Dad?' asked Megan, 'and one for Jason.'

'I'll have one too, thanks,' said Josie who was feeding Benjamin.

'Of course.' Charles escaped to the kitchen to make the drinks and let the girls entertain their visitors.

The washing machine was on almost permanently now, with another load in the plastic basket waiting to go in. The kitchen was a shambles; baby feeding bottles lined up to be filled. Other, used ones, were waiting to be washed and sterilised. His usual tidy, immaculate kitchen, the place he called his "happy place" was under siege.

Yet, despite the mess, Charles had never been happier. He'd underestimated how much work the twins would cause. He'd forgotten how demanding tiny babies could be. And Megan needed support with Grace. Even though she was doing remarkably well, she was still a teenager herself and sometimes she found it all too much and he had to step in to help out.

They were all on a steep learning curve and there were times when he was almost at the point of calling Eloise and asking her to come back and help. But they needed to do this. There were three adults and three babies, they should be able to cope. But some things had to be shelved. Things like the housework.

Charles made the tea and returned to the fray.

Jason was sitting on the floor at Megan's feet which was fitting as far as Charles was concerned. He should be worshipping at her feet. Megan was far too good for him. Josie was still feeding Benjamin and Clarissa was perched on the edge of one of the armchairs. Todd was still standing and looking extremely uncomfortable. He had never had children of his own and was obviously not happy around babies. He wondered if Clarissa would get broody, but one look at her body language told him her baby days were over, except as a grandmother.

Charles put the mugs of tea on the coffee table, after shoving everything already on it to the floor.

'Thanks, Dad,' said Megan.

'Yeah, cool,' said Jason.

'Thank you, my love,' Josie said. Charles watched Clarissa's face which had turned to a thunder cloud. Or a smacked arse as Josie would have said.

'Wow,' said Jason as he stared at Grace.

'What do you think of your daughter, Jason?' asked Charles.

'Oh wow, yeah, cool.' Jason couldn't tear his gaze away from her.

'Don't let your tea get cold,' Charles said.

'Look at her hands, they're so...'

'Tiny?' asked Megan.

'Yeah. And her fingernails are like...'

'Tiny as well?'

'Yeah. She's...'

'Amazingly beautiful just like her mother,' Charles couldn't help adding.

'Yeah, cool.'

'Megan, now that you've had the baby and are feeling better, your mother and I thought it was time for you to come home.' Todd hadn't even mentioned Grace. Had barely looked at her. Charles felt a wave of anger wash over him.

'Dad, is it okay for Jason to stay for a few days to get to know Grace?'

'Of course, you can stay for as long as you like, Jason.' It would do him good to get his hands dirty and change some nappies. See what looking after a baby was really all about. But the way he gazed at his daughter was encouraging. Maybe he'd turn out to be a responsible father after all.

'Megan, Todd is speaking to you, didn't you hear what he said?' Clarissa asked.

'Have you held Grace yet, Jason?'

'Yeah, sit down next to Josie and I'll put her on your lap,' said Megan.

'Wow, cool,' said Jason and leapt up to do as he was asked.

Megan stood up and put Grace on Jason's knee. 'Support her head, that's right.'

Only when her baby was safe and happy on her father's lap, did Megan look at her mother.

'Yes, I heard what he said.'

'Well? Would you like to come back with us today? Jason needs to get used to looking after her. It's about time he took some responsibility for the situation.'

'Grace isn't a situation, she's like, our baby.'

'Yes, I know that. Please don't be pedantic.' Clarissa was not in a good mood thought Charles. He wanted to intervene, but this was Megan's call. She needed to make the decision.

Charles caught Josie's eye and she shrugged. He winked at her.

'I'm staying here. We're going to buy a house big enough for all of us. Aren't we, Dad?'

'We are, indeed. I've taken the liberty of signing on with some estate agents so we should get some viewings soon.'

'Cool,' said Jason. 'Can I come and stay?'

Megan looked at Charles who nodded. 'You're welcome to stay whenever you like, and for however long you like.'

'Thanks, Dad,' said Megan. 'Grace needs to get to know you, Jase.'

'Yeah, that'd be cool.'

'Jason can get to know his daughter in London. That's what we planned, don't you remember, Megan? After the baby was born, you were going to come home.' Clarissa was sounding anxious. She hated not being in control of the situation.

'This is my home now. I want Grace to grow up with the twins. We're a family.'

'That's ridiculous,' Clarissa said.

'No it's not,' said Megan. Charles was worried that Megan would get upset but she seemed to be keeping her cool and was standing up to her mother well.

'Why ridiculous?' asked Charles.

'I'm talking to my daughter, it's none of your business.' Clarissa sounded like a petulant child and Charles said nothing, not wanting to start a row.

'Yeah, Mum, why is it ridiculous?' Megan seemed as irate as Charles felt.

'Because they're not your family, we are.'

'They are my family. I'm sorry, Mum, but we're staying here. You can come and visit though if you want.'

Just then Benjamin, who Josie was trying to burp after his feed, started crying and Charles suddenly wanted them out of the house.

Josie handed their son to him with a towel to put over his shoulder. Benjamin had a habit of regurgitating some of his feed and the smell of stale milk was strong despite the use of plug-in air fresheners. They had got used to the smell, but Todd and Clarissa were obviously aware of it as they both looked as if they had a bad smell under their noses.

'There you are, mate, you're okay.' Charles talked softly to his son and walked slowly up and down to stop his crying. Charles imagined that Benjamin was making his feelings known about the two people who didn't belong in his home.

Clarissa was watching him with a strange look on her face. Perhaps she was remembering the times he had done the same with Megan when she was a baby. He turned away so he didn't have to look at her.

'Come on, Clarissa, let's go. Megan—if you change your mind or need some respite from this madhouse, give us a ring, okay?'

'I won't, but thanks for the offer.'

'Jason? What are you going to do? Are you staying here or coming home?'

'Staying.' Jason didn't look up to answer. He was too busy falling in love with his daughter.

'Fine.' Todd made his way to the door and Clarissa got up and stood in front of Megan.

'Goodbye, darling. I do love you, you know.'

'Yeah, me too.'

They hugged briefly and then Clarissa followed Todd. As Charles listened to the sounds of their departure, he realised that Clarissa hadn't cuddled Grace or shown any interest in her at all. Jason, however, was still under his daughter's spell. It was good to see.

Once Clarissa and Todd had gone, the atmosphere in

the house lifted. Charles had succeeded in getting Benjamin to sleep and Bethany hadn't woken up for her feed. They still hadn't managed to synchronise the twins' schedules. It appeared they travelled to the beat of their own drums. But they weren't giving up. They'd read all the literature on bringing twins home and the first year of their lives though Josie preferred to talk to her mum, who had first-hand knowledge.

'Right,' said Charles, 'I'm going to clean the kitchen while it's quiet.'

Nobody answered him. Josie had fallen asleep. Another piece of advice was to sleep when the babies did so she did right. Megan and Jason were sitting side by side on the couch and Megan was telling him the details of her labour. Poor lad. But he looked happy enough.

Charles returned to the kitchen, realising his happy place had changed. It was now anywhere his family was.

Epilogue

The O'Connors had to buy a bigger table. It filled the dining room with just enough space for the adults to pull their chairs out safely. But it was the only way to get everyone around a table at Christmas. Their family had grown this year to include two more adults and three babies.

Josie gazed around at her family. Her father was having the time of his life pulling crackers with everyone and reading the silly jokes inside. He appeared to be wearing two paper hats. Whether this was by accident or deliberate Josie wasn't sure. They'd sensibly chosen crackers without any small plastic toys inside. Ones that were safe for children under the age of three.

Her mum was also watching everyone with a smile on her face. Josie caught her eye, and she smiled back. She had Bethany and Benjamin on her knees and looked as happy as a dog on a beach.

Riordan had Abigail on his knee, and she was trying to feed him the sprouts that she had refused to eat herself. He was pretending to eat them, but secretly passing them to their dog, Luna, who sat expectantly under the table, waiting for a morsel to come her way. She didn't care what it was, as long as it was edible.

Casey was talking to Tom, man to man, about sport or something else equally manly. Tom idolised his uncle Casey. Lexi and Zoe had their heads together, swapping toddler stories. Jay held Lucy on his knee and Caitlin sat next to them with her arm around Jay. Josie wondered if Caitlin would be next for motherhood.

Jade, who considered herself quite grown up now, even though she still wore her princess dress and tiara, was entertaining Charles with a story of a friend from school. Charles was listening attentively.

Josie and Megan sat next to each other. Megan was quietly feeding Grace a bottle and Josie wondered if she was feeling a bit overwhelmed.

'You okay?' asked Josie.

'Yeah. They're cool, your family. I've never had a Christmas Day like this. Is this what it's always like?'

'Pretty much,' said Josie, 'although there's never been as many children as there are now.'

'I hope we get invited next year. Maybe we can bring Jason.'

'You don't need an invitation, Megan, you're family. And Jason.'

'Thanks. That means a lot.'

'I better go and rescue Mum.'

Josie got up and took Bethany off Eloise's knee.

'Thanks, love,' she said as she handed Benjamin to Charles. 'Who's for tea? Or are you still on the booze?'

As Eloise, Jay and Caitlin cleared the table, Charles and Josie wandered into the living room.

'A bit different to last year,' said Charles as he stood in the middle of the room and rocked his son.

'Do you know, I was just thinking the same thing,' said Josie who stood next to him with their daughter. 'If it hadn't been for Brenda and Mike and a snowstorm, we would never have met.'

'You would have spent last Christmas with your family and I would have got drunk in the cottage. What an awful prospect that seems now.'

'You wouldn't have come to Leytonsfield to work and I would be still single and childless.'

'Life happens to you when you're busy making other plans.'

'I love you, Charles. I know it took me a while to realise it, but you and the twins mean everything to me now.'

'I love you too, my darling. Last Christmas you saved me from myself and this Christmas I'm the happiest man alive.'

They kissed gently. Josie thought she heard the sound of clicking. Like knitting needles. She turned around to see what it was, but the room was empty except for herself, Charles, and the twins. Then a picture came to her of Gran, sitting in a rocking chair, knitting baby clothes. The ones she had already made were in a neat pile on her knee. Two pink jackets for every blue one. Gran was knitting for Grace as well. She was singing quietly to herself. Josie joined in. 'Away in a Manger.'

When the carol had finished, Charles kissed her again. 'It's lovely to hear you sing. You've got a beautiful voice.'

'Thanks, love.'

Then, one by one, the O'Connors wandered into the living room, talking, laughing, hugging. Three generations of family, united by love, together forever.

'Happy Christmas, Gran,' Josie whispered.

More by Jax Burrows

vinci-books.com/lostforwords

Love might set them free...

Dr. Joel Whittaker wants a new beginning. Esme McBride stopped believing in those long ago. But when the guarded nurse and grieving doctor collide, long-buried emotions resurface. Can two people haunted by the past find the courage to let love in?

Turn the page for a free preview...

Lost for Words: Chapter One

It was Monday morning again. Esme McBride stepped through the door of the medical centre with a familiar swirl of anticipation and dread in her stomach. She shook her head a little. Dread was too strong a word she told herself sternly. But sometimes the anxiety she'd been suffering with for the past ten years made things feel worse than they were. Her heartrate increased as she nodded and smiled at the two old ladies in the waiting room who greeted her.

'Good morning, Sister,' they said cheerfully.

'Good morning,' she replied before continuing down the corridor to the treatment room she used to see her patients.

The feeling of anticipation was always there, however, as she loved her job as senior practice nurse at the medical centre. With each day being different, she never knew what was in store.

When she reached the kitchen in the middle of the corridor, she heard laughter emanating from the propped open door. It should be shut when the clinics were running, to keep the noise level down. But, propped open, any loud laughter would be heard by the two patients already in the waiting room.

The laughter continued. It was obviously a very funny joke. Should she ignore it and get ready for clinic? But the professional Esme was annoyed and she had to speak out.

She walked through the open door to the sight of Patricia, one of the registered nurses, Sally, the youngest receptionist, and a man she had never seen before standing in the middle of the kitchen. The laughter died as soon as they saw her. She must have had a serious look on her face to match her mood. Granted the clinics didn't start for another half an hour, but the staff knew better than to behave like school kids on a day trip when they were on duty. They were professionals and should behave with decorum at all times.

'Morning, Sister McBride,' said Sally as she squeezed passed her to return to the reception desk carrying a mug of coffee in each hand.

'Good morning, Sally.'

'Esme,' said Patricia, 'good timing. This is Dr Whittaker, our new GP. He was just telling us a funny story of when he was a medical student. Right, I'll leave you in Esme's capable hands.' Patricia left the kitchen and Esme turned her attention to the man who was standing in front of her with his hand out to shake and a smile on his lips.

'Good morning, nice to meet you. Shall I call you Esme or Sister McBride?'

Esme looked at his hand—strong with beautifully manicured fingernails—then took it in hers. He was looking directly into her eyes, his blue eyes seeming to reach into her soul. She dropped his hand quickly.

'I'm old school, Dr Whittaker, I think we should be professional at all times, so Sister McBride will suffice.'

Esme knew that many nurses her age weren't concerned with titles but she preferred to be called by hers. She may be only thirty-two but she was an old-fashioned girl at heart and she'd worked hard for her title.

'Absolutely,' he said with a smile. An open, happy smile which reached his blue eyes. Esme imagined that Dr Joel Whittaker smiled a lot.

'But welcome to Leytonsfield Medical Centre, we're very pleased that you're joining us, and I hope you'll be very happy here.'

'I'm sure I shall.' Dr Whittaker spoke slowly, enunciating each word clearly and he hesitated slightly before he pronounced some words.

Esme hoped she hadn't annoyed him, that was never her intention. She came across as quite stern and serious—she'd been told enough times by both her family and her colleagues to lighten up—but she was serious about her job and liked things to be done just so. It was unfortunate that, in the modern world in which they were all forced to reside, most people preferred informality. She'd lost count of the number of times she'd had to complain about the receptionists using their mobile phones when the clinics were running. It created such a bad impression for the patients.

'Would you like me to show you to the room you'll be using today?' Esme asked in an attempt to make up for her earlier abruptness.

'Thank you, that would be very kind.' Dr Whittaker spoke politely but Esme couldn't lose the feeling that he was laughing at her in some way. It wouldn't be the first time someone mistook her desire to behave appropriately for stuffiness. His blue eyes were twinkling far too much for her liking.

As they walked down the corridor to the room Dr Whit-

274

taker would be sharing with two part-time GPs, she realised
that she had to look up to meet his eyes. At five feet eleven
inches tall, Esme towered over most women she met and a
lot of men too. But Dr Whittaker must have been over six
feet tall. It made a refreshing change. Not that she had a
problem with her height, she rather liked being tall.

'Right. Here we are. Georgina, our practice manager,
will be along before clinic starts to show you how to navi-
gate the patient software and set up passwords and the like.
I can give you a brief tour before she arrives.'

Dr Whittaker sat down and Esme stood next to him,
leaning over slightly to use the mouse and show him how to
move from one piece of software to another. She was aware
of him as he stared at the screen, a tiny frown creasing his
brows. It had been a long time since she had been this close
to a man and she knew her cheeks would be cherry red if
she didn't back off and keep her distance. Damn these
blushes. She'd been plagued with them all her adult life and
wished she knew how to control them. No matter how cool
and detached she wanted to be, her red cheeks always gave
her away.

'Good. It looks similar to the one I used at my last place,
so I'll be able to hit the ground running.' He turned his
head to look up at her and the smile was back in place.

'Where were you working before?' Not that she really
cared but small talk had never been her strong point.

'A small health centre in Manchester.'

'Oh, so what made you move to Leytonsfield? It'll be a
lot quieter here than what you were used to in the big city.'

'Peace and quiet sounds good at the moment.' He
sighed and looked away, staring at the computer screen
again. 'I've moved in with my brother who is a psychiatrist
at Leytonsfield General. He bought himself a fixer-upper

and finds now that he has neither the time nor the skills to do the place up. I needed a change, so I offered to help him.'

She was tempted to ask him why he needed a change but feared it might be too personal a question. Stick to the mundane and avoid affairs of the heart.

'Do you know anything about house renovation Dr Whittaker?'

His smile this time was barely perceptible. 'I did a lot of work on my own house in Manchester, so I'm not a complete novice, and anyway, there's plenty of advice on the internet.'

Esme had run out of questions to ask him and was keen to get ready for clinic. 'I see. Well, good luck with it all.'

'Thank you.'

The door flew open, and Georgina, the practice manager, rushed in. 'Sorry, sorry… the bus took ages this morning. I'm here now anyway and I'll take over. Thanks, Esme, for looking after Joel. I'm so sorry I wasn't here to welcome you. Well, I'm here now.'

'Right.' Esme backed away from the desk to avoid Georgina elbowing her out of the way. 'I'll go then.'

'Yes, go, clinic's starting soon and some of your patients are already here.'

Esme left the two of them together, Georgina still talking and Dr Whittaker—Joel—frowning at the screen, trying to keep up with the cascade of information Georgina was no doubt imparting.

As Esme reached the small clinic room she used to see her patients, Patricia was coming out of it.

'Esme, I'm sorry, I forgot what day it is. No wonder you were a bit tetchy earlier on. Are you going to the…?'

Tetchy? She was merely expressing an opinion. But at

least Patricia had the grace to apologise. 'Yes, I'm going after work today. Thank you for remembering.'

'Oh, you're welcome. It must be… well, I know how hard this day is for you. If there's anything you need, please just shout.'

'Thank you, Patricia, I will.'

'Right, better get on.'

When Esme was alone, she took a deep breath and closed her eyes, trying to calm her thoughts and her fast heartbeat. Then she turned her attention to the list of patients she was seeing that clinic. Professional at all times. Personal things would have to wait until later.

After spending the morning performing routine procedures such as cervical smears, pregnancy tests and dressing changes, Esme took a quick break for lunch.

Two of the younger nurses were in the kitchen as Esme made herself a coffee and ate her sandwiches.

'What do you think of the new doctor?' Matilda asked Ebony. 'Bit of a hottie, eh?'

Ebony glanced at Esme. All the nurses knew that she disapproved of gossip, especially when they were discussing other members of staff. Idle chat about which reality show or soap opera they had watched the previous night, or something equally innocuous was acceptable. But talking about colleagues behind their backs certainly wasn't.

On this occasion, Esme said nothing and pretended she hadn't heard. She continued to eat her sandwiches and scanned the front page of a tabloid newspaper that someone had left on the table.

'I've only seen him briefly so I couldn't really say.'

'Oh, go on, you have seen him. I think he's sex on legs. What do you think, Esme?'

'I think you shouldn't be having this conversation, you know how I feel about gossip. But if you must know, I think he's very pleasant and yes, he is also attractive, but whether he's a good doctor and will fit in here remains to be seen.'

Esme had her back to the door and hadn't heard it open. She did, however, note Matilda's eyebrows rise almost as high as her hairline and her eyes widen. Too late, Esme realised that she was trying to signal the need to stop talking.

'Right, come on Ebony, back to work.' The two nurses rushed out of the kitchen as if devils were chasing them.

Esme felt the heat rise to her face and knew, without having to look in a mirror that her cheeks would be bright red. She also knew who she would see behind her. She turned around slowly but couldn't meet his eyes.

'Ah, Dr Whittaker. I'm so sorry you had to hear that—'

'You surprise me, Sister McBride. This morning you were telling me how you believed in being professional at all times. And now, I find you gossiping about me with two nurses.'

'Dr Whittaker, I don't know what to say.' Esme's face burned with humiliation. She felt sick and stared at his shoes.

When Esme finally forced herself to look up, she expected to see thunderclouds, but the doctor was smiling, the skin around his eyes crinkling attractively and his blue eyes shining with mirth. He was enjoying her discomfort, that much was obvious.

'I think you've probably said enough. It's gratifying to know you find me attractive and I'll do my utmost to prove to you that I'm a good doctor and can fit in here.' His tone of voice was almost gentle as if he knew how bad she must be feeling. But also slightly mocking as if he found the whole thing a hoot.

'Dr Whittaker... please accept my apology...'

'Apology accepted. Enjoy your lunch.'

Then he was gone, and Esme was alone. She threw her sandwiches in the bin. She had lost her appetite. After making herself an extra strong coffee, she took a deep breath, then groaned. *Damn the man.* Today of all days she had to make a complete fool of herself. Maybe she should have asked for the day off, but then she would have been moping around at home feeling sorry for herself. Since it happened Esme had taken refuge in work, finding the act of helping others went some way to allay the pain that she carried with her constantly.

Esme went back to her office and her next patient.

Joel survived his first day at the medical centre without any mishaps. The patients he saw were a mixed lot; elderly people with arthritis, heart conditions and diabetes, a young man with suspected gall bladder problems, a child who had got a bad cough and a runny nose, and a woman in her forties with a lump in her breast.

Joel had written prescriptions, referral letters to specialists and listened to the patients closely to ascertain their real problems. Sometimes they were too shy or embarrassed to tell the doctor what was really troubling them. Occasionally they only got to the point of their visit when they were about to leave the surgery. They'd say things like, "While I'm here, doctor, I thought I should just mention..." then they'd admit to a lump, or rash in an intimate place, or bleeding and try to shrug it off as not really worth mentioning, or they'd look at him with frightened eyes and Joel would know that, really, they were worried sick. It was part of a GP's role to recognise the serious symptoms.

It had been a long day and Joel was glad to head home. As he was saying goodnight to the receptionists, he bumped into Esme, who was also taking her leave.

'How was your first day?' she asked as they walked towards their cars.

'It was fine, actually,' Joel said, 'I think I'm going to like working here. And I hope I can prove to you that I'm a good doctor.' He smiled to show that there were no hard feelings about the earlier incident.

Sister McBride blushed which softened her features and made her look more vulnerable. Joel felt strangely protective of her.

'I am sorry about the gossip in the kitchen, it's not like me at all.'

'It's fine,' said Joel, 'I've forgotten about it already.'

'Good.'

They stood together, Esme looking at the ground and Joel wondering if he should ask her if she fancied a quick drink in the pub at the end of the road, which, he had been told, was the medical centre's local. She intrigued him and he'd like to get to know her better. Just as colleagues, of course. But Sister McBride was clutching her car keys and looked eager to be off.

'Right then,' he said, 'I'll see you tomorrow. Goodnight, Sister McBride.'

'Yes, goodnight, Dr Whittaker.'

He walked away and got in his car. Sister McBride did the same and she pulled away from the carpark, turning right. Joel turned left heading for his brother's house. They had an exciting evening planned—stripping the old wallpaper. He knew from the experience of doing his own house up how thrilling that was. But Noah was letting him live there rent free. It was a fair exchange.

He wondered what Esme McBride would be doing tonight.

Lost for Words: Chapter Two

'Hello, David, I'm here again.' Esme took the dead flowers out of the vases and replaced them with fresh ones. Gerbera, dahlias, allium and rudbeckia or black eyed Susan. There was also some white gypsophila which reminded Esme of weddings. She had bought them from The Little Flower Shop, her favourite florists. She usually bought David's flowers there. Occasionally she brought flowers from her own garden, from the house she shared with Scarlett and Maria.

Once the fresh flowers were arranged to her satisfaction, she stood in front of the gravestone and wondered what to talk about this time. This was a special visit as it was the anniversary of David's death. It had been ten years to the day since the road traffic accident that Esme had survived and her fiancé had not.

'We have a new doctor at the medical centre, and I made a complete fool of myself today. He overheard me telling the nurses that I thought he was attractive. Well, he is. Not that looks matter. He didn't seem annoyed, just amused. I have a feeling I'm going to struggle to get him to take me seriously now.'

Esme usually found a lot to tell David and had got used to their one-sided conversations, so they came naturally to her. She didn't even care if anyone walking passed heard her talking to his gravestone. She missed him so much and longed to hear his voice again. The next best thing was being able to talk to him as if he could hear her. It may be daft, as several members of her family thought, but it had always brought her comfort and kept the connection with him alive, even if that was only in her mind.

Today, however, she was finding it hard to focus on David. All she could see when she closed her eyes was Dr Joel Whittaker and his sparkling blue eyes. When she added in his sexy smile that made her heart race faster than she was comfortable with, she realised the truth of what she had said to the nurses in the kitchen. Their new doctor was an incredibly attractive man.

But David had been her fiancé, the only man she had ever loved, and she missed him like crazy. She shouldn't be thinking of another man when she was visiting him. She needed to concentrate on him and think of how happy they had been together, at least at the beginning.

Esme shivered, even though the air was warm. She glanced at her watch and saw that she had been standing at the graveside, daydreaming for nearly half an hour. It wasn't like her to feel sorry for herself and she stood up straighter and smiled.

'Right, David. I'd better get back before they send out a search party. Goodbye, my love.' She walked briskly back to her car.

Joel cursed and brushed bits of plaster and dust out of his hair from the large piece of wallpaper he had ripped off the wall, the plaster coming away with it.

'There's no doubt about it, Bro, you'll have to get these walls replastered before you do any decorating.'

'Yes, I know. I don't think anyone's changed the décor since the house was built in 1899. Or it seems that way. This wallpaper's awful.' Noah coughed as the dust settled on both of them. He brushed the dust from his short, dark hair.

'Strange how fashions change. Anyhow, more importantly, when are we stopping for tea? My stomach thinks my throat's been cut.'

'Me too. Right, which would you prefer? To nip out for fish and chips or stay here and finish stripping this room. We've nearly finished here anyhow. Then we can start on the floorboards. Another dirty job.'

'It's a dirty job but someone's gotta do it,' Joel said in his best American accent.

Noah laughed and put down the steamer he was using to loosen the wallpaper.

Joel looked his brother up and down, then glanced down at himself. 'Seeing as I'm the one who's copped for most of the plaster and other unidentifiable muck, I think you should go and get our tea. I'll just finish up here, then have a wash and put the kettle on.'

'Sounds like a plan. What are you having? Fish, chips, and mushy peas?'

'You know me so well. Lots of salt and vinegar on mine.'

Noah laughed and went into the kitchen to wash his hands and face.

When he was gone, Joel got stuck into removing the last

of the wallpaper. He sang as he worked. It had been the right decision to come to Leytonsfield and help his beloved big brother rather than stay in Manchester moping because Julie hadn't wanted to marry him. Joel hoped he'd be able to carve out a brand new life for himself in the Cheshire countryside.

Joel triumphantly pulled the last piece of wallpaper off the wall, then started clearing up. By the time he had done this as best he could, Noah was back with the food.

'Ah, that smell! The best aroma in the world—fish and chips with salt and vinegar—heavenly,' Joel said.

'What, better than the smell of roses or coffee, bread fresh out of the oven?'

'Sorry, Bro, but they're a poor second to fish and chips when a man's hungry.'

Noah laughed and Joel was reminded how much he had missed the company of his brother after Noah left Manchester. The easy banter, gentle teasing and shared confidences had been the background to his life, and he missed all that. It was great to be living with Noah and he was determined to help him turn the old house into a palace.

They sat down at the small pine table in the almost empty kitchen. They were definitely roughing it while the renovations were being carried out. Only essential furniture, bare floorboards, bare lightbulbs, cheap and cheerful crockery; a plate, bowl, and mug each.

Joel sighed with pleasure as he savoured his first mouthful of food. 'This is good. We'll have to eat there again.'

'One of the best things about living in this town is the amount of great places to eat, including the fast food joints.'

'I'm looking forward to having a good look around. I'm liking what I see so far.'

Noah took a drink from his mug of tea. 'How was your first day in the medical centre?'

Joel took a swig of his own tea before answering. 'It was good. Everyone seemed friendly and welcoming. All except one, that is.'

'Oh, who was that?'

'Her name's Esme McBride, she's the Senior Practice Nurse. She was quite standoffish at the beginning of the day. She said she believed the staff should be professional at all times.' Joel couldn't help smiling as he pictured Sister McBride trying to put him in his place, then blushing like a teenager when he caught her gossiping about him.

'Weren't you being professional? What the heck were you doing?'

'I had just met another of the nurses and one of the receptionists and I was telling them the story of my first day as a junior doctor. I was just trying to break the ice and be friendly, but Sister McBride didn't approve.'

'You'll win her over. Just use the old Whittaker charm and she'll be putty in your hands.' Noah stuffed more chips into his mouth.

'Well, listen to this. I went into the kitchen to make a coffee and she was gossiping about me with two other nurses. She knew I'd heard her and did have the grace to blush. Fire engine red.' Joel had felt quite sorry for poor Sister McBride.

'Terrorising the nursing staff on your first day isn't the way to make friends in a new job.' Noah scrunched the chip shop paper up and threw it into the bin. 'Slam dunk.' He grinned.

'I'll make it my business to be extra specially pleasant to her, whilst being professional of course.'

'There's a nurse in the unit called McBride—Scarlett. She's got sisters who are nurses. I wonder if they're related.'

'It's a common name. You could ask her though.'

'Yes, I will.' Noah looked away then up at the ceiling. He usually did this when there was something he didn't want to talk about. Or someone.

'So Scarlett is a friend or something else?'

'She's a colleague.' Noah wouldn't look at him.

'Is she pretty?'

'Extremely. Red hair, green eyes, alabaster skin, always laughing.'

'And just a colleague?'

'That's right.'

'So why don't I believe you?'

Noah was quiet for a while, staring into space. Then he sighed. 'No comment. Right, I'll wash up, then we can make a start on the floorboards.' Noah had always loved red heads. But he wasn't going to get any more out of his brother tonight. The floorboards awaited.

'Whoopee do,' muttered Joel.

Lost for Words: Chapter Three

When Esme arrived home to the house she shared with Scarlett and Maria, she expected to be able to smell the aroma of food cooking. They knew she was visiting David's grave that afternoon and she had been sure that one of them would have, at least, started preparing the evening meal.

Scarlett came running down the stairs as Esme was about to go upstairs to get changed.

'Hi, we've been summoned, so you've just got time for a quick shower. Maria's home, so we can all go together.'

'I do wish she'd give us more notice. It's lovely to be invited for a meal, of course, but I could have made other plans for tonight,' Esme said irritably. Then she sighed. She should be used to Mum and her impromptu gatherings by now.

'But you haven't though, have you? I mean, you never do after you've been to the cemetery. You never go out on the anniversary, do you?'

Scarlett studied her face as if searching for clues. Since

becoming a mental health nurse, her sister was acutely aware of people's "tells", the little clues that gave away how they were feeling, or whether they were telling the truth.

'No I haven't but that's hardly the point. I'm going up for a shower.'

'Okay, Esme. I'll drive so you can have a drink.'

Esme got into the shower and let the hot water run over her. All she wanted at the end of a busy Monday that just happened to be another anniversary of her fiancé's death, was the chance to chill. She wanted to get into her PJs and slump in front of the telly, then have an early night and cry herself to sleep. But instead, her mother decided to host a dinner party. Well, okay, it was just the family and perhaps Dot, her mother's best friend, but still. It would involve polite—or not so polite—conversation, being interrogated about the slightest detail of her life, and hearing about how wonderfully well everyone else was getting on.

Esme stepped out of the shower and wrapped a towel around herself. She wiped the condensation on the mirror so she could see herself through the narrow gap. *I'm being a bitch aren't I?* She studied her reflection. *It's okay, you can be honest.* Her reflection nodded mournfully. Esme sighed. She needed to stop feeling sorry for herself and count her blessings.

When they were all ready, they piled into Scarlett's car. She loved big, powerful cars, that she drove far too fast for the family's liking. When she traded her last car in, she compromised and bought a second hand Honda Accord. Scarlett had confided in Esme that she had her heart set on a Ford Mustang that cost about two year's salary. Esme promised not to tell their mother.

When they arrived at the house, Esme hung back while their mother hugged and kissed Scarlett and Maria.

'Here's my girls, come and give me a hug.'

'Hi Mum,' said Maria wrapping her arms around Candy.

'Hi there,' said Scarlett and hugged them both which made them laugh.

Esme took deep breaths and plastered a smile on her face as they all made their way into the house which had been the family home for thirty-five years. All four of the McBride girls had been conceived in this house, although they had all been born in the maternity unit of Leytonsfield General Hospital.

The house was full of memories, but instead of calming Esme, it reminded her of everything she had lost. The innocence of childhood, her father, Frank McBride, who had died five years previously of a heart attack, and David. Always David.

'Aren't you going to give me a hug?'

Candice McBride, who liked to be called Candy, was nearly as tall as Esme and at fifty-seven, was an extremely attractive woman who made the best of herself. Her ash blonde hair was cut in a fetching bob and her blue eyes were framed by false eyelashes which, on some older women would have looked silly, but on Candy looked chic.

'Yes, Mum, of course. How are you?' Esme, not being fond of public displays of affection, put her arms around her mother as they hugged each other, but was the first one to break the hug.

'I'm fine, dear, but you're looking a bit peaky. Are you getting enough sleep?'

'It's the anniversary of David's death. Had you forgotten?' Esme snapped at her mother.

'No, darling, of course I hadn't forgotten, but it was ten years ago.' Candy moved to hold Esme, but she avoided her and stood with her face averted. 'Don't you think you should be trying to move forward? I know you'll never forget him, as you loved him so much, but you're wasting your youth mourning him after so long. It's time you started living again.' Candy reached out to her eldest daughter, but she backed away.

'You don't understand. Just because you've managed to get over Dad so quickly, doesn't mean we're all cut from the same cloth.'

Esme turned away from her mother and went into the living room. Scarlett followed her in.

'That was nasty, Esme, I think you should apologise to Mum. She hasn't got over Dad, she just keeps her feelings to herself. Next year will be their thirty-fifth wedding anniversary. You were only with David a matter of a couple of years. There's no comparison.'

Esme turned on Scarlett, her face hot and no doubt as red as a pillar box. 'What difference does that make? Love isn't measured in years and anniversaries. I will never get over him no matter how long I live, and the thought that I can just move on like that, as if I have the choice and can turn off my feelings…' Esme couldn't say anymore as the tears came, fast and hot. She wished she could make her family feel what she felt and understand the depth of despair she experienced, especially on the anniversary of the accident.

She sat down on the couch and sobbed. Scarlett was beside her immediately.

'Oh, my darling, I'm sorry, please don't cry. Forgive me. We all need to stick together, that's what Dad would have wanted.' Scarlett rocked her, and Esme cried harder to think she had upset her darling mother who she loved so much.

Mum came into the room and sat on the other side of Esme. Then Maria came in and sat quietly in the armchair, not speaking, but looking anxiously at Esme.

Esme felt as if she was at the bottom of a dark pit and a tiny beam of light was drawing her upwards out of the pit, back into fresh air and sunshine. Her family was the light and Esme shuddered to think of how she would have coped without them over the past ten years.

Surrounded by her family, all loving, concerned, and supportive, Esme slowly calmed down, then felt stupid for losing it with Mum. She didn't deserve to be spoken to like that.

'Come on now, dry your tears,' said Candy, 'we all know how much you loved David, and it's admirable that you still have deep feelings for him, but I'm your mother and my concern is for your happiness. I hate to see you tearing yourself apart year after year. You're such a lovely young woman, I want you to be happy, that's all.'

'We all do,' said Scarlett.

'I know. I'm so sorry. Sometimes I get these feelings and I can't control them.' She knew her family wanted the best for her and she vowed that she would try harder to keep her darkest feelings hidden from them to prevent her lashing out and hurting the people she loved the most.

The sound of footsteps running down the stairs and the door bursting open announced Connie, the baby of the family, although she was twenty, who still lived at home.

'Hi! I'm starving—oh, what's wrong?' Connie came and knelt in front of Esme and tried to hug her. 'Are you okay?'

'It's the anniversary,' said Candy, holding Esme's hand in her own and stroking it gently.

'Oh yeah, sorry Esme. I'm really sorry.'

Esme sighed. 'It's fine. I'm okay now. Thanks everyone and I apologise for acting like a complete fool.'

'Well, not a *complete* fool,' said Scarlett and Esme smiled.

'Right, let's take our seats shall we before the meal is ruined?' Candy got up and held her hand out to Maria. 'Would you help serve? You can open the wine.'

'Of course,' said Maria who took her mother's hand, and they left the living room.

When they were all seated around the dining table and were enjoying Candy's homemade chicken and asparagus pie, with steamed vegetables, Esme silently gave thanks for her family. They were always supportive and loving; no matter how appallingly she behaved, and she knew she did, they understood and forgave her. What would her life have been like if she'd had to endure the last ten years without them?

When they were eating their dessert of Eton mess, Candy asked, 'Dot's spending Saturday with her family as it's her daughter's birthday, so if any of you can spare a few hours to help in the shop I'd be grateful.'

'Working, sorry,' said Scarlett between mouthfuls. 'This is gorgeous, Mum, is there any more?'

'There's some left, yes. I'll get it in a minute.'

'I'll get it.' Scarlett left the dining room.

'I'm working, too, Mum, sorry,' said Maria.

'I'll do it.' Esme enjoyed working in the cake shop. She was a reasonable baker, having been taught by the best— her Mum—and liked the idea of the two of them spending some time together without her sisters there too.

'Thank you, sweetheart, that's kind of you.'

'You're welcome.' Maybe it would make up for being cruel to her earlier on. Guilt weighed heavily on her for hurting her mother. She knew how much her parents had loved each other and that her mum kept her grief hidden to protect her daughters.

Scarlett came back carrying a plate with what was left of the Eton mess and fresh strawberries. 'Right, who wants seconds?'

Grab your copy...
vinci-books.com/lostforwords

About the Author

Jax lives in the NW of England with two cats - George and Cloud. She spent the last twenty years working in a cancer hospital as a secretary and retired in the middle of the pandemic. Her colleagues still managed to give her a decent send off.

Jax writes contemporary romance novels set in a small fictional town in Cheshire. All her stories have a happy ending which is hard won. She doesn't shy away from serious subjects - her characters have a lot to cope with! But that makes their happy ever after all the sweeter.

When Jax isn't writing or plotting a new series, she listens to music or reads. She can sometimes be found doing a sneaky cross-stitch whilst listening to an audio book.